# Jersey Smith

Ordering Information:
Special discounts are available on quantity purchases by
corporations, associations, and others.
For details, contact the publisher.
Orders by U.S. trade bookstores and wholesalers. Please contact:
www.Sales@GlynnLSimmons.com

Printed in the United States of America

# Jersey Smith
## *The Wild, Wild East*
### by Glynn L. Simmons

1.—Novel—Action/Adventure/Thriller/Suspense
2.—American Fiction set in the
      1850's/Frontier/Pioneer/Western
3.—Inspirational/Historical

ISBN: 978-1-7353217-0-7

FIRST EDITION

Cover by GLS Books

*gls*

For Janene,
The Love of My Life

# Jersey Smith

BY GLYNN L. SIMMONS

# Part One

South West Pennsylvania
1849

The bodies lay near thorn bushes and blackberries, under a string of trees at the water's edge. The river turned there, forming the west and southern boundary of Jersey's land. He had just crossed the same river a few miles away in the foothills. While his father-in-law Hamish made his way through the loose shale rubble, Jersey leaned on his saddle looking over a ledge down at the water below. Eager for level ground, he glanced back at the old man taking his time through the shifting shards of stone.

He waited on the opposite bank. The river flowed from the mountain above, and burst powerfully between ancient stones before dropped forty feet into the deep pool. So clear was the water below it seemed to magnify everything; what looked to be three feet deep was really ten or twelve. He'd fished the pool often, it was a productive spot. The falling water was so loud there he often found himself in fear of a silent attack by bear or the now rare cat. When the water level was lower after the spring thaw, he'd position himself on the large flat rock out in the pool. He had to swim there, but it was safe. Occasionally he'd see Indians fishing with spears in the shallows, shaking his head at their accuracy. He was taught to spear fish when he was young by a few Mohegans in his home town of Anchor Bay Rhode Island. It was a lot of work for the results. For him a pole and worm seemed to land more fish. They also taught him how to throw a knife, that skill he picked up quickly.

The river moved on from the pool into the valley, past the trading post, and another mile or so before turning at Jersey's place.

Today though, he wasn't fishing. He and Hamish were returning from a long day of small game hunting with a week's worth of meals. He pulled the reins and held up his hand as they both stopped at the sound of a distant gunshot.

"What?" the old man said.

"Sounds different."

"It sounded far away and the sound of the river is still ringing in my ears."

"I 'spec."

Jersey sat up high in the saddle looking in the direction of his place, but they were lower now, the trees blocked his view.

They stopped at the Trading Post for flour and sugar in trade for a large rabbit. They talked with Ed the owner. The old man drank mountain water and Jersey had a beer, cold from sitting in the river box. After a while Jersey became impatient, if he wasn't there to stop them the two would go on all night.

"My how that story gets better every time I hear it."

"Aye Jersey, after tell'n it a few times a person just gets good at it," said Hamish.

"Hmm," Jersey nodded and looked around the room.

"Okay," Hamish said, lifting from the bench. "Let's get. Bye Ed."

"That's good Hamish, see you Jersey."

Life was never the same after that, a short mile away was a devastating truth. Nothing could repair their broken hearts after finding the bodies of Catherine and Marie. Jersey searched for two days for Martin's little body. When he returned, he'd brought a Sheriff and a deputy, but no Martin.

"I'm sorry I left you with all of this Hamish," Jersey said.

It was the first time in a long time Jersey called him by his real name and not 'old man'. Hamish was sitting in a corner of Catherine's flower garden on a chair brought from the house at the foot of the graves he'd lovingly prepared for his daughter and granddaughter.

I understand son, it was the hardest thing I ever did," he said.

Jersey and the two officials stood silent near the graves while Hamish read out loud from his Bible. Jersey seemed to want time alone at the graves, so Hamish and the two officials walked to the front porch. They went inside when they saw him fall to his knees and bury his face in his hands.

"Can you tell me what happened?" the Sheriff asked.

"Hmm?"

Hamish was looking out the window at Jersey and thinking about how a few days ago this house was full of girl's laughter and that little boy asking one question after another.

"When you returned from hunting? What you saw?" the Sheriff asked.

"Oh, aye. Ah..."

He sat down in the window seat and motioned for them to sit. The Sheriff sat, crossed his legs, pulled a small cloth bag from his pocket and rolled a smoke.

"They were near the river," he pointed through the glass, "where you crossed, and Marie was on top of Catherine, it looked like only one shot killed them both," he said.

The young deputy walked to the open door looking out at the river.

"And the boy was gone?" the Sheriff asked.

Hamish nodded. "There were two scrape marks in the dirt that led into the river that looked like the toes of Martin's boots," he looked up, "you know like he was dragged to the water."

"Hmm, any other marks in the dirt?"

"No boot marks, it was like he stayed on his horse the whole time."

"Then what?"

"Ah, I sat with the girls and Jersey ran downstream lookin' for the boy. After a bit Jersey came back, he went behind the house, got a fresh horse and headed north. Later, he rode past-across the river head'n the other way. He slowed near where it happened and after lookin around he rode off."

"Well, he must have come back by in order to get to us up north."

"I think I heard him that night ride past, must have been him."

"So he left you to take care of the, um, well..."

"Yes. Had to. If the boy was in the river he could be way downstream or caught up along the shore," the old man whispered, "and the animals..."

His eyes were tearing up as he looked around the room, he twisted back to the window.

"I had Ed, and his oldest, from the Trading Post help dig the..." he continued by motioning a pointed finger at the garden and the graves.

"I hate to ask you this, but I have to. If you think the man didn't get off his horse, then he didn't physically..."

"No," Hamish stopped him. "He didn't do anything like

that, but Catherine had bruises on her arm and her little knife was on the ground with blood on it."

"So, she cut him—good, and if he was on his horse that means it was most likely a cut on a leg."

"Well—could be on his arm, if'n he was pull'n on her," the deputy said.

They all nodded.

Jersey stepped through the open door, standing large near the threshold, dust swirling in the sunlight around him. He felt out of sorts, as he looked around the room it all seemed to hit him. Exhausted, he stumbled to a chair, wiped the sweat from his forehead—knocking his hat to the floor.

The Sheriff stood up. "Well, we're gonna head south towards Spring Valley pay a visit to Ben, the old friend I told you about—Sheriff Ben Jenkins."

He looked at Jersey but got no response.

"Well, he's a good man, if someone strange passed through he'd know. We'll come back if we find anything. If we don't, we'll head across the valley a ways and head back north to Johnstown."

Hamish nodded. Jersey stared into the cold dark fireplace.

The Sheriff and Deputy walked their horses to the murder scene, they looked the area over closely.

"How can a man kill a young girl and her mother?"

"Murder like that, man has to be cold to the bone."

They saddled up, crossed the river and turned walking along its far bank—heads down looking closely at everything. They ruled out Jersey's horse marks with its distinctive style. Almost a mile upstream they found tracks of two horses that stepped out of the river. They almost missed them but were riding wide apart, and the young Deputy spotted them in the rough.

"Where did these come from? Looks like two of 'em."

The Sheriff looked at the area, he turned his attention to the river's edge.

"They could have come up through the river and stepped out here, and brushed away their tracks from the path."

"I think they're head'n southeast along the foothills," the Deputy said.

"That's good work."

The Sheriff crossed the river, it was wide and four feet deep at its center. He rode along the bank, checking for tracks.

"Nothing over here," he yelled. "He must have been walking in the river all the way from the murder, I think we found him, I mean them. I'll check a ways farther just to make sure. You follow them tracks, I'll catch-up. But don't ride through the tracks, I want to see 'em first."

"Right," the young Deputy said.

# Chapter 2

Jersey was gone for another five days searching for Martin and the killer. When he returned he was a different man. Hamish had wondered if he was coming back at all. Catherine and Jersey had been together from childhood, this kind of loss was life changing. He rode up tired and dirty, he sadly shook his head and crawled in bed, where he stayed for nearly two days.

Hamish woke to the smell of coffee and found Jersey sitting on the porch step. His dog had come back after a few days wandering and was laying close by. Jersey was whittling, and by the amount of the shavings at his feet—he'd been at it for a while. It was a way he had of working through something before committing to it.

"What ya working on?"

Jersey looked out at the river as he'd done all morning, and as with every other time his eyes were drawn to the line of trees and berry bushes.

"I'm moving out," he said.

"Oh—where you head'n?"

"To the hunt lodge, you can come if you want."

The old man looked out at the river, his eyes were drawn to the berry bushes, "call'n it a lodge doesn't change the fact that it's a shack," he said.

"Yeah, I was going over the work needed before winter. I figure we take the boards off the new stable, load the wagon, and keep it at Ed's behind the post.

We can come down for more as we need it," Jersey said.

"I guess that can work—when do you want to start?"

"If you get some bacon and biscuits on, I'll find the bar and start pry'n boards."

"There's lots to go over," Hamish said.

"Yeah, I know, let's do that on a full stomach."

Hamish turned back inside, stoked the stove's fire, moved the coffee pot next to the flue and put the big pan in its place. Jersey stood, snapped his fingers, as the dog followed him around to the back of the house. He led the horses into the corral and stood looking at the little building for a moment, as he started tearing it down he thought of the day he and the old man finished it.

Hamish wondered if heading into the mountains was the right move, but all the hard work could help get them through. We have to start over whether we want to or not, Hamish thought. They each moved slow, almost clumsy at times, the sense of loss was overwhelming.

# Chapter 3

It was dark by the time they got to the trading post. They slept in the small out-building where Ed had bunks that he charged strangers a few cents a night for. Jersey's hunt lodge wasn't too far up in the hills, but it was steep and the trail was winding. The terrain limited the amount of wood they could move at a time. They each hauled as much as they could and pulled a third horse heaped with more supplies. Slowly they made their way up to the turn off path, along a level section to his place near the river.

The building was in worse shape than expected. Hamish looked it over for priority fixes to start on. Jersey took care of the horses, the lumber, and started repairing the little corral. It was connected to a shed big enough for two horses, which was connected to the house. He watched small animals exit the house as the old man screamed a few times. Things started flying out the front door onto the yard. Hamish hung every piece of bedding and cloth from a rope between trees. He slapped them with a broom and left them to air out. When he felt like it was time for a break he walked out to the pen, leaned on the fence post, and ran down his list.

"Well, the fireplace flue had a nest in it, I cleaned it out. It'll work but it needs a good clean'n. When did you get that little stove? You know it's got a broke leg. We need glass for one of the window panes. A few nests were around, but the birds seemed to have moved on, probably on-a-count of the family of red squirrels that moved in. Them's some mean little critters Jersey, they tend to get angry and fight back. Also, lots of mouse droppings but no mice in sight."

"Yet," Jersey said under his breath.

"What?"

"There's a rock near the stove that fits under it, that will be fine for now. Let's use a shingle for the window until tomorrow."

"We head'n down tomorrow?"

"Yeah, we got the money let's get Ed Junior up here for a week, give us a hand," Jersey said.

"Oh, that would be good," Hamish said.

Hamish started feeling better. At seventeen Junior was tall, strong and as likable as his father. Now things should move twice as fast. He stood there for a while looking around. The ever present muted sound of the river through the trees filled the clearing. Jersey must have burned out the big tree stumps at some point, it was all nice and flat out front. He could see it now, what Jersey saw before, and why he would call it a hunt lodge. He knew Jersey had planned to spend time here with Catherine, he'd told him when they started to build it, 'at some point we'll leave the kids with you and come up here for a few days once in a while.'

He'd helped put the frame up, but that was it, all the other work Jersey did on his hunting trips. He'd cleared the little sucker trees from the woods and fern had taken their place, stretching to the big trees in the distance. The river was to the south. To the west, from the front of the lodge, the forest floor slowly sloped downward to an abrupt drop off. Below that was the winding trail down to the Trading Post. To the east, behind the lodge fifty yards or so, the mountain incline took a serious turn upward. From out front looking over the roof the steep tree and rock filled hills looked impossible to traverse, but there were winding trails and paths throughout. It was really a beautiful spot, he thought.

"Well?" Jersey said.

"Looking around, get'n hungry. You know that root cellar needs a lot of work too," Hamish said.

"Yeah, remind me to get another shovel tomorrow. Hey, if you can get the stove going I'll go catch us a few trout. You'll need to use the ladder to get the burlap off the top of the flue."

"Oh—I'll get it going. We got some cornmeal and powdered milk, think I'll batter fry-um," the old man said.

Hamish hurried off. Jersey walked to the fence nudging a horse out of the way. From his hanging saddle bag he took a string and hook, strapped on his gun and knife belt, and walked to the river.

# From the Journal of Hamish Maguire
5th of August 1849

Been a while that I wrote down anything and I don't plan on writing about what happened to Catherine and the children. Someday I might.

We moved into the lodge up in the mountains, we boarded up our house on the river and left. Hoping to let the sadness of what happened fade. After a lot of work the lodge is tight and ready for winter. Jersey increased the size of the stable to fit four horses inside, out of harms way. It's connected to the lodge wall so we can check them without go'n outside. We only kept three horses, the rest we sold with the other livestock to Ed at his trading post and we gave Ed Junior a horse along with some cash for helping with the fix'n of the lodge. Jersey is now spending more time hunting and fishing and trapping and is making some good money do'n it. We don't have much to spend it on now though.

A friend of Jerseys stopped by and is stay'n till November. Fixed him a small bunk near the fireplace, while Jersey and I share the bedroom. Planning another room on in the spring. His name is Earl and those that know him call him Trapper Earl, as he's a very good trapper and hunter. He's taught Jersey a lot over the years, but this is the first time I met him. He lives over the ridge on the other side and farther north in the highlands. I guess he lives in a cave or gorge and rarely comes this far west or south. He calls the mountains here abouts hills and says the real mountains are out west, and he plans on going back someday. The man is a bit loud, he's either talking or snoring. I have to say he's kinda fun to be around. Tells a lot of jokes, most old but still funny.

This mornings scriptures seemed to be saying something to me, something fateful, must keep my eyes open. It was in Isaiah 13:11.

# Chapter 4

Trapper Earl was following Jersey along a narrow path that hugged the steep hills high above the little lake village. Through the trees the sunlight flickered off the water far below.

"Why, I remember once shooting a bobcat in the head in mid-air as he was a jump'n for a friend's dog. Amazing shot—must have been 50 yards away. He was..."

Jersey interrupted. "That was me," he said without turning around.

"What?"

"Yeah, remember you was fiddling with your rifle so I had to shoot it with my new Colt Navy before it got Duke. I teach my dog better now, like my horses, besides it was more like 50 feet and it took two shots to hit him."

"Oh—yeah, I remember now that was in the fall of 46' we met that spring, yeah—huh, funny how I remembered it."

Jersey's horse made a little start and his ears turned. He leaned over and rubbed his neck below the mane and said softly, "someth'n out there Blue?" He eased off on the reins and sat up. He was a large animal of 16 hands and speckled gray. The rancher called him a Blue Roan, so Jersey called him Blue. Now Jersey heard something too and put his hand up as they stopped. Earl knew it was time to stop talking and listen. Some distance ahead came a scream. Jersey made two distinct clicks Blue did the rest. They were twenty yards down the path before Earl even got started. The horse knew this path all too well, Jersey let him run it, though at times he felt out of control. The scream came again; it was faint through the wind in their ears. He kept off the saddle and leaned in close, talking as calmly as he could to him.

They twisted through a few tight turns, inclines, and down around a large tree. They reached a clearing where everything had recently rolled over and slid down the mountain. Blue's legs tightened and locked, pushing down together bringing them to a fast stop in the soft ground. They stood and listened to get a bearing. Jersey lifted up listening, but Blue heard enough and leaped forward. After twenty feet into the clearing Blue turned down the steep open ground.

"You trying to kill me?" Jersey yelled.

The incline was so severe Jersey had to stand in the stirrups leaning back, far back, as the big horse took giant strides, kicking up dirt and debris. They knew this area, but only from the crossing paths, never straight down the side. Jersey couldn't see below, the ground ahead was ending. He saw the horizon – the far shore of the distant lake in the valley below, and the vast blue sky spotted with clouds. They were coming to an even steeper drop, possibly the big drop-off, but as foreign as the recent ground shift changed things he was sure they hadn't come as far as the cliff. Jersey started to pull to the right on the reins, and Blue turned a bit, but still jumped over the edge to whatever was beyond.

They seemed to fall, then they merged with the steep soft slope, front hocks deep, Blue's tail and back side dragged in the loose dirt, which helped to slow them. They practically fell when they slid down onto the wide lower path. Jersey was jerked around, but relieved to be on the main trail. Blue hit the ground square, got his balance, leaned north and pushed off, running along the steep wall of loose dirt and stone. It was the old path, but it was very different because of the avalanche. Jersey gave him a nudge with his heels and leaned forward to let him know he was doing good. That was enough, as in the past, with a bit of encouragement Blue poured on his last bit of power. The bright sun flashing through the trees as they were once again in the lush green forest flying down the well used lower trail. Long shadows crossed the path hiding possible holes and rough spots, scaring Jersey—but Blue was determined and unfazed.

Jersey would remember this as the moment he questioned Blues motives—was he really that smart? Could he detect peril? He's just a horse, this has to be a game to him, something he can excel at. Maybe to him it's the best part of his job. They often ran down prey, but Jersey didn't teach him to run towards danger, this had become an acceptable, maybe even enjoyable part of Blue's life.

Ed Junior had tied his horse off, when he heard someone coming. He turned to see a huge horse moving fast, it pulled up skidding. Jersey was off before Blue was fully stopped. The scream came once more but muffled this time.

Jersey looked at the young man. "You stay here. If I need help, I'll call for you."

The boy nodded as Jersey ran off, lifting his waistcoat up over the Navy Colt and large knife. They were both sheathed and strapped to the back of his belt, they crossed each other, the gun's butt for the right hand, the knife handle out for the left. Ed Junior reached for his rifle, then noticed the large handgun in Jersey's saddle. He grabbed it, stood for a minute, then decided to follow.

Jersey saw a few colors through the dense young trees, then movement. He slowed, careful not to make a sound, he watched each step. He found an old path which led up behind them. There were five armed men standing in an opening around a half-buried, waist high chunk of flat shale. They had a young woman stretched across it.

One man had put a gag on her, he watched the young woman as he walked backwards up next to his friend. They were the closest, Jersey moved his head to see around them. Two others were holding her down. The nearest, his back to Jersey, wore white under-all filthy with stains and sweat, his suspenders hanging at his sides. Jersey needed to keep him in the sight line of the man across the stone. That man wore a red bandanna and his hat was hanging on his back from a strap at his neck, greasy long hair pulled behind his ears. Both men at the stone were struggling at times to hold her down, though she was showing signs of exhaustion.

"Oh—she's a real beauty boss, ain't she," bandanna man said.

The boss was dancing around at the girls kicking feet, which hung over the end of the stone. He was showing off for his men, and they were laughing, but all eyes were on her.

Red bandanna man ripped the last bit of under clothing off, tossing it over his shoulder. When he put his hand back on her leg Jersey stepped out into the clearing. The girl turned her head like she knew someone had come for her. Jersey saw the face of Catherine, the eyes, the hair, to him they were holding down his woman—this time he will stop it.

Knife in hand, Jersey edged up to the two closest men. The girl started kicking again and while the two men at the rock were bent over holding her down. Jersey edged closer still behind the watching men. The man in charge was dancing in a circle, hands raised, his hips swinging to a song he was loudly singing. The two watching men laughed at the dancing fool, they smiled at each other but noticed something over their shoulders.

When they turned, Jersey was in motion, one pulled his gun but it was too late. He grabbed the man's gun hand twisting it while his big knife penetrated up to its steel guard. He quickly pulled it out as the other man leaned in, lifting his gun from his belt. Jersey's elbow slammed back square in his face. The man's head shot back, blood came instantly, he dropped to his knees, the jolt shook his gun from his hand. Jersey squeezed his knife's bone handle tight, as the man tried to get up, he hit him hard, the man bent sideways. Jersey caught his hair at the back of the head and pulled him up and close. He quickly looked to see if his presence was known but they were still laughing, then he saw red bandanna glance around the other man. Jersey slammed the man's bleeding face down onto his rising knee, quickly turning his full attention to the men at the stone.

Seeing his friend on the ground, and a strange big man looking at him, red bandanna stepped backwards fumbling for his gun which was hanging from a low tree branch. The man across the stone saw the look on his face and turned. The last thing he saw was Jersey Smith moving at him, gun raised. The first shot buzzed past his ear, red bandanna fell back bleeding in the tall fern. The second shot he didn't hear, he fell on the big stone, the woman kicked him to the ground. She rolled off the far side of the stone and lay stunned looking up at the bits of blue through the treetops.

Jersey walked through drifting gunsmoke. The man in

charge turned at the sounds, then stepped backwards, away from the large man approaching. He was astonished at what had happened and how fast it came down to just him. He took a wide sweep with his knife, then a few more awkward steps back, until he hit a tree.

Jersey put his gun away. He held his knife up as he watched the man take a few more wide sweeps with his own large blade. He took a step closer catching the man's knife hand on the next swing. Holding it high he pulled the man up with it, stuck the tip of his own big knife a half an inch into the center of his throat.

"There's something I've wanted to ask a madman like you," he said. "You have one second—start telling me what it is that makes you more important than anyone else?"

The man couldn't move back so he started to sink, but Jersey pulled him back up by his hand squeezing until he dropped his knife. Jersey's knife moved a bit, and the man stopped fighting.

"What you mean by that?" the man said.

The sweat was dripping down his dirty face, he was frantically thinking of a way out, his eyes darting about, escape seemed impossible.

"You know what I mean—how can you do this to another person and think it's okay? You must believe you're better than the rest of us. Right?" His voice was low and rough, but calm, not out of breath. The outlaw could see in this stranger's eyes that he was working through something.

"I mean look at you men, you're the lowest of the low, if you didn't travel in a group and didn't have guns, people would toss coins to you outta compassion. No—the worlds better off without you roaming around."

The boss looked around, if his fallen men were any indication he hadn't much time left.

Jersey couldn't shake the vision of the bodies at the river, two innocent, defenseless loving... He tried to put it out of his head or he might just kill this man for the murder of his family. He thought of Martin and how he was just gone. Now this—it was happening again, but this time he's here in time. He never found the monster responsible, and it left a hole in his heart, right now his blood was boiling over, he was seeing red, it was dripping down this animal's throat.

"Well—are you better than everyone?"

The man didn't know what to say to save his life. He saw the look in Jersey's eyes, a look that told him this was the end. He felt the knife move at his neck. A gunshot made them both jump and turn. Ed Junior was standing in the rough at the clearing's edge, Jersey's saddle Colt was in his hand, it's smoke drifting through the thin green saplings. Jersey looked back at the man he was holding. He hit him hard in the face with his knife in hand knocking him out, he fell sideways to the ground.

Jersey looked around to see what Junior had shot, the only man he hadn't killed on his rampage was now face down with a bullet hole dead center in his back. His gun in hand stretched out aiming in Jersey's direction. Ed Junior had saved his life, he'd never forget that. He looked at Ed who was looking around for the girl. He looked over at Jersey who was staring at him, then raised his shoulders practically to his ears and said, "I heard gunshots, and you said if you needed help."

Jersey looked down at the man with the hole in his back, "I did need help."

The young woman moaned, Jersey snapped out of it, he moved quickly around the large rock, took bandanna man's coat and placed it around her. Ed ran to the stone calling out, "Abby!" Jersey stood between them until the jacket was covering her.

She looked up at him whispering faintly, "thank you."

Jersey saw how young she was and how pretty, he stood so Ed could get to her, they both started crying.

"Junior, can you help her out to the path?"

Ed Junior looked up at Jersey confused. "Hmm? Oh, okay."

He helped her to her feet but she limped, hugging they walked slowly away.

Trapper Earl walked into the clearing past the young couple and stood looking around.

"As usual just in time, see if you can find her dress," Jersey said.

Jersey rolled the man in charge over, tied his hands behind him and his ankles together. He walked to the marauder's horses and brought them back, tying the reins around a tree near the bodies. He made a pile of things he found from the men and their horses. Trapper found the dress. They walked to Ed Junior and Abby where they were sitting quietly on a smooth rock waiting. Her long legs were exposed, and she was shivering.

"If I hold a blanket up can you get into your dress?"

She nodded. Jersey took his bedroll from his saddle, rolled it out as he walked to her, then held it high. Ed and Trapper looked everywhere but in her direction. It took a while and she moaned a few times then she asked Jersey to help her, he lowered the roll peeking over then put the blanket under his arm and loosely laced up her dress tying it off.

He checked her condition, moving her arms and asked her to lift her legs. He decided she had a broken rib, probably two, but besides all the bruises and what was going to be a bruised eye and cheek, she seemed okay to take on a slow ride down the steep trail home.

Jersey looked at Blue's hind and got his canteen,

unfolded a leather cup and gave his horse some water.

"We'll get Hamish to get a poultice on your backside when we get back." He rubbed the top of his snout.

He said to Ed Junior. "You stay here with Abby, Earl and I will get the bodies on horses and tie them behind your ride to take down."

"You not come'n Jersey?" Junior asked.

Jersey shook his head then poured water sparingly onto Blue's hind to clean dirt out of a few scrapes. He nodded to Earl and they walked back to the clearing. When the bodies were tied over their horses and the leader tied in place in his saddle, a few of the village men showed up. They were shown around and told what happened. Two of the men led Junior and Abby home.

"You see dee's men before Jersey?" one of the men asked.

"No."

"I ain't neither," said Earl.

The men went through every pocket, the head outlaw jerked away as a man felt through his coat and pants. He found a few papers, his eyes got big as he said something in Swedish, then he signaled for the others to see what he'd found.

"Ah, Jersey this here's Bucky Murray."

Jersey looked up from a gun he'd picked up. "Good, tell the Sheriff."

"He's a bad man."

Earl looked at Jersey then at the gang of men. "Well hell gents, we know's they's bad men. You forget'n what they was try'n with that sweet innocent, right here?"

Jersey and Earl looked at the men like they were crazy.

"Bucky Murray—you not heard about him?"

Jersey and Earl looked at each other and shrugged.

Another man spoke up. "Dis big Jersey, dat man's wanted in tree states, head of a bad gang of bad mens—dis a few of em right here, dead."

The man swung his hand out at all the dead bodies across their horses.

"Bound to be a reward, might be a big one," said another.

"Good," Jersey said. "Put it in the village chest, fix a road or somethin."

"Now wait Jersey," Earl said. "Could be some real currency involved,"

Jersey gave him a look.

"Yeah," Earl said. "Little village could use it more than us." He felt sick as he turned and walked slowly away.

As they led the horses away one of the men said, "what's all dat?"

He was pointing to a small pile of things Jersey had taken.

"That's spoils, it's mine, if the Sheriff has a problem with it tell him where I live."

"You not coming down wit us?"

"No need, you and Junior and the girl know what happened, they were evil sons-a-bitches and we stopped em," Jersey said.

They all nodded in agreement, then walked the string of corpses to the path while the tied man begged to be let go. Trapper Earl walked to the small pile of knives, guns and leather goods, then looked up at Jersey smiling.

"What's in the box?"

Jersey said, "a Samuel and Charles... It's mine."

Trapper lost his smile and he looked back down. "Okay, I want the Sharps. What's a Samuel and Charles?"

"It's a fine shotgun from England," Jersey said.

"Ain't you from England Jersey?"

"I was born there, don't remember much."

# From the Journal of Hamish Maguire
14th of November 1850

At the trading post today and I was sitt'n at one of the outside tables and Ed asked how was Jersey, so I was tell'n him and a few Indians was at the other table and they started talkin loud and moving around and looking at us and one of them said something to the n'other and he said in pretty good English, that they know Jersey, and they all nodded and looked at Ed and I. So we nods back and the others coax him to tell their story and he went ahead and did.

Seems they was in a hunting party up along the upper ridge and this Indian he pointed up at the mountain behind the trading post, "heard a big gunshot," he says, "went to see, we found a white man sitting on the ground next to a bear," he motioned that it was a very big bear and his friend said something to him about the size and he kept talk'n. "We talked to him about the bear and told him we wanted the bear because it was so big we could go home early. So, we said we would take it, and Jersey put up hands as this," the Indian put his fists up in a fight'n stance and the others laughed. So, he pointed to one of the others there and said, "he (meaning his friend there) pulled out a knife and showed it to Jersey, hoping to scare him off. Jersey looked at the bear for a spell then back at the Indian with the knife, so he stood up slow like pulled out his own knife from his back." He held his hands apart to show the size and a few of the others laugh't and corrected his estimated size of the knife so he moved his hands apart more. So he said Jersey stood ready to fight, but then Jersey smiled, like he wanted to fight. He used his hands to show a big smile and the others broke into even bigger laughs, "but when he stood he was a big man, bigger than they knew from him sitt'n, and no one wanted to fight him. so we rode off, but he called to us, help butcher it and you can take half, but Jersey got to keep the skin too. We skinned and split and salted and wrapped it." He was stopped again by the others, he nodded and looked back at Ed and me. "Jersey showed us some new ways, but we show him some old ways, old ways better. He gave us rest of his salt too and now Jersey Smith is a friend."

I reckon that was a year or two back cause Jersey tells of a few Indian friends he has. As I was leaving I heard Ed tell'n the Indians another Jersey story. He's becoming well known here bouts, but I don't think he knows it, he doesn't go down much any more. I make the trips to the trading post myself. He hunts, traps and fishes and trains his animals and practices shooting with all his different guns, he's been readin a bit more lately too.

Ed Junior brought us a pot of meat in some white sauce, which he swears is not gravy, and some bread from Abby's mother, the pot was so full I spill't some and Duke ate it up in a hurry. Not sure how the young man got it up the path without spill'n more of it. It was different, but it was very good. Junior say's Abby's family are always ask'n about us, Jersey in particular.

Good verse today about sow'n seeds, it reminds me to prepare seed from a few things in the root cellar for spring also to give a good amount to those who needs it. It was in Leviticus.

# Chapter 5

Hamish was staring into the flames of a burning stump standing across from Jersey warming his hands and switching his weight from one foot to the other. Winter was in full swing, the snow was a good foot deep and the gray sky had been dropping powder off and on for a few days. A dark dreariness had descended on them and standing at a burning stump seemed an inviting change. Hamish heard a noise he looked over at Jersey, his gun was already out and he was looking up the hill. It surprised Hamish how fast he'd pulled his gun; he kept it high inside his coat in such weather.

From behind the hunt lodge up the mountain through the leafless trees they saw what looked like a bear; it was having trouble controlling its speed down the steep path. Soon its momentum was too much—it fell and started rolling down the trail clipping a few small trees which kept it on the path. It was big, furry, and picking up speed. When the path turned the big fur ball took to the air, as a voice was heard, "Oh no!" Trapper Earl landed butt first in the snow-covered debris pile. Fine snow and a few dead leaves swirled in every direction. Without missing a beat Earl bounced up and rolled off the pile.

Hamish looked at Jersey who was smiling and back staring into the fire; he'd slipped his gun back in place. Trapper brushed himself off, walked wide gate and awkward to the fire. He pulled off his big mittens placed them under his arm and rubbed his hands together over the burning wood.

"Gents," he said.

"Where's your horse?" Hamish asked.

"Well boys that's a bit of a story, you see the Lord called him home and the biggest bear I ever seen did the deed."

He looked at Hamish. "Do horses go to heaven old man?"

"I'd like to think we'll have their comfort in the hereafter. Now, tell us what happened?"

"I walked here from my place," Trapper said.

Jersey and Hamish looked at each other and Hamish started walking to the lodge and said over his shoulder, "I'll put more wood in the fireplace, you get him inside."

"A walk that distance in this weather can kill a man Trapper," Jersey said.

He nodded. Jersey helped him inside brushing him off. He had a rifle strapped across his back that looked bent. He was wearing a few layers of clothes and two coats then a hooded fur cape that usually fastened around him but for his current girth.

After some time in front of the fire Hamish said, "well?"

They sat in the small room, the fire had made it almost too hot for Jersey but Trapper was feeling better.

"That bear."

He rubbed his foot with his hands close to the fireplace and rocked slightly front to back on a folded blanket across a log ottoman.

"He was massive Jersey, hit us from outta nowhere. Kill't my new horse and Jimmy the mule. I ran while he was killing, and then he come after me. I got to that gorge, you know near my place," he looked at Jersey, "slipped in as far as I could and he was a reachin for me but he was too big to come in. I watched him walk away, so I ran home."

"To your cave?" Hamish said.

"So now, this is a black bear right?" Jersey said.

"I know, but he was as big a blackie ever I'd seen, and meeean."

"What then Earl?" Hamish asked.

"Yeah—So I did some fixin' at my entrance, cause of this bear's size and attitude and I was need'n to sleep and all. I re-fastened all my pointy rods and traps. Anyways, I went to my animals the next day, but he was there in the hills and he saw me and made a roar like I ain't never heard. I ran back..." He looked up at Jersey, "my Sharps and Colt are lay'n there in the snow under my horse and all I gots this little pea-shooter," he pointed to the gun leaning near the door, Earl tilted his head seeing it looked bent, "believe me that gun will do it but I don't want to get that close to him, might just piss him off, and that bears already pissed off at somethin. So—I couldn't get out to get food or firewood and yesterday when I saw him walk by in the direction of my animals I skedaddled and headed here."

Hamish took his empty cup and handed him another.

"Hm, black bear," Jersey said.

"Maybe he's got the fever or rabies or somethin worse," Hamish said.

"I reckon. Well your feet and hands look okay, let's give it a few days and head over there, kill us a bear," Jersey said.

Trapper looked at the fire silent for a minute. "Naw. Naw—I'm heading down."

"Movin away?" Hamish asked.

"Yeah, not given up you see, just done with it, been at it for years. Try my luck on level ground for a while."

"Well no one would hold it against yah—you held your own here for what ten years? But, it's a different world down there Trapper, different from when you came up," Jersey said.

"Yeah, I got some money saved, ready for somethin new, maybe find a woman that can put up with me."

"Well Trapper that's the best reason to go, man needs a woman," Hamish said.

"Gonna miss you up here old friend," Jersey said.

Trapper nodded and kind of got emotional and sniffled a bit, he held his cup with two hands and leaned down to sip from it.

After resting for three days Trapper Earl paid for, then mounted the horse called 'Number Three'. He was heading to Ohio or somewhere else in a westerly direction. Hamish gave him a wreath made of sticks and dried red berries to put on the graves as he passed the house on the river. Jersey and Hamish said their goodbyes from the porch. When Earl got to the path's edge he turned saying, "guess I'll be join'n the human race, if-en they'll have me," and slowly descended.

# Chapter 6

North of the lake village above sloping squared rock on a high outcropping Jersey Smith sat eating breakfast. He enjoyed this spot often; it was a narrow ledge with a shallow pocket of soft grass and a stone wall slanted at just the right angle for leaning. He was watching a hunting party below as they sat around a fire talking and laughing. He shook his head thinking, a hunting party that makes enough noise to scare off its prey is just a party.

Wanting to learn more about the mystery man below, he'd watched them all morning. He knew he didn't like him; the man seemed to have a plan of disruption and an attitude of self importance, which always rubbed Jersey the wrong way. After buying up half the valley and every remaining inch of lake property, the man was making a move to take some land from a few of the lake people that wouldn't sell. Jersey felt he knew many types of men and he liked most of them, at least he could put up with them. A man like this seemed more common in stories he thought. Where someone seemingly important rushes in and plunges a rod in the spokes of a growing community. All attention is turned to him as everyone watches in disbelief as the destruction plays out.

His father would tell him stories of England and his namesake island in the channel or of the countries he'd been to. Some in Europe where it was usually governments or royalty that would overstep, it was one of the reasons the family came to America. He'd tell him how in all the places he'd been the people were usually good, friendly, and willing to help anyone in need—God's people. It was always governments and politics that messed things up, and most likely under the guise of helping—for the betterment and good, but he rarely saw any good come from that kind of help. It always helped them, the so called powerful. It was about getting more control; more money which always leads to even more power.

In areas like this where men and women have a beautiful arrangement with their creator and his bounty—this is it for them. They set up their life and legacy. They work hard to relax completely. To just look out the window of a house they built and see what they've done and be proud, and God willing, that will be their destiny. Of the many types of men Jersey had known, men with money were the hardest to figure out. Most that he knew where he'd grown up were good men. He felt it was all about the man they were to begin with; if they were rich jackasses, most likely they were jackasses before the amplifying properties of wealth made them worse.

He tapped salt on a hard-cooked egg and took a bite of bacon jerky while watching from above. One of his Indian friends was leading the group below, he watched him walk into the woods and out of view. The party sat around the fire as two men started cooking from a chuck wagon. The money man stood at the fire talking to the group getting a few laughs out of them. The party was made up of strangers he must have invited from where he came, a few looked influential, at the very least well off.

"Jersey, com'n in." A voice came from the woods down a nearby path.

"Come in, Roger," Jersey said without seeing him.

His name wasn't Roger but his real name sounded close to that and he never complained about it.

"So, they pay'n well?" Jersey asked.

Roger came close and Jersey tossed him a large piece of jerky. He knelt on the grass and looked out at the green valley and deep blue sky, then he shook his head at the men around the fire below.

"Yes, good money," he said, "I see you up here, told him I was scouting a better place."

They smiled and looked down at the city people thinking they were roughing it.

"What do you think of the man?" Jersey asked.

"Don't like him." He paused then looked at Jersey. "Like his money."

Again they smiled and looked down at the city people.

"He's fat and slow," Roger said.

"Yeah, I crossed paths on the road when they was head'n in, a few months back. Something was odd about him, also he was wearing suspenders and a belt, I didn't trust him on that count alone," Jersey said.

"He's not a good shot, no," Roger said.

"I saw that. You know he's makin trouble in the village, fraid I may have to step in."

"Mm—Need help?" Roger asked.

"Well, that would be mighty neighborly friend."

Jersey held up a hard-cooked egg and Roger cringed, he nodded to the last piece of bacon.

# From the Journal of Hamish Maguire
12th of May 1851

Haven't written in a while so I'll catch up. Spring came and we got started on all the plans we'd made all winter while sit'n at the fireplace. Jersey was away a lot trap'n and hunt'n we made a lot of money this year. I read until I ran out of books, then I swapped a few with a new friend from the lake that I met at the trading post. I think I added another ten pounds on, but already lost a few chopping wood, as we were running low.

Jersey was practicing his shoot'n out front all winter, the noise was driving me crazy and I can't think how they hated it down below. He used to do that stuff a ways up in the hills, not sure why he changed it. He'd shoot 6 shots with the one then 6 with the other, then come in and reload as fast as he could. He's got a nice little measure that he turns downside up and it gives just the right amount of powder for each chamber. It's fascinat'n how times have changed. I got to shoot Jersey's new shotgun; it has quite a kick that gun does. Should be a fine bird gun.

Everything is green now, and we have lots to do. Weeks ago we filled the chute behind the root cellar with the last bits of snow and ice. It's a Jersey invention where the snow and ice goes down this deep hole with wood sides and it's vented near the bottom and runs under the root cellar floor which is wood slats. As the snow and ice melt it fills the under floor with very cold water and keeps it colder for longer into summer (we hope) we should be able to store fresh meat longer in there in the summer, well we'll see. We put a hole in the slats so milk and a few beers and such can sit in the cold water. My worry is that we may see too much mold down there when all the ice melts and summer comes on strong.

Before the snow even melted a new neighbor down below started putting up fences all around the lake area. The village was all a buzz with frustration. Then the big house goes up and people are very interested in it, some even sat in boats and watched the building of it. It's a three story place with a big porch around and plaster walls and wainscoting and lots of fancy things. They must have had 40 men come to build it, brought everything they needed and put it up in no time. Then when it was done the new owners showed up. Name of Tom Monrow and family.

So, they had this big party and the whole village went and everyone was excited, well not everyone. At the party he asks a few men by name to come into his game room or his office (not sure which, conflit'n stories) and the men are happy, think'n they were gonna play some pool, until he tells them they have 3 weeks to vacate their homes. It seems they were a little late on a few payments and he bought their mortgages. He wants their land because it's the best in the valley for grazing. (But it's a big valley and that's hard to believe, I'm think'n he just wants to cause trouble) two of the men leave say'n they will be going to Johnstown or even Pittsburgh to straighten things out, but the other guy, old Lars Koskinen well he just punched the man square in the face. The party was over at that point. The men say they were never more than a week or two off on payments.

This is the first spring that Trapper Earl hadn't stopped, I miss the man, all those funny stories. I hope and pray he's doing well. Summer is the best season here in the mountains. The windows and doors are open and the breeze is cool and the river is over full, rushing and loud.

Read a meaningful verse this morning and a few Psalms, feeling up-lifted.

# Chapter 7

Hamish rode up the path to the hunt lodge in a hurry, he was pulling the new horse 'Number Three', she was bred for mountains, or so Ed was told. They ordered it first of spring and it wasn't cheap but she was a beauty. He ran in looking for Jersey but he wasn't there. After unloading and bedding down the new Number Three he sat on the front porch and read until he couldn't see, at dusk Jersey road in.

"Did you hear the news?" Hamish asked.

"I don't know, what is it?"

"Lars Koskinen is dead, face down in the lake near his house. Betty and the family are grieve'n somethin awful. He had two daughters you know, they's married with kids."

Jersey said nothing but Hamish could tell he was thinking as he lead Blue to the big bucket of water on the corner of the porch then unloaded.

"Coffee on?"

"Yeah, well what do you think?" Hamish said.

"I didn't know Lars very well, but I think the first move was just made."

"I think so too. Well Lars threw a good punch at that party, but that man was try'n to take his land. So, what can we do?"

"Hey, we get the new horse?" Jersey asked.

"Ah, yeah she's a beauty."

Jersey stepped sideways looking into the pen.

"Oh, she looks very good."

"What can we do?" Hamish asked.

"Train her."

"No, no about Lars Koskinen."

"Eaten yet?" Jersey asked.

"No wait'n."

"Good, let's talk while we eat, I'm empty."

Jersey sat at the fire running a wooden spoon through the hanging pot of beans.

"These look good you can go ahead and toss the fish on."

Hamish cooked the fish in butter, adding a few of the early herbs in the mix.

"Well?" he said.

"You remember that drawing of me that was in the trading post?"

"The one you made them take down and never ever, ever put back up?"

Jersey rolled his eyes and said, "yes, that's the one. Anyways, who drew that, it was pretty good wasn't it?"

"This is what you been think'n on? We need to come up with some kind of revenge for Lars."

"Are you say'n he was murdered? Do you know that for a fact?" Jersey asked.

"Well not for a fact. I guess we need to find proof, but what if we can't find any? It can't be happenstance, not after he punched Tom Monrow in the nose." Hamish said.

"So, who drew that drawing of me?"

"Abby, okay—Abby drew it, would you like me to get it framed for you? We can put it on the wall, or better yet how about the mantle?" Hamish said.

He held out his plate and Jersey scooped beans onto it then put some on his own plate.

"Was Abby at Tom Monrow's party?"

"I believe so."

"Good, let's take a ride down there tomorrow," Jersey said.

Hamish shook his head, "I hope this is part of a plan."

"It is," Jersey looked up.

"Old man this fish is perfect."

"So," Hamish smiled then said, "wall or mantle?"

"I'm think'n mantle."

# Chapter 8

After looking over the murder scene and giving condolences to the widow, they went to Abby's house and found her hanging laundry in the breeze off the lake. Her father was just heading out in the boat with a friend and waved. She smiled, big eyed and happy to see Jersey, she credited him with saving her life—at the very least her innocence.

"Abby, do you think you could make a drawing of the new neighbor Tom Monrow? Just his face. Do you think you can remember his face to make it look just like him?" Jersey asked.

She picked up the empty basket and turned to them, tilted her head thinking.

"Yes I think so. It would be better if I could see him again. But, why would you want a drawing of that man? He's bad," she said.

Well, I want to get a few of them delivered to the nearby law offices, to see if he's on a list, you know a list of bad men."

Her small collar was slightly open, and the wind blew her long blond hair off her shoulder and both men were smitten. Hamish sucked in his stomach and thought of how one year can change a young woman so much. Ed Junior called from the street between houses and she lit up like a sunny day, waving to him. When she turned back she looked a little embarrassed. "Oh—ah yes, I'll start on it today, if it looks good enough I'll leave it at the trading post for you. Did you say you want more than one?"

"Yes please, three would be good," Jersey said, "Oh, and don't tell anyone and wrap them up so they don't know what it is at the post. It's important not to let it out that a drawing of him is being sent out."

The back door of the house opened, Abby's mother came out determined rushing to Hamish.

"Now Hamish I ask you to get Jersey down here a year on now."

She had an accent from Sweden or near there; she held a measuring tape in one hand and a notebook in the other.

"Abby you take down dees numbers as I calls dem out," she said.

"Yes'm,"

Abby took a lead pencil from her mother's hair and stood ready. The woman looked up at Jersey for a minute, then said to Hamish, "We will need a bit more leather than I thought."

She reached up to Jersey's chest and stretched the tape from shoulder to shoulder and called out a number in another language. Jersey looked at Hamish with his, it's time to go face.

The woman looked at Hamish, "you don't tell him?" she said.

Hamish dropped his head a little and said, "no ma'am."

She stepped back and looked way up into Jersey's eyes and told him she was going to make him a very nice coat, she'd seen one on a lawman back east and it was fancy but manly and rugged. Jersey looked back at Hamish who nodded and smiled. The woman was back to calling out numbers and roughly handling Jersey's arm.

"Well that's very nice ma'am but..." he said.

"No—no but!" she practically yelled.

"Not fancy ma'am, please—not fancy," Jersey said.

"He would like it practical, Jersey's not the fancy type," Hamish said.

She started to twist him around but decided to just walk to the other side and called out a few more strange sounding numbers.

"Okay, no fancy—practical. Yes? Practical?" she repeated.

Jersey looked over his shoulder at her. "Yes, thank you."

# Chapter 9

Hamish was at the trading post, he'd just settled up with Ed when they heard the news about the Smith home on the river.

"Jersey's gonna be angry," Ed Junior said.

"That'd be truth," Ed's wife said.

Hamish felt sick, conflict was a day or two off.

"Someone should warn him," Ed Junior's brother said.

"I guess it'd be the Christian thing to do, but I doubt he's a Christian."

Everyone mumbled in agreement.

Junior's brother looked around the room. "Yeah, he's been up in the hills and doesn't know what Mr. Monrow's like."

"Wait—you," Ed chuckled. "You mean warn Jersey?"

Everyone laughed.

Jersey and Hamish sat on the porch of their old house on the river; there was a notice on the door that informed them to keep out and that Tom Monrow & company now owned it. The door had been opened but nothing seemed to be out of place, all the window boards were still up. Apparently they had two weeks to vacate. Hamish could tell Jersey was steaming mad, but as usual he was holding it in. Jersey took the notice down, folded it, and put it in his saddlebag.

They'd visited the graves but now it was getting cold. They didn't want a fire for fear of smoke being seen. The sun was setting, and a few stars were shining through the darkening sky. It was one thing Hamish missed living in the hills, all the trees seem to keep them closed in up there, not like here in the wide open. There were trees and little hills out here but far enough away that you could see around.

"I miss this Jersey," he said.

"Yeah, me too. Used to enjoy sitting here with the kids play'n or Catherine reading a book to them."

"Heck, she was reading to all of us," Hamish said.

"I reckon she was," he started to tear up, "what a woman," he said low and soft.

They were waiting for Roger and his friends to show up. Hamish started to say something but Jersey raised his hand and turned his ear to the open yard, the river and beyond.

"They're coming," he said.


By the next afternoon word had spread that miles of fencing had been cut, and not just taken down, but taken away. Cattle and horses were roaming freely through the valley. They offered a reward for information, everyone knew who did it, but they would never tell. They weren't sure how he did so much damage in one night, but if anyone could do it, it was him. Jersey knew the man would figure it was him, he counted on it. But he worried that the man would use Hamish to get to him. He needed to stay close to home, ride along with him to the trading post, and keep his eyes open.

That morning they'd gotten in early when the sky was dim and the sun was still below the horizon. They slept for a few hours but were too worked up to sleep more. They knew the gossip would be spreading, so they went down to the trading post for afternoon coffee and a beer.

Ed brought out a package for Jersey and they sat at an outside table in the little courtyard and looked at the drawing. They both agreed it was a very good rendering and called Ed out.

"Look Ed," Jersey said. "We got a situation here."

He nodded to Hamish who slid the folded wrapped paper across the table to Ed.

"Ah, we was wondering what was in this," Ed said.

He pulled out the drawing and said, "well that's Tom Monrow, what the hey Jersey."

"We need to get these to Johnstown and Union, and any other Sheriff's office as far as Pittsburgh if we have to. Problem is we need to find someone to take them, in fact I think we need two men," Jersey said.

"So, you think he's a wanted man?"

"Don't know, worth a try," Jersey said.

"He has to be, you can't be this awful and not have a past," Hamish said.

"Well I can get two men, hell we'll send Junior, then we only need to get one more."

"We can't let anyone know about this," Jersey said.

"If Tom Monrow finds out, and if he is wanted, no tell'n what he'd do," Hamish said.

Three men from the village rode in, tied their rides off, and came up to the table. Junior came out to see what was going on. They were smiling and looked at Jersey and he smiled and nodded to them.

"Well, what's the latest men?" Ed asked.

"Tom Monrow and five men are riding through looking for the people responsible, go'n door to door."

"Responsible for what?" Hamish said with a straight face.

Everyone looked at Jersey, he almost spit out his beer and they all laughed.

"Can I use your telescope Jersey?" Junior asked.

Jersey nodded, and he ran to Blue and got it from a small case stitched to the saddlebag. Ed Junior ran up the side stairs to the valley overlook which was on top of the trading post, he aimed his view down the little hill at the lake village.

"Yep, they're at the Johnson's place," Junior said.

"Hmm, could be head'n here next," Ed said.

The men and Ed walked away from the table talking, then they came back.

"You two should go," Ed said.

"I think maybe they're right Jersey," Hamish said.

"Think I'll finish my beer."

He rarely had more than one beer in a sitting and was stubborn about finishing this one.

"Yeah, but we need to get, here let me help with..."

Hamish reached for the beer but Jersey gave him a look.

"You head back old man," he said, "in fact that's the best thing, I got a few things to say to this guy."

Junior came down the stairs and said, "yeah they're a com'in here, on the way up the path now."

The locals almost bumped into each other looking for a place to sit. They needed a spot where they would be out of harm's way, look natural like, but still have a good view of the goings on.

Jersey asked Junior, "when you put the spyglass away can you bring my saddle Colt back with you?"

Jersey stood leaning on the end of a long outside table which was against the side of the trading post wall. Ed's wife came around the corner with a tray of drinks when Tom Monrow and his men rode in. They kind of stopped for a moment, surprised to see Jersey leaning there. They continued past the hitching post scattering chickens and clopping loudly on the stone walkway. Ed's wife dropped the tray on the men's table then rushed back inside. The riders all looked at Jersey as they slowly moved in, they were huge in the enclosed area.

"I know you're upset Mr. Monrow but you need to tie your horses off at the hitch there," Ed said.

Two of the men rode a few feet past Jersey, they stopped, and all turned to face him in a kind of half circle. The large patio area seemed small now, filled with mounted horses. They were very close to Jersey, so a few of them backed up, their hind quarters hovering over the tables opposite, and the men had to reconsider their seating arrangements.

"What's all this?" Jersey said.

He took a long sip and looked at each man carefully from between his beer tankard and his hat's brim.

"I got some missing fence..."

Jersey interrupted the man. "No..." he looked concerned, "that a fact?"

Jersey set his beer on the table and stood upright, his left hand hung by his thumb in his belt near his front gun and his right was mighty close to the back gun.

"Well, how can we help?" Jersey asked.

"I'd like to know who did it," Tom said.

"Well—if'n I hear anything I'll let you know."

Tom Monrow revealed a small nervous smile and said, "I think I've had enough of this."

He nodded to the man on the end, the one Jersey had picked out as the first to go down. The man sat up in the saddle his hand sliding for his gun. When Tom Monrow turned back, Jersey had both guns out, one pointing at his head and the other at the man on the end.

"I'm detecting some hostility here, how about you old man?" Jersey asked.

The sound of a shotgun's large hammer locking into position came from behind.

"I'm feel'n something," Hamish said, "I'm start'n to question these men's intent."

"You know, Hamish has been dying to try out that new shotgun."

Everyone was still for a moment, one of his men started to say something, they heard another hammer clicking into place.

"Oh yeah, it's one of them double barrel guns," he looked at the row of men, "if any of you survive this you can say you had a friend who was shot by a fine English Samuel and Charles ten bore game gun," Jersey said.

"State-of-the-art," Hamish added.

Tom held his hands out to calm his men down.

"Well," he paused, "if'n you hear anything you come'n tell me, okay?" Tom Monrow said.

He nodded to his men, they slowly turned and rode to the end of the patio.

"Oh Tom," Jersey said.

He walked to the nearest man as he unfolded the notice from the door of his house handing it to the man.

He looked at Tom Monrow with anger, "this won't do." Jersey said.

The young man tried to hand the paper to Tom, but he hit it to the ground and gave him an angry look as he nudged his horse on.

On the way back Jersey told Hamish how surprised he was that Tom Monrow took it that far in front of witnesses.

"You know, after killing Lars Koskinen you'd think he'd lay low a bit. But, I'm glad it was just us that pulled guns today, it does put us in his sights, but only us," Jersey said.

"So you think he'll be coming soon?"

Jersey turned in his saddle, "Very soon."

# Chapter 10

They stacked firewood around the porch just high enough to see over from a chair and boarded the windows. Outback they cleared a path for a run to the hills with scattered woodpiles for added cover on the way. They took turns sleeping four hours at a time, while the other watched from the porch, only coming in to refill coffee, eat, and warm up at the fireplace. Duke came walking up after two days gone, and stood watch with them.

After four days on the lookout, Hamish woke Jersey. "Someones come'n."

Jersey sat up quickly, "how far out?"

"Just made the turn off the main trail."

They followed the agreed upon plan then waited. Nothing was going on out back as best they could see. Five men rode in, each had a badge on his lapel and they didn't seem at all stealth-like. The oldest of them yelled out. "Is this the place of Jersey Smith?"

They weren't familiar, so Jersey waited.

"We're looking for Jersey Smith, anyone in there know where he is?"

"Who's ask'n?" Jersey said.

He was behind the house but with the steep incline back there and with the sound of the river in their ears they couldn't tell where he was. Their horses shuffled as they looked around, some even looked up at the mountain beyond the roof of the house.

"Marshal Wagner—I am, and these four men are sworn deputies."

"What do you want with Jersey?"

They were surprised and kind of taken-a-back to see a man standing just off the corner of the porch.

"Ah, Mister Smith we're glad to see you. We're on the trail of a man you know as Tom Monrow," the Marshal said.

He was very fit for his age and well dressed, a younger man might look a dandy in the same clothes, but he looked to be a man tried, tested, and come out on top. His gray hair trimmed tight under a round and low crowned dark gray hat with a similar colored handkerchief tight around his neck. He reached inside his light gray vest and pulled out a piece of paper, unfolded it, and held it out for Jersey to see. Hamish came out from the other side of the house, the shotgun across his chest. Jersey walked in front of the men and took the paper.

"It's a legal warrant for a man," he said to Hamish.

Jersey looked back at the Marshal. "This man is a Tom but it says nothing about Tom Monrow."

"No, Monrow's not his real name, a Sheriff in Johnstown matched your drawing to a man in a warrant from back east," the Marshal said.

"Why are you up here and not after the man, whatever his name is?" Hamish asked.

"Well sir, he saw us coming and high-tailed it with a few of his men, ran to the hills. We were told if we want to get him outta there we should seek your assistance. So, we would like to ask you to give us a hand, we can pay you for your time. Seems like these hills are full of ambush points," the Marshal said.

"Where did he enter the hills?"

"About a mile north, it was a winding trail where we ran into a man that pointed us here."

"I'll get him," Jersey said, "and I'll bring him down to you, but I'll do it alone, it's faster this way,"

"There's six of 'em."

"Only one of them worth worrying about, besides they'll split up," Jersey said.

"You know that for a fact?" one of them asked.

"I would, wouldn't you," Jersey said.

"I spec," the Marshal looked around thinking, "at least take Jim here he's the best we got."

Jersey looked at the man they called Jim, he looked capable enough.

Then he said, "no complaining."

"I won't, if'n you won't," Jim said.

Jersey liked that answer but tried not to show it.

"How's your food supply?"

"What?" Jim said.

"How many days of food do you have with you?"

The Marshal spoke up, "our supply horse got loose in the chase, take a few hours to retrieve it."

"Okay, we got food," Jersey said.

"One of them has a distinctive crack in his shoe," Jim said.

"And you saw this in the tracks?"

Jim nodded. Jersey looked at Hamish and said, "old man," he looked back at the Marshal, "I don't mean you sir." He looked at Hamish, "can you get us two days of trail food and water together? While I get Blue saddled up."

"For how many?"

"Better make it three, I'm hope'n we run into Roger," Jersey said.

Hamish walked to the front door when the Marshal spoke up, "that's a mighty fine shotgun you have there."

Hamish turned slowly and said, "it's Jerseys"

Jersey stood up straight, took his hat off and scratched his head, put his hat back on, looked at the

Marshal then said, "is there anything you want to say about my Samuel & Charles?"

The Marshal stared at Jersey for a few seconds then smiled and said, "I always enjoy seeing a fine gun like that."

"Well, thank you. Now we're fix'n to get, so—is that all you got to say on the subject?" Jersey asked.

The Marshal took an uncomfortable swallow and said, "ah, yes—yes it is."

Jersey nodded to Hamish who then went inside to pack food for the trail.

Jersey walked along his porch looking at each man's setup and told one of them to give Jim his bed roll.

"What?" the young man said.

"Just do it son," the Marshal said.

"Now you men can head back down the path you came, turn left at the first trail..." he paused. "No wait, take Hamish with you he'll show you. It's the trading post, they have bunks and food and we'll bring Tom Monrow back there."

"I want him alive Jersey, I heard tell of some of your adventures," the Marshal said.

"I never killed a man that wasn't try'n to kill me or someone else, and I never will,"

The Marshal saw the look on his face and said, "okay—okay, the stories never said you were a murderer. Still, I'd like to talk to this man, he has a great deal of cash hidden somewhere and the owner would like it back. I left two men at his ranch looking for it, but he's a smart man I don't think it's there."

"Most likely spent, he's been buy'n up the valley and built that over-sized house," Jersey said.

"I spec that's possible."

"I can't guarantee the condition of Tom Monrow or whoever he is." He looked up at the Marshal, "I'll do my best," he said.

One of the other men spoke up, "well what are we here for? We came to help get this outlaw."

"And that's what we're doing," the Marshal said. "Jersey you head'n over the top?"

"I am."

"We'll cover this side along the foothills, they may come back down—not go over at all," the Marshal said. "We'll keep to the foothill all along here, and in the hills to the south."

Jersey nodded, "this next trail over, that you just crossed, it winds its way to the top and there's a well-worn path up there, but be careful as you said lots of good ambush spots. And take enough food and water, and keep your eyes peeled for bear, they're usually fine but don't get betwixt mother and cub. Also, there's a group of Natives in that area, they're good men, use my name. Ask for Roger, if he's there send him in my direction," Jersey said.

He looked at the group as they scanned the steep hills beyond the roof of the house. Everyone but Jim, he was smiling at Jersey Smith.

# Chapter 11

They took the little path east behind the lodge winding up the side for a while, turning north onto the halfway trail.

"This is very beautiful country out here," Jim said.

"Yes, it is. Can you use that gun?" Jersey asked.

"Yes."

"How about the rifle, is it sighted in?"

"Yes."

"Well, if Tom Monrow is as smart as the Marshal says he is, and if he has five men, I'm think'n he'll try to set a trap using a few of those men. Keep your eyes wide and ears open," Jersey said.

"You think we'll have to spend the night up here?" Jim asked.

"Probably, I hope not, but track'n a man ain't easy up here and you can't rush it."

Jersey turned in his saddle, looked at Jim to give importance, "you need to keep look'n around even behind us. Never stop look'n in all directions and if you see anything, *anything*, just say my name and the direction for me to look. Got it?"

"Yes sir, I got it."

"If they think we see them they'll start shoot'n, so we keep rid'n like we're unaware till we have cover then we'll dismount," Jersey said.

"I understand," Jim said.

They traveled north for a while, as they got higher the trail took a sharp turn south as it twisted up the side of the mountain. Jersey thought about a pass or two that went over the top farther north, and ruled them out as too far away. He thought he knew where they'd go over because of a few good ambush points, and it was nearby.

"There it is," Jim said.

He jumped off his horse and knelt down touching the dent in the hard ground with his finger.

"We found them," he said.

"Very good Jim, only one trail from here going in that direction," Jersey said.

Jersey got down and took a close look at the mark on the ground. He looked in the direction the print was heading and had a good idea where they were going.

"Well, let's go."

They turned up another rung where there was a stretch of fairly level ground heading directly east. After a few minutes Blue's ears perked up. Duke was up the trail he twisted his head looking back at Jersey, who raised his hand, they stopped. He let out a low deep whistle and Duke came back looking up at Jersey; he sat for a moment but anxiously turned his head in the direction of their distraction. They were on a section of trail that had the advantage of being a bit more level. It headed straight for a while too, but ahead the terrain got steep and the path went up, it had a hard turn north along one of the top stone ridges.

"What is it?" Jim said.

"Not sure yet, noise is bounce'n off the rocks."

They sat listening for a minute, Jersey heard something. Duke stood up turning in the noise's direction, but he kept looking back at Jersey to get the okay to run after whatever it was.

"Keep look'n around, could be an ambush," Jersey said.

Jim sat silent, looking intently in every direction.

They got off the horses. Jim tied his to a tree just off the path and Blue stood next to it.

"Better bring your rifle," Jersey said, he looked at Jim's rifle, "better yet, grab my Sharps it has a strap, and get the little box next to it, it'll fit in the stock wrap."

Jim looked at it for a minute then slipped them together and over his shoulder. Jersey nodded acknowledging he didn't have to instruct him. They walked a ways up the path with Duke on a leash, Jersey stopped looking at the terrain. The trail went up out of sight under and beyond the trees ahead. Above the trees though was a high cliff formation that Jersey recognized, it was an area he avoided.

"The path ahead takes a hard turn north where it meets the wall," Jersey pointed. "It's where I'd guess they'll be waiting."

He looked through the trees at the high rocks near the top and shook his head. Jim could see he was thinking about something. Jersey looked across the path up at the ridge just to the south.

"I think we got an ambush up there," he paused looking close. "Hard to tell through the trees," Jersey said.

He pointed, and Jim looked.

"Lot a places to hide up there," Jim said

"Yeah, we need to keep those trees between us and the ridge. I'm gonna climb a tree and get a better look, stand ready in that direction."

Jersey looked the ground over and carefully stepped off the path where he thought he would make the least noise and started up a tree. At each foothold he looked in every direction before moving farther up. He saw them, ducking his head down, he moved to a lower branch, sliding to the other side. Slowly he peeked up over a branch, they were on the next plateau just after the turn where the steep path ended. They sat talking low in a small pocket at the base of the wall. Jersey was lower than them and farther away than he'd expected. He couldn't be sure but it looked like them. He climbed down to a low branch.

"I think it's them," he said quietly down to Jim.

"How about over there?" Jim asked.

He was pointing to the high ridge to the south where an ambush was likely.

Jersey said as quietly as possible, "Too many trees, can't see that way, keep your eyes over there."

Jersey looked back down the path and made a few clicks with his tongue off the roof of his mouth and Blue started walking up the path to them.

"Get my spy glass from the small case on the side of the saddlebag and toss it up."

Blue walked up next to Jim and he found the telescope. Jersey let out a very low whistle, like blowing over the top of a bottle, Blue walked backwards a few steps and waited there. Jim carefully got under the tree and tossed it up.

Jersey could see them clearly and Tom Monrow was not there, just two of his men. It was a trap. He climbed down and talked with Jim as they walked back to Jim's horse.

"The only way up is the path, any other way is through the rough and they'll hear us come'n. We need to take out the one on the cliff first," Jersey said.

"Are you sure there's someone over there?"

"Yeah—has to be, this is the only path, and it turns right into those men. Why else would they camp next to a turn in a trail like that? Once we made that turn they'd have us."

"How many are up there?" Jim asked.

"Just two, Tom Monrow ain't one of them, but they are his men.

"Why don't I sneak up and take out whoever is over

there, while you ride in and nail them two, or we could wait till dark?"

Jersey was thinking through things.

"Wait'n for dark's not an option, Monrow's already covered too much ground and we're just standing here. Na—the longer we wait the farther away Monrow is get'n," Jersey said.

"Okay, how do we get up there?" Jim asked.

"Well, let's head back down the path a bit, fifty yards or so, so's they can't hear us trudge through the rough, we'll head over to that clearing, you can just see the light through the trees."

Jersey pointed into the forest to the south as they started walking.

"It's where a big section of rocks fell and took down everything in its path. We can make our way to the top of that ridge, from there we can see over them find out how many there are and come up with a plan," Jersey said.

"Leave the horses on the trail?"

"Yeah."

They tied Jim's horse and Duke to Blue's saddle horn, watered and fed them so they wouldn't make too much noise.

"So, what's the Samuel and Charles Smith shotgun like?" Jim asked.

"What?"

"The Samuel and Charles, must be nice," Jim said.

Jersey was folding Blue's leather drinking cup inside out and putting it away.

"The one they talked about in court."

"What are you on about?"

"Yeah, at the trial of Bucky Murray."

"Buck Murray, the molester?" Jersey asked.

They stepped off the path and headed south.

"Now don't step on any sticks, the sound carries,"

"Yeah, they's only a few of that gang left now. You know, his brother was at the trial, course we didn't know it was him at the time. But after the verdict was said, that night he got drunk at the Red Dog and started talking out loud about killing you and getting Samuel and Charles back. Course I didn't know Samuel and Charles was a gun at the time, thought it was some of their friends. Oh, and..." Jim paused.

Jersey stepped over a fallen tree and turned to Jim. "And what?"

"Well, he was say'n how he was gonna cut you up in little pieces."

"Hmm, did he say how little?"

"Nah. But then he said he was Bucky's brother. Well, the men with him pulled him out'a there in a hurry, and by the time the Marshal found out they was gone."

"What was this brother's name?"

"Ah that was Robert, but I hear'd one of them call him Bobby."

"How many men were with him?"

"Oh, not sure, maybe four. They say they's six left in the gang."

Jersey looked at the treetops and shook his head. "Great, why didn't the Marshal say anything about this?"

"He told us not to say anything till we was done, I guess he didn't want you distracted."

"Hmm, I think a warning would just be common courtesy. Distracted huh."

"Oh, also there was of talk of sending a few men from court to come for the bandits guns-n-such, I guess they sell'em and that's how the judge gets extra money for judge'n, but no one wanted to face you after the stories they heard in the courthouse."

"Stories?"

"Yeah, the kill'n and all. Oh, and they heard you said someth'n bout, 'if the Sheriff has a problem with it tell him where I live.'"

"Mm?" Jersey turned and looked at Jim. "Well, the way you tell it, it does sound a bit intimidat'n." Jersey looked at him for a long second, "let's keep moving."

Jersey turned and moved quickly, Jim took a few big steps to catch up.

"Can you climb?" Jersey asked.

"I guess—will we need to?"

"Yes."


The clearing was a cut through the mountainside, everything got bright and open. Light gray shale pieces in every size spread across from the tree line on both sides down a few hundred yards where it disappeared over a cliff. A small creek ran down the middle and boulders were strewn about.

Jim looked up at the high outcropping where the rubble had fallen from. "Hmm, I guess we are going to climb."

"I know this section here, it gets steep but I think I know a good way up," Jersey said.

Jim was unsure as he stepped on loose shale chips. He followed Jersey across the creek as they headed up the incline.

"Stick to the grass over here and off the loose rocks, but keep watch for bears, they like this area, caves-n-all."

Jim got more attentive. After a while Jersey looked down at him and signaled to keep quiet. They'd reached an area below the ridge where things had become very steep. Jersey moved around a small waterfall, then a few boulders and found a well-worn path. They zigzagged around and under thick stone slices until they got to a plateau. Jim looked out over treetops at the vast valley below and distant mountains.

"We should be above and just south of where they are," Jersey said.

They walked along a rock ledge, a steep drop-off was on the left and the mountains top section to their right almost within reach. They hunched over, moving fast and quiet, until Jersey stopped. He lifted his hand then moved the rest of the way on his hands and knees. Jim crawled up close, as they both looked over the edge.

There was only one man down there. They rolled over onto their backs resting, looking at the sky, and talked over options.

"He's in a tight little spot there," Jim said.

"Yeah, in a pocket of rock but low enough to see over. Guess I'll..."

The man below said something like 'who's that,' they heard a whistle. They rolled over took off their hats and moved to the edge. The gunman stood up and stretched, his arms reaching up high and head leaned back, they ducked for fear of being seen. They heard talking, so they moved back, one of the other men walked into the lookout area.

"My turn."

"Bout time dam-it."

He picked up his gun and started to leave as the other one moved into position. The new man set his rifle against a boulder and lit a smoke.

"I thought we wasn't to smoke over here, just at the fire."

"I do what I want. I'm sick of this job. Get'n chased down for noth'n and now were pertect'n him while he gets away."

"Yeah but we're meet'n back up, get'n paid."

"Yeah, I'll believe that when I see it."

Jersey and Jim rolled away from the edge.

"You stay up here, keep the rifle on him, if I get in trouble kill him. Can you do that?"

"Yeah but I thought we weren't shoot'n?"

"I'd rather they get shot than us," Jersey said.

"Oh, right."

"If'n that happens, have at the other two but just wing um, remember we need to find out where Tom Monrow is heading," Jersey said.

Jersey made his way back down, Jim found a spot a few yards farther, he stood between two small trees with the Sharps aiming down. After a few minutes Jim saw the man move quickly and become alerted by something. The man looked over the edge, he said in a loud whisper, "who's down there."

Another whistle came from farther below and the man seemed to ease up and leaned against the rock wall. He was lighting another smoke when Jersey stepped into the little recess. He raised his hands and turn to yell but was stopped by a big knife in his side thrown from twenty feet. He let out a moan as Jersey ran to him, put the man's hat on, took a pull off his cigarette and stood up to be seen by the other men. He blew smoke in the air and looked at them. They were now standing looking in his direction, Jersey held his hands up like 'what's the problem' and they sat back down.


Jersey turned and wiped his brow, he knelt at the hurt man and sat him up as best he could. He looked under the man's shirt; it was a terrible wound.

"Now you know, this is the end," he said.

The man nodded, he was sweating and having a hard

time keeping his eyes open.

"You can do something good right now by tell'n me where Tom Monrow is head'n."

He seemed to want to talk but Jersey could hear gurgling as he spoke.

"Take small breaths," Jersey said.

He labored to speak. "Tom said to meet at the next town, just over this here top, in the valley."

He coughed blood and his eyes rolled. Jersey recognized him from the beer garden at the trading post.

"But," he coughed again, "he's a lie'n S.O.B. and he could be anywhere. I think he's head'n east, make a new start."

Jersey took a rolled cigarette from the man's shirt pocket, lit it and put it in his mouth.

"You're just an outlaw."

The man's eyes looked down at the ground, "Yeah—I did some bad things."

"Well, you work for a man like that you can expect no good to come from it. Why work for him?" Jersey asked.

The man shook his head. "Mmm—money." He was slurring his words, it was hard to talk, "my last mistake."

He chuckled, spit more blood, leaned on his side and moaned, "Oh Lord."

Jim whisped from above. "Should I come down?"

Jersey was feeling the man's pulse at his neck and held a finger up to Jim. After a minute Jersey stood, motioned as shooting a rifle at the other two men, then pointed to Jim.

Jim nodded, "I got a clear shot."

Jersey lifted the man up between two rocks and put his rifle in plain view. He cupped his hands at his mouth and said up to Jim, "Drop your sidearm down."

Jim pulled his gun, held it by the barrel and let it fall, Jersey caught it, looked at it and placed it in his belt.

He looked back up at Jim. "This will take a few minutes."
Jim nodded again then left for his new spot.

Jersey found the path that led to the main trail. When he got to the turn he could see them sitting at the fire talking. He moved closer slowly stopping at each concealing tree. He made it to the place where he would make his move and pulled both guns. They were facing each other on either side of the fire, one's back was to Jersey. When he stepped out in the open, one of them stood up walking to a pile of collected wood. They were now apart which made for a more difficult situation. Jersey worried if the man at the pile of sticks was even visible to Jim now, but he had to say something before he turned and saw him standing there.

"It's over boys," Jersey said.

They jumped a bit. The man at the fire stood, they each touched their guns, they heard Jersey's guns click ready for action; they froze. Jersey was standing with arms outstretched and a gun aiming at each man.

"Now I'm tell'n you, don't be stupid, your friend up there is dead."

They both looked to see.

The man at the fire spun around yelling. "You killed my brother?" He bent down low and drew.

In the tick of a time piece Jersey squeezed back on the trigger of his Colt Navy which let loose the spring held hammer, it hit the powder cap with force and the cap caught fire. The 20 grains of black powder exploded in the small chamber, the round lead mini ball had only one way to go. Its path was determined its mark was met. The man lifted over the fire and spun to the ground. Blue-gray smoke puffed cloud like, hanging in the still air around him. Jersey was looking at the other man before the recoil was done. The man's gun was half raised as

Jersey redirected his aim, giving the man a determined look. But smoke pushed out from the outlaw's barrel it briefly followed a speeding lead ball. Jersey heard it go by as it plowed through the brush behind him.

Before the man could bring his gun down from the recoil Jersey had both guns on him. "Well, this would be a good time to toss that gun away, and—make it slow."

The man had stopped cold, gun still aiming at the treetops. Jersey could tell he was thinking about making his move.

"If by some fluke of nature you hit me before I hit you, I have a friend up there on the ridge with a Sharps aimed at your head."

The man didn't move.

"Jim!" Jersey yelled.

"Yeah," came the reply from above.

By the time Jim got there Jersey had both men secure on their horses and was dragging the lookout man by the boots down the path from the ridge.

"Trouble get'n down?" Jersey asked.

Jim nodded, "I almost died twice."

"Help get this one over the saddle and tied off."

They walked to the trail, turned down to the steep incline, and Jersey made two short but loud whistles. After a minute they heard, then saw the horses and Duke running up the path.

"You have to head back down with these," Jersey said.

"What? I don't want to, you need my help," Jim said.

Jersey was checking each horse's shoes.

"Yeah I truly do, but we can't leave-um up here, bear country and we can't take um with us."

"Can't you have Blue lead'm back?"

"You've been a good man to have along." He paused. "Well, no offense but I'd rather have Blue along than most any man, he's saved me a few times over."

"Yeah," Jim held his hat up and scratched his head.
"Guess I'd do the same."

"Time you get back it'll just be get'n dark, by then I'll
be over the ridge."

Jim pointed to the horses. "One of these with the
gouge in its shoe?" Jim asked.

"No, we got lucky," Jersey said.

"You think you know where Tom Monrow is head'n?"

"That outlaw said he'd be wait'n on them in a little
town in the next valley. I been there, it's called Milford. If
I'm not back in three days, tell the Marshal to head over
there, then up to the pass and follow the tracks due east."

# Chapter 12

It was dusk when Jim rode into the village. The distant sky over the lake was deep red, long thin clouds were bottom lit and glowing. He came off the hills from the north where Tom Monrow had gone in. He talked with a few people on the way through the lake village; they led him to Ed's Trading Post.

Ed walked out smiling. "Where's Jersey?"

"Still up there, these here were try'n to ambush us."

"Mm—still up there huh?" Ed said.

He looked up at the mountain behind his building the last rays of sun lit its upper most trees.

"Marshal here?"

"Nah."

"Did the Marshal find the money at the ranch?" Jim asked.

"No, they tore that place apart. You know it wasn't even his family," Ed said.

"What?"

"Yeah, they was get'n paid to act it out. So after believing that they knew nothing about his villainous ways the Marshal let all the house people ride on out."

"I hope Jersey gets him, only a few left," Jim said.

"He will, outta all the men he's gone after, only one he ain't caught," Ed said.

"Yeah, who was that?"

"Oh—that's the one story we don't talk about," Ed said.

Ed looked beyond Jim up at the north star, bright in the dark blue sky. The sun was below the horizon now.

He looked at the dark hills and thought about Jersey having no problem sleeping up there, he got a chill and looked at Jim. "Help me get the dead in to the root cellar."

The Marshal was still out searching the foothills and valley to the south, two of his other men were up in the hills heading in a southward direction. Ed booked Jim a bunk and got him dinner and put it all on the new account for the Marshal. The Trading Post was glowing in lantern light, Ed had the center stove going to take the nip off. The prisoner sat at a central table cuffed to a thick chain which was wrapped over a log rafter. A few regulars from the lake came and looked him over as they talked, drank, and listened to Jim's account of the days chase and capture.

The Marshal returned around noon the next day and was glad to see Jim but disappointed that Jersey was still out there and Tom Monrow was still at large. He was considering wrapping it up and heading back empty-handed, at least without Tom Monrow, but Ed and a few locals told him of their confidence in Jersey. They offered him a vacant cottage on the lake for his service as a lawman while he waited.

He accepted and over the next two days he'd ironed out every argument and disagreement they had. He took a liking to one of the single women and his men wondered if he was heading back at all. But he needed to get the bodies and the captive to an undertaker and a jail. So he had his men take them back, all but Jim.

The Marshal roamed around the area helping and talking with the people. He spent late afternoons watching the sunset on the lake with new friends. Evenings were spent at the Trading Post talking, sipping coffee, and snacking on meat pies. When Jersey didn't get back by the deadline, the Marshal give him one more day.   Well—maybe two.

# Chapter 13

Jersey stood near the top of the eastern slope at dusk. He hoped Roger had heard the gunfire earlier, so once he found a spot for the night he signaled to him one last time. It was a long shot that he was within seeing or hearing distance.

The little town of Milford was miles away, north through the valley. He lit a fire and sat with Duke sleeping at his side. Blue was eating from a feed bag hung between trees and the stars seemed as close as they'd ever been. As with times alone like this he thought about Catherine, the kids, and his other life and how different things would have been if not for men like the one he was chasing.

A noise came from up the hill, Jersey hoped it was a friend. He heard a strange whistle, like no bird he'd heard before.

"That's funny Roger."

"Don't want to get shot," Roger said from a ridge above.

Jersey stood up trying to see him, then he nodded and clicked to Duke who ran off.

"Killer dog on the way," Jersey said.

"Killed by famous Jersey Smith's dog," Roger said as he and Duke walked into the camp.

They sat at the fire, and ate then planned the next day.

"Reward," Roger said.

He drew a square on the ground with a stick and looked at Jersey, then he tapped on the square,

"Reward," he said again.

"Yeah, there's a reward."

Roger drew a line across it and pointed to the smaller side and then pointed to Jersey with his finger, "You," then pointing to the bigger side he motioned with his thumb to himself.

Jersey smiled and shook his head. "I'm think'n no."

"So, famous huh? Where d'you get that?" Jersey said.

"Famous means a lot talked about?"

"Yeah, spec so."

"Then famous," Roger said.

"If that's the truth and I think it might be, could be time to move'n on. Change my name and get. You know I have men come'n after me now, I could get Hamish or others hurt," he said.

"Just kill'm," Roger said.

"Well, thanks for the advice."

"Friend," Roger shrugged.

Jersey nodded, "I guess that's what friends do."

Jersey took the stick from Roger and drew a circle, he dragged the stick across the center and pointed to it saying, "friends."

Roger smiled and nodded, "friends."

The tracks led to the small town. They stood on a high point in the valley looking the area over with telescopes before riding in, Roger with the telescope Jersey had given him after he purchased his new longer one. A few buildings had gone up in the year since he'd been there. Back then it wasn't much more than a stage stop with a mercantile shop. Which is why he'd stopped, occasionally he and Roger had off loaded some skins and meat to make the trip back less burdensome. Also, the big public-house called Charlie's Still, now sat between two new buildings.

"Looks bigger," Roger said.

"You not been back since we were here last?"

"Mm, last spring, still bigger."

It was close to noon when they rode in. They went directly to the back of the livery, unseen. A few new houses were scattered around town. More were under construction in the cleared area just beyond town near a stream, and a church was half built farther downstream. The only law was men that took turns sitting with a shotgun on one of the porches along the only road in town, but usually they would be near Charlie's where everyone congregated.

Jersey hoped they were at the public house and had a few drinks down. For reasons of smell the livery was at the far end of town, it was a little walk north from there. Roger walked across the street and Jersey walked down the west side to the lawman of the day, he was sleeping. The man looked up from his leaning chair startled, but Jersey smiled at him.

"Oh, hey Jersey."

"Hey."

"Well what's this?" the man asked.

"We think you got some undesirables here in your little town."

"Really?"

The man looked concerned turning his head side to side. "Undes-whatables?"

"Seen anyone new in town?"

The man nodded. "Yeah, in Charlie's."

"Look, you can sit here and watch or you can help, but I have to warn you about getting in the way," Jersey said.

"Ah, yeah, ah—I guess I'll watch."

"I think it's fair that I tell you again," Jersey got very serious, "don't get in the way."

"Oh yeah, consider me a by-stander. Say—is that Roger over there?"

The man lowered his chair onto all four legs waving to Roger. Roger started to wave back but thought better of it and nodded instead, he stood ready on the narrow boardwalk across the little alley from Charlie's.

Jersey signaled that they were in there. Roger stepped off the walk, crossed the few feet between buildings, stepped up onto the boardwalk and peeked in the window of Charlie's. Roger turned and sat on a bench near the door and looked at Jersey who was walking across the street. He nodded to Jersey as he stood and went inside.

Roger stepped into Charlie's, he put his hands on his hips, and looked around the big room. There were six at the bar and a table of four in front of it, the rest was empty. All eyes were on the Indian as he walked through the room to the far wall and turned when he got under the stairs. Everyone was watching as he raised his hands high over his head and with a wide swing brought them back down to his sides resting on his leather belt. The people in the room were perplexed and watching close.

"Oh, I think that's them," he said.

Roger moved his hands behind his back and held the bone handles of his two knives, they were crossed—Jersey style. He said, "what do you think, Jersey?"

Heads snapped to the front of the room where Jersey Smith was standing big and dark in the blinding sunlight at the open door. He had a gun in each hand cocked and aiming at the floor, as if daring them to try something—one did.

It was the gunman he knew from the Trading Post beer garden, the one he expected trouble from. He was fast and Jersey shot short hitting him in the leg; he dropped his gun and grabbed the bar top in pain. He hugged the bar moaning for a few seconds. He looked at his gun on the floor and up at Jersey. Slowly he reached around his back and with two fingers he pulled a large knife out and dropped it to the floor. Looking at Jersey he pushed off the bar and hobbled to the door while quickly stripping his black bandanna from his neck and holding it on the wound. He looked unarmed so Jersey let him pass for now, as the man next to Tom Monrow pulled his gun. Jersey used both of his to put him over the bar. Tom Monrow pulled at his gun but a large knife entered his upper arm near the shoulder. He jumped up screaming as he skipped across the room.

Smoke filled the room, the sound of Jersey's large saddle gun still ringing in their ears. Jersey nodded to Roger who went to Tom Monrow to get his knife back, he picked up loose guns on the way. Jersey looked around the room. When he felt they'd gotten all the outlaws, he went to the door thinking the gunman would be there on the ground but he was nowhere in sight. Blood led his view off the side of the porch. He carefully opened the door the rest of the way, stepped out, and looked around—but nothing. He looked at the man in the chair across the street, he was motioning up the street with his gun. Jersey stepped out walking slow following the blood of the hurt man. He heard a horse, it was hard to tell where it was coming from. He turned looking east up the street as the gunman came riding fast from between buildings behind him. The rider raced crossed the street, Jersey snapped around firing twice hitting a porch post then the corner of the building, as the hurt man rode behind them. They heard the man stop back there and yell, "I'm gonna track you down and kill you Jersey Smith."

As he raced off Jersey looked at the ground and

shook his head, he turned to go back inside. Roger was out front with Charlie. They'd dragged the dead man out and was tying Tom Monrow to a hitching post.

"Go after him?" Roger asked.

"Nah, we gotta get Monrow back before the Marshal leaves," Jersey said.

"Mm, nother killer gun'n for you," Roger said.

"Well, if he lives, and doesn't bleed out, he'll never walk again—not without help. I guess I should start a list though."

Charlie looked up from Tom Monrow, "I gotta guy run'n for the doc—get this one wrapped up for the ride."

"This place has really grown, you gotta doctor now?"

"Well, he's the barber, but he knows some stuff."

"Mm. Well we gotta get," Jersey said.

"Coffee and steak first?" Roger said.

Jersey shook his head. "Are you always hungry?"


It was a day and a half later when Jersey, Roger, and Tom Monrow rode into the lake village and headed to the trading post. The Marshal walked out from a small house and stopped them.

"I almost gave up on you."

He looked around. "Where are the others?"

"Got away—one did, and the other we had his body sent by stage to Johnstown," Jersey said.

"Well, you got Tom here, and that's what matters."

"Marshal, this here is Roger, he's a good friend and helped, he's in for half the reward," Jersey said.

The Marshal nodded. "Okay. Roger, I think I've seen your friends at the trading post, leastwise they dress like you."

Roger nodded.

"Tom here needs a doctor, took a knife to the shoulder, been cry'n like a two-year-old," Jersey said.

Tom perked up. "Was not."

"Get to the Trading Post and I'll be there shortly with help," the Sheriff said.

# From the Journal of Hamish Maguire
2nd of November 1852

Glorious morning today.

Jersey was get'n gifts of food and such from the lake people for weeks after his return with the villainous Tom Monrow or whatever his name ended up be'n. He also hasn't shaved or cut his hair, he's start'n to look like a mountain man from the books.

Abby's mother finished his coat. Abby and Ed Junior delivered it, Jersey really liked it. It's just right for most of the year, sep'n winter and midsummer. He hasn't taken it off. Abby made him a very fine leather waistcoat, golden brown in color and he kind of teared up a bit. After that he got a few pairs of pants and shirts for the come'n winter. The lake people really took him in as an honored friend.

Jersey was attacked in the hills on two occasions while hunting, second time must have shook him a mite, he came home empty-handed. Then we heard at the trading post that Bucky Murry was killed in prison and his brother Bobby was shoot'n for Jersey. He's been staying close by lately, he has some plan of move'n away, he's worried about get'n others hurt on-a-count of the bad men after him. I told him to give it a little time, but I think come spring he's gonna leave. He hid a lot of money in the crawl space of the river house. "To improve the place someday," he said.

The Marshal from the Tom Monrow problem was offered a job by the lake village and he accepted it. He said he was ready to retire, and this was as close to that as he could get. Also, he was smitten with one of the lake widows. He was a little ticked at Jersey because he didn't show up to the trial, but I was at the trading post when he told Jersey to "be there" and Jersey said "no" and after a few minutes of tell'n him how important it was Jersey said, "okay," but then the Marshal asked Ed if'n he thought Jersey would show and Ed said, "no." I'm think'n Jersey feels better about leaving now, because of the area people being in the Marshal's good hands and all.

Autumn colors were amazing this year. The colors were why we stayed here years ago when the plan was to pass through. If'n we'd come any other season we might have missed it. Catherine said she could live a lifetime here, and I guess she did.

Tear'n up, time to stop writing.

Read Revelation this morning, went to a few Psalms to cheer up.

# Chapter 14

It was deep winter, and Jersey was heading home when he saw what looked like another attacker. He was leading horse Number Three laden with pelts, along a low ridge north of the lodge. He saw movement down in the valley; he looked closer. It was a man in black on a light-colored horse racing down the river trail. Through his spy glass something told him the man was trouble.

Hamish was up early, it was the second day at sunrise and Jersey would ride in soon with a load for the Trading Post. He'd done his chores and saddled up. His horse was tied out front, ready. Like every other time, Jersey would hit the hay while Hamish took the trail down the hill and negotiated with Ed.

Duke ran from the fireplace to the door, he barked once and anxiously looked at Hamish.

"Jersey back boy? Okay, give me a minute."

Hamish poured a fresh cup of coffee, put his coat on and went to the door. Duke took off fast tossing up fresh snow as he rounded the yard to the trail. Hamish closed the door sat putting his boots on while glancing out the window, Duke walked out from the path followed by Jersey on Blue.

"Coffee?" Hamish asked.

"Oh yeah. Any trouble?" Jersey asked.

"No, why?"

"Just wonder'n. You ready to head down?"

"Ah, I was gonna change—why you come'n?"

"Think I might."

"Leave now?" Hamish asked.

"Soon as you're ready."

Hamish handed Jersey the cup of coffee.

"Well, no need to change I guess, I'll just put the gate on the fire."


At the Trading Post Hamish took Number Three around back where Ed could go through the load and add things up. Jersey walked up the side stairs to the look-out scraping snow off each step as he went. He looked down at the lake village for anything out of the ordinary. It was a quiet winter morning, there was a small fire next to the village pump and two boys were there filling buckets. The new Sheriff came out, jumped on his horse and sped off around the lake to the northwest. Jersey saw smoke over there. He pulled his spy-glass to length; it was an outbuilding at the little boatyard. The town bell rang, and soon the town was in motion. Men with buckets loaded into a large pump sleigh heading to help out, Jersey was closely scanning the area. When he didn't see the stranger in town, he looked in every direction.

He walked to the end of the platform, looked down at Hamish and Ed at the back of the building, "we could be in for some trouble."

They looked up at him; he was looking out and around.

"You mean the town bell? What's go'n on down there?" Ed asked.

"I knew someth'n was up," Hamish mumbled.

"That's a fire at the boatyard, think it's a diversion."

"Yeah, I bet two of my boys are head'n over there, are they safe?"

"Ah," Jersey was scanning, "the outlaw is going to be wherever I am. Better get inside."

"What outlaw?"

"Dark man, ride'n a white horse," Jersey said.

"Uh-oh." Hamish stepped back and looked up. "You say a pale horse?" he asked.

Jersey was still looking around, wishing they would get inside, he looked down at Hamish nodding. "Yeah."

Jersey took one last look around before he started down the steps. He saw the Sheriff ride back into the village; he was suspiciously looking around. Good, Jersey thought, he knows something was odd about the fire. He was off the look-out platform standing on the uppermost part of the steps, taking one last look around. He fired a shot into the air and waved down to the Sheriff. When he had his attention Jersey signaled with a flat hand over his eyes like he was looking around, he acted like he couldn't see anyone. Jersey felt better when he saw Sheriff Wagner start slowly making his way in the direction of the Trading Post while cautiously looking in every direction.

Hamish and Ed were in the Post looking over each accessible gun. Lizzie had locked the back door and kept an eye out the windows. They saw snow drop past the window from the steps as Jersey came down, he didn't come inside. They heard him ride off.

"Where's he going," Lizzy asked.

"Probably drawing him away," Hamish said.

"Why is someone after Jersey?" she asked.

"Could be from the time when he saved Abby," Hamish said.

"Or could be from Tom Monrow, I hear'd rumors of that," Ed said.

"Well, two have tried recent like and Jersey said they were from that gang of outlaws that took Abby."

"We never here'd about any attacks," Ed said.

"Hmm? Yeah ah, Jersey said not to mention it."

"Well, what happened?"

"They's buried in the hills."

Ed scratched his head. "Mm."

Hamish walked to the front window near the door and looked out. "I looked and behold, a pale horse; and his name who sat on him was death and Hell followed with him."

"Revelation," Lizzy said.

She was visibly shaken as she stepped away from the window.

Hamish turned to them. "Has to be more than one man out there. Jersey said next time they'll send a few because the last two never came back."

The door swung opened; they jumped back guns out, Lizzie hit the floor. Sheriff Wagner stepped in, his gun in hand. He looked around, everyone lowered their guns. When the Sheriff saw Hamish he quickly walked to him.

"What's going on?"

"It's another... Ah, we think it could be a ambush. Jersey came back from trap'n act'n strange and when we got here he went to the look-out. Not long after he called to us that there could be some trouble. So we come in here and got ready for trouble," Hamish said.

The Sheriff looked around. "Where is he?"

"We heard him ride off," Lizzie said.

"Probably drawing the outlaw away," Ed said.

"Mm, sounds about right." Sheriff Wagner scratched his chin. "Okay, I'm gonna go find him, see if I can help. You all stay here, lock this door, don't open it unless you know who it is. That fire on the other side of the lake has to be out by now so you're gonna have guests soon."

The Sheriff moved for the door handle.

"Be careful I'm think'n there's more than one," Hamish said.

The Sheriff nodded, opened the door, looked in every direction then left.

"Can we get to the look-out or the roof from inside?" Hamish asked.

"With some effort we could, have to move some snow."


The Sheriff rode in a circle around the Trading Post looking in all directions. He found Jersey's tracks behind the bunkhouse leading into a forest of evergreen and large spruce, he followed. As he moved into a clearing from the corner of his eye he saw a man in a snowdrift aiming a rifle. He quickly turned and rode back, but he thought that man looked familiar, at least the coat he wore was familiar. He turned back and edged closer to the open area. Between trees he could see the man hadn't moved. He rode in and saw it was a scarecrow Jersey had made with clothes from the bunkhouse and a broomstick. From the other end of the clearing it would look like a man in a snowbank aiming a rifle.

He ran into two more similar scarecrows that were aiming into other small clearings. He found Blue tied to a tree, but no Jersey. He dismounted and walked cautiously past Blue trying to see through the dense snow-covered trees. Slowly he moved into an open area.

"Hey Jake."

The Sheriff spun around fell backwards with his gun drawn. He looked around but nothing.

"Keep that gun outt'a the snow," Jersey said.

He looked up in a tree, Jersey's face was between snow filled branches looking down at him.

"What the hey Jersey, I nearly shit."

"Sorry."

"Well? What's go'n on?"

"Bad element, he's come'n this way maybe fifty yards out."

The Sheriff scrambled to his feet and backed into his horse.

"How do you want to handle this? Sure there's only one."

"No, I spotted one from up in the hills, he was riding alone but now I'm thinking there could be a few."

"Hamish seems to think there might be more."

"Mm," Jersey jumped down. "Let's head back to the scarecrows." He nodded to the side, "keep to the center of the trail."

They mounted and headed back the way they'd come.

"You got a plan?"

"Well, one is smarter than the others," Jersey rubbed his lower lip, thinking. "Could he have..." He scratched his head.

"What others?" the Sheriff asked. "Has this happened before and you hadn't told me?"

"Yeah."

"You should have said something, I have the safety of this village to think about."

Jersey said nothing, they kept moving through the deep snow.

"What makes you think he'll come this way?"

"It's where I am. I rode out looking for him and left tracks all the way back."

The narrow path led to an open area surrounded by dense spruce where two of Jersey's dummies were at the far end.

"When we get just past that big Blue Spruce we're

jumping off I'll go first then you pull up and step in my tracks."

Jersey hurried down, took a rope, tied it to Blue's saddle and made him move forward, and tied the Sheriff's ride to it. He made a whistle and a low noise—Blue took off down the path taking the other horse with him. They moved to the back side of the tree.

"Quick under the tree, careful not to hit too many branches, let's keep the snow on them," Jersey said.

He found a wide bushy branch and used it to dust away their tracks as best he could.

Jersey moved under the canopy at the tree's base, it was a tree he'd spotted earlier; it had fewer branches at the ground in the back, where deer had lain. It was dry and soft with a few inches of pine needles. They sat quietly for a few minutes listening.

"I don't hear him," the Sheriff said.

"Or anything else."

"That's true," the Sheriff propped his gun on an eye level branch, then looked around. "Think he's nearby?"

"Right over there," Jersey pointed across the opening. The Sheriff scanned the area but saw nothing.

"But," Jersey said.

"But what?"

"I don't think he's the dangerous one."

"The dangerous one?"

"The smart one."

"Are you saying you now think there's more than one?"

"Yeah, I'm thinking at least two behind us, they're apart by twenty yards or so, I just hope the horses got through," Jersey said.

The Sheriff nervously looked around. "What did you mean the smart one?"

"The one whose idea it was to set the fire and this

here trap we're in. He must know I saw him from the hills, that had to be part of the plan to lure me down."

"Oh, perfect. Just when I was getting used to sit'n around and enjoy'n this relax'n job," he leaned against the tree's trunk. "Well, I been hear'n bird song that I thought had all headed south for the winter—you think that's them?."

Jersey nodded.

"I got six shots. You?"

"Here," Jersey handed him a small Colt from inside his heavy bearskin coat. "Now we both got eleven, let's make 'em count."

"Hear that bird call, they're close'n in."

The sound of a stick underfoot came from a ways behind.

"You keep looking across this here clearing, I'll work on the other two."

Jersey took off his coat spread it over a low branch, put one gun in the holster at his back then edged out from under the big tree. The Sheriff moved behind the coat and watched across the snow filled clearing.

Jersey moved hunched over in the direction he thought the men were. At the next open area he stepped up to another spruce. The bottom of this tree had no open area, and snow covered the branches. He pulled his shirt out covering his gun and knife in back, put the other gun in his front belt under the shirt, tightened his hat strap, and stepped into the tree a few feet. Snow fell on his head and shoulders, as he edged in farther more snow fell. He stood still until he was sure the snow was done falling, he slowly pulled out both guns.

The Sheriff looked around his area, pulled the big coat closer to the tree's trunk, and knelt there hoping the shooter would aim for the center of the coat giving him time to see where he was shooting from. He was right—the shot pierced the coat dead center. The sound was loud but thud-like softened by the snow. He kept still, moving only his eyes looking between the dense horizontal branches. When he saw the gunsmoke he let out a gasping cry and waited for movement looking where the smoke had drifted from. It took a minute before another shot hit the coat this time lower almost at ground level. The Sheriff didn't move but made a gurgling noise. The gunman stood and walked hunched over into the clearing, he looked around as he took a few steps, then he saw one of the scarecrows. He jumped sideways shooting, but missing twice, the next shot took the dummy's hat off. Not knowing if he killed the man, the gunman started running for the Sheriff's tree. At twenty feet the Sheriff fired one round with each gun, laying the man out in the snow.

Jersey stood still. After the gunshots pierced the cold air, he heard movement coming from two directions, he waited. Two men came slowly through the brush and saplings, one of them was the man he saw from the hills. Jersey looked like part of the snowy tree. He slowly raised his guns, they hovered, hidden between dense horizontal snow topped branches. He heard another man on the other end of this little opening, but he couldn't chance turning his head.

The first one to go had to be the man he saw earlier in black; his gun and holster was of quality and strapped on low, he looked dangerous. The two saw their friend step out in the open at the other end of the clearing. They also saw something different about the tree in front of them; they looked closer—pulling their guns. Jersey opened fire as one of them panicked turning into the dangerous man in black, he took the led ball intended for his friend, and they both fell. Jersey quickly stepped out of the tree turning to the man at the other end of the open area. He hit him off center sending him spinning to the ground. He quickly turned back to the two men on the ground, but the dangerous one was now sitting up and shot first. It connected, sending Jersey's shot wild and throwing him back into the tree. Half of the tree's snow fell covering most of him as the branches sprung back up.

The outlaw in black helped his friend up. Blood dripped down his left arm, they walked carefully to the tree, guns out. A large section of branches were now exposed—thick and green hovering over Jersey. All they could see of him were boots sticking out from under the big tree.

"Let's just shoot him again and get."

"We were to give him a message remember, besides I think he's dead, that shot looked center. You grab his feet, pull him out while I cover you."

The man's left arm hung useless. He was sweating as he looked closer into the base of the tree, he could see Jersey's still face, eyes open.

"Looks dead."

With effort he put his gun in his belt and grabbed Jersey's pants at the boots trying to pullhim out with one good hand. The other man rolled his eyes, he looked close at Jersey through the branches, bent down and grabbed a handful of pant leg and they both pulled. As Jersey's body moved out a few feet, he raised both guns from under the snow. The man in black flew backwards as the recoil flipped that gun out of Jersey's weak hand, his other gun misfired. The man holding Jersey's pant leg was surprised glancing at his friend dead in the snow, Jersey took another shot at him, another misfire. The man yelled, "Ah!" dropping Jersey's boot and jumping back he fumbled for his gun, Jersey took another shot, nothing. The man from the other end of the clearing ran by holding his side. Jersey shot again, and again a misfire. The powder had gotten wet. He felt for the fallen gun but could only move so far. Reaching caused his head to spin, he looked up through the dense tree as he gave up, dropping his hands he passed out.

The man standing at his feet smiled, looked at his other friend running away.

"Hey, I got him, wait for me."

His friend kept running, the outlaw looked down at Jersey

"This is from Bobby and Bucky Murray, them which you wronged,"

He took aim. Several shots exploded through the little clearing; the man lifted sideways sliding across the frozen ground leaving a wide red trail in the deep snow. Sheriff Wagner, Hamish, and Ed ran to Jersey, followed by a few other men.

## A Letter from Hamish Maguire
to: Aaron Maguire
Maguiresbridge, Ireland


Greetings from America.

Hello son, I hope all is well with you, thank you for your last letter, your beautiful description of the countryside made me homesick for the first time since I was a boy. Please say hello to all my relations (and any old friends you may see).

I saw your name in a magazine about your last book, they seemed to like it as much as I did. Also, about the new one you recently sent, I only got halfway through when I had to sit down and write this letter to tell you how good I find it. It's very well written and it reminds me of a story you once told me of your days as a Marshal with Jersey's brother James.

I have some news I thought you should know, your old friend Jersey has been shot. He's doing fairly well considering where he was hit, but the shot did miss vital internals and he's a tough man, as you know.

There have been other attempts to kill him on account of him saving a young woman from molesters, he killed a few bad men in the process. Turned out they were from a gang of marauders, very bad men indeed. Seeking revenge they sent a few men after him. At first it was one at a time but this last time it was a trap set by four men and one of them got away to tell the tale. Jersey had put a note for me on his horse then sent it back to the trading post from the woods, if we hadn't seen that note he'd be dead. We got to him just as an outlaw was going to kill him. Five of us shot at once, two connected.

It's been a long winter, what with Jersey on the mend. We are still in the mountain lodge, it's become a nice (little) home. He's getting around now, but still can't ride in these hills, he found that out the hard way. I was much obliged when the village men took it in turns, watching our place while Jersey recovered. They sat in pairs at a fire and walked the hills, at least until Jersey found out and could walk outside that's when he asked them to go home. The women from the lake village I've told you about have been visiting with food and books and clothes. A few of Jersey's Indian friends have also been by.

I fear he'll be leaving soon, he talks about it but won't tell me where he's going, or when he'll be back. He thinks me, and the locals are in danger as long as he's here. He says he will be back and wants me to hold most of his money. You may not know it but when their parents passed, Jersey, James and Josie got a lot of money left to them, Jersey's is still in the bank back in Rhode Island. He never really seemed to be interested in it, he's always been able to make what he needed.

When are you coming home?

If Jersey leaves, I'll be moving back into the big house on the river, plenty of room for you.

Christmas will be here soon, when you get this note it will have come and gone. I hope you had the best Christmas in that beautiful part of God's creation.

Joy to the World,
with Love, your father.

# Jersey Smith

## Part Two

# Chapter 15

Three Years Earlier

"Cane! We gotta be come'n up on that trading post soon, if we don't get outta this river and head south we're gonna be seen." Kaden looked down at the rear hooves as they splashed through the cold mountain water. "Besides these here hocks have to be freezing up some."

"Not yet! Hell—if it weren't for you, we wouldn't be in this water at all," Cane said.

They were riding through the shallows near the banks of the river. The boy was across the murderer's saddle, it's horn was bumping and rubbing his side and stomach. After several hits to the head, his crying had become a whimper. He couldn't stop the awful scene from playing out, slow and horrible, over and over—mother and sis are dead. His tears falling in the river only a mile from where it happened.

"Look, we gotta start head'n south."

Cane saw the ground ahead was turning into foothills, the riverbanks were getting high and they were now in the shadow of the mountains. He looked around for a good place to pull out. With effort his ride turned in the moving water stepping up onto the bank, they continued across the river trail to the field where he turned and looked down at Kaden.

"Well?"

"I gotta stop this bleed'n before I pull out."

"What the hell were you think'n, if you weren't an old friend you'd be dead right now and laying back there with the others."

"Well Cane," Kaden lit a smoke, he leaned on the boy's back and looked up at Cane, "I'm think'n if you pull on me you're the one go'n down."

Cane knew Kaden was better with a gun and he'd never want to fistfight the mean bastard, but if it ever came down to that, Kaden would never see it coming. He was an old friend, he'd be hard to replace, but killing a mother and daughter like that and this close to home, well that was just stupid and stupid was the direction Kaden's decisions had been leaning lately.

"Look Kaden, you know how much money those two were worth, they were top-notch."

"Well, she bit me."

"So you killed her, and the girl too?"

"No. Then she stabbed me in the leg."

"Well, you can't blame her."

"I reckon, but the little one just jumped in while I was shoot'n, just got in the way is all."

"Still you know the rule, break no laws close to home."

"Well, this ain't that close to home."

"Close enough to stop and think about it. Hell, I guess we need to set some actual boundaries of where we can and can't break the law, and stick to 'em," Cane said.

"Boundaries... it's not like the old days."

"Be'n careful is how we made it through the old days, most everyone else is dead."

Kaden pulled the boy up by the back of his shirt, lifting him to his face.

"You still alive boy?"

"More than you'll be when my paw gets hold of ya," the boy said.

The man had a thin scar from his mouth to his ear where its lobe was missing. Seeing him up close Martin looked shocked, the man undid the boy's belt and pulled it through its loops, whipping it out. He dropped the boy in the shallows near shore and the boy took off running; he jumped to shore and headed quickly into the field. Kaden pulled his gun and took aim.

"Quick little bug," he said.

"Don't," Cane said.

The shot rang loud; the boy heard the bullet buzz past his head, he stopped, the sound echoed off the mountains. The boy hung his head and turned; he walked back mumbling words his father insisted he never use, while kicking at the ground. Kaden lifted his leg moaning as he slipped the boy's belt around just above the knife wound, he tightened it down slipping the loose end back under itself. Blood soaked his pant leg and boot and he wanted to pull the boot off and drain it but he felt they should move on farther first, besides he needed help to do it and didn't want to ask Cane. To keep the blood from dripping to the ground, he tucked his pant leg into the boot as best he could , moving to shore he crossed the trail stopping next to Cane.

"How bad is it?"

"I'll live, have to see how it feels to walk on."

"We need to cover our tracks back to the river, brush the ground with some branches. Let's stay in this rough, head in and out of the foothills a few times, the loose gravel will hide the tracks. When we get closer to home, I have a few extra shoes I could change out for any that could be easy to follow us by."

"Fine."

Kaden moved into heavy brush twenty feet from the river trail and looked down at the boy.

"Boy, get that branch there and brush the ground, cover all those tracks up where we crossed," he said.

When they were happy with the boy's work Kaden took his gun from his side, put it inside his coat then held his hand down to Martin, "you ride in back now boy."

He pulled him up and said, "hold on."

They took off at a gallop through the open field.

After meandering through the foothills they stopped five hours south where a river poured out of the mountain and ran fast into a green forest pointing the way to Spring Valley. Kaden waited while Cane found the shoe that was leaving a characteristic track and changed it out. They brushed away all tracks from the area with bush branches and tossed them into the river where the current carried them away.

"I'll be back in a few days for the meeting."

"Anything you want done?" Kaden asked.

"Make sure we have enough food for the weekend, get on the women to make something good."

"What if we need more of something?"

"Well, ride in and let me know or send Clayton but be discreet, in and out, you know the routine."

"Okay," Kaden said.

They separated but Cane turned in the saddle. "And Kaden, the boys mine, I want him in good shape when I get there."

"Mm—hm, fine."

# Chapter 16

Cane Gannon rode into Spring Valley as usual, out of sight. He took a wide sweep out through the woods behind the few houses that sat along the river to the north of town. At the west end he crossed the river, dismounted and walked his ride behind the Valley Blacksmith to the Stable. He grabbed his saddle bag, nodded to Harry Junior who everyone called Little Harry, and tossed him a coin.

"Take care of him good Harry."

"You ride'n out tonight Mr. Gannon?" Little Harry asked.

"No, he's been ridden hard for a few days, just needs to be bedded down good tonight," Cane said.

He walked up a side ally to the street where a few people passed by. Leaning against the corner of the stable's storage building, he rolled a cigarette while looking up and down the street, seeing no one of importance he crossed. Cane walked between a house and the new land office which was under construction, though the area was quiet now. He turned, walking along the back of the buildings to the Public House called The Highlands, and entered through the back door.

Howard was behind the bar standing under a huge moose head talking to a customer. Cane walked along the storage room wall which was a back hallway, it opened into the big room; he sat at the back corner table. It had a permanent reserved sign on its front edge; always reserved for him. He set his bag in the corner behind his seat, moaning as he sat down. Cane looked the room over as he pulled his gun, placing it on the little shelf under the table. He dropped the belt and empty holster to the floor, kicking it to the corner. Exhausted, he put his head in his hands.

"Hey, Mr. Gannon," Howard said.

He approached the table with a glass of water and set it in front of Cane.

Cane looked up and smiled. "Hey Howard, how are you?"

"Oh, I'm just fine—Sir, just fine. What can I get for you?"

Cane pulled a pocket watch from his waistcoat snapping it open.

"Well, I guess I'll just have an ale," he said.

"Hungry at all?"

"Ah—yes, I think some hard sausage and cheese and maybe some bread," Cane said.

"Anything else?"

"Yes, a washing bowl and a towel."

"Have it shortly," Howard said.

Cane reached for a deck of cards from a box on a bookshelf and started counting them, hoping the Sheriff would walk in and see him all casual like. It felt good to be back. This place was home. Being back gave him a sense of relief, he felt safe. The strain of traveling with Kaden was finally over. One thing was sure, he didn't want to get back on that horse anytime soon.

# Chapter 17

Martin thought they were riding in a round-about way through a swampy lowland and into the valley, only to turn back down again. They passed through a few large boulders which turned into a crevice where tall cliffs of shale rose on both sides. Large rocks were scattered, and the area looked as if it had been excavated with explosives. Rubble was pushed along the sides revealing a hard narrow road.

"Are we lost?" Martin asked. "Cus, it seems like we're lost."

Kaden wanted to twist his elbow back and knock the boy off, but they were almost home.

A man with a rifle appeared high on a ridge. He leaned over looking down at them.

"Well, welcome back," he yelled down.

After a few turns things opened up, and they rode straight, stopping at a tall fence with a wide door. The fence was more of a wall of logs standing on end with their tops chopped into points. It ran level and tall up to the mountainside where it was fastened tight against it. The door was framed in with thick lumber and positioned closer to the mountainside. The log wall continued in the other direction to a level open area, where large half buried boulders and stones were scattered under scrub and pitch pines. Some tree roots were exposed, appearing to claw over large stones, pinning them to the ground. The log wall turned a corner there, extending out of view. Martin could see the valley and far in the distance were more mountains, it was a familiar sight; the hilltops were like the ones he saw from his porch. He looked at the gate and the tall wall—a feeling of doom rushed through him. He wondered what was on the other side, and if this could be the last time he saw the outside.

The man on the cliff appeared again high above them on a narrow ledge. He yelled to someone inside. "Open up, it's Kaden."

The door opened and they rode into a very large compound that resembled a quarry. Behind the large open door was a small guardhouse which stretched back to the stone wall, and above that was the narrow ledge where the guard had walked to. He was looking down at them. The whole area was beneath the steep mountain wall which ran to a far corner where a narrow waterfall fell, disappearing behind a ranch house. The house looked out of place. It had a small horse pen between the house and the wall. It was a big house but looked small in the shadow of the massive stone corner. The tall rock wall turned there, continuing from the corner and waterfall out thirty yards where it connected with the log wall which ran back to the front where the gate was. This formed the boundary of his new life.

Along the mountainside of the compound were small workshops, storage buildings and a few bunk houses. Past that was a large fenced garden of corn, in front of a large house. On the log-wall side was a horse pen and stable, it sat across from the gatehouse in the opposite corner. There were more gardens along the log-wall where people were chopping at the ground and picking vegetables. An old man was carrying a bucket of water from a small pond at the far end. The waterfall poured down behind the house in a high corner cut from the mountainside. It's water flowed along the section of wall behind the house until it pooled at the far corner's log fence. There the log-wall acted as a dam forming a pond, letting some run under a small section. An old woman was washing and hanging clothes and sheets.

Martin looked back as the big door was shut and a large bolt was dropped into place. The man ran a chain around it and put a large lock on it. The man walked to the little guardhouse and sat next to a shotgun picking up a newspaper. Kaden rode up to a long bunkhouse. He twisted around quickly and elbowed Martin to the ground.

"Susanne!" he yelled.

A voice came from inside. "She at the house."

"Here, take this kid and get him familiar with things, find some work for him."

The woman walked out on to the porch; she was in her early thirties and sickly.

"Yes sir," she said.

An older man walked out through the open door wiping his hands with a dirty cloth. "Hello Mr. Kaden."

"Jamie, where is everyone?"

Kaden sat up in his saddle and looked around. The old man looked around as well.

"Well—you and Mr. Cane done sold-um off."

"Yeah, I guess we did. Do you have enough to get the work done?" Kaden asked.

"Just," Jamie said.

Kaden rode off as the old man helped the woman get Martin inside.

Once inside Jamie woke up a few men that were sleeping in bunks and made them leave.

"Boss is back boys, have to get back to work," he said.

They looked at Martin shaking their heads, mumbling as they pushed a few boards away and edged out through the back wall. Two of them crossed the road to the garden, one went into the blacksmith building and started hammering.

"What's your name boy?" Jamie asked.

Martin edged behind the woman and grabbed her apron strap. He'd never been around so many black people before. He remembered his mother's teaching on the subject.

"I'm not the one to be afeared of boy," he said.

"I ain't afraid."

Jamie looked at the woman. "Well, tell him what's—what," he said.

She grabbed him by the arm and pulled him around and knelt down, looking him square in the eyes.

"We all in jail here and now you are too. Ain't no way out, so we have to do as they say. If you try to run they'll kill you, we seen it happen. This is Jamie, and he's in it with us and you can trust him, okay?" she said.

Martin nodded. "When my paw gets here he'll fix things."

"Okay boy, that will be real good. Now..." Jamie stopped and looked around. "Where do you want him?" he asked.

"In Andy's bed on the end," she said.

"You're here boy, ah—Martin," Jamie said.

He led the boy to a corner bunk.

"You're on the bottom. No clothes I reckon."

Martin shook his head.

"Who's Andy?" Martin asked.

The two looked at each other, Martin had seen that look before on the faces of his mother and father when he asked something they didn't want to talk about.

"How old are you, Martin?" Jamie asked.

"Nine."

"A mite small for your age?"

"My paw didn't shoot up till he was fifteen," Martin said.

Martin turned when a woman came to the door. She stood in the sunlight her hands were touching the sides of the open doorway. She leaned in looking around the dark room, when she saw him she hurried in kneeling close.

"Well, who is this?"

"I'm Martin, who are you?"

"I'm Susanne and I'm going to look after you."

She was slim and pretty, and he thought of his mother until she got close and out of the sun.

"Let's go for a walk and have a talk," she said.

Susanne nodded to Jamie as she took the boy by the hand, leading him outside.

They walked around to the back of the bunkhouse and sat on a large flat rock at the base of the tall stone cliff, Martin looked up amazed.

"I ain't never been this close to the mountain before, my paw is up there a lot," he said.

She nodded, then the smile left her face.

"Martin, where is your father and mother?"

"They killed my sister and..."

He cried, and she put her arm around him. "Sis is dead, he killed her."

"And your mother..."

She could see he wasn't going to talk much. "Did the man kill her too?" she asked.

He nodded and hugged her tight.

"What about your father?"

"He was hunt'n with grandpa," Martin said.

She held him close for a while; it was a comfort that

she missed very much. In a selfish way she was glad he was here with her—finally someone she could love again. She missed holding her daughter. The closeness, the happy loving bond as warm as the sun. So natural a thing it was given that it would always be there until it was taken. Susanne looked around and realized she had a lot to tell the boy, but feelings were coming forward, things she'd kept buried for so long started to surface.

Becky's smile and laugh burned in her memory, but she'd been away so long she felt the image of her little girl starting to fade. The nonstop abuse was taking its toll. It was changing her into a cold, hard woman. A necessity for survival had kicked in. Unlike many here she hadn't given up, she was determined to make it through alive, to do whatever she had to do to see her little girl again.

Now this little boy arrives—she thought about it. Maybe she should keep him at a distance, not show weakness to Cane and the others. Those animals would use him against her if they thought it would motivate her, or just to be mean. She needed to stay strong. If she was to give-in to his needs, and hers to have someone close, it would change everything. This little boy could be her downfall.

Looking down at the crying boy, she started to cry. She held him tight thinking of Becky, of flowers, of cooking, and of her laugh and the happy times. Now after so long she wasn't alone, but saving the two of them would be a lot more work. Seeing him every day would be one hopeful and shining thing to look forward to. She could watch over the boy. She had a new purpose. Susanne decided to commit to it—whatever it takes, she would get him out alive.

# Chapter 18

Rebecca looked up from her McGuffey Reader. "What's Pompey's Pillar?"

Sheriff Benjamin Jenkins thought for a few seconds and said, "now if I give you all the answers you won't learn noth'n, will you."

He leaned back in his desk chair and continued to read the newspaper. She was sitting at the small desk he'd built into the front of the office; her back deliberately in the corner to keep her away from the distractions out on the street. She shook her head and looked back down at her book, mumbling something about him 'not knowing'.

The Sheriff heard her but ignored it. Mostly because he didn't know it, but also because he'd asked her to please let him get a paragraph read before she asked him another question. As she got into the higher level books there were more and more questions he couldn't answer. She was already smarter in arithmetic, and she could spell an awful lot of good-sized words. Now he needed to find out about this Pillar thing, and bring it up casual, in a conversation, like he knew it all along.

Two men rode up and secured their rides to the front post. Rebecca started up, but Ben pointed to her chair.

"They'll be come'n in," he said.

She was up leaning over the desk trying to see out the front window, her long hair draped across the smooth oak planks. The Sheriff walked outside; he seemed to know one of them, they were laughing. She stood, walked around to see better, and casually leaned back on her desk. She picked up her book acting like she was reading. The young man was very good looking, she thought, but he needed a bath and some clean clothes. They walked in and filled the room with loud laughter and talking but Rebecca acted like she hadn't seen them.

"Oh—this is Becky. She stays with me and she needs to be finishing her school'n."

He nodded for her to get back to her seat.

"Becky, this is Marshal Jackson and his deputy. The Marshal is an old friend, and he's helped us out..." he paused for a second. "Ah, in the past."

"Speaking of that," the Marshal spoke up. "How did that all turn out, with the disappearances?" he asked.

The Sheriff looked uncomfortable and nodded to Rebecca.

"Not so well, never found em."

It got quiet. Rebecca looked up from her book to see the men staring at her.

"What?" she said.

She looked down at her dress and patted her hair as if she looked funny, she wiped her nose with her sleeve. "What?" she said again.

They started looking around the room to change the subject. Their attention landed on the large map on the wall near the girl.

"That a young George Washington's map?"

"Yeah," the Sheriff said. "Let's take your horses down to the stable then get lunch at the Sunny Side."

"I want lunch," Rebecca said.

The Sheriff looked at the clock. "Well, finish that page and you can go get lunch."

"I was think'n Sunny Side for lunch today Ben," she said.

He smiled at her. "Okay, sweetness—lunch at the Sunny Side, but finish that page."

"Yes sir," she said.

Spring Valley was a small town, and its main street ran straight through but for a side street that branched off midway forming a long U around a fenced public island of trees and grass. That little side street was narrow and held a few businesses, and one of them was the Sunny Side cafe. It was a warm calm day, people were walking in all directions and some hammering was coming from both ends of town. A new building was going up next to the Highlands, and they just started on a new church at the very east end of the main street.

"So Ben, was that the woman's daughter?" the Marshal asked. "The one that went missing?"

"Yeah, she stays with me now, but the whole town took her in," the Sheriff said.

"Mm,"

They walked back through town to the little cafe. Becky was sitting at the counter looking at a menu and talking with the cleanup boy Harry, one of the many Johnson children that roamed the town looking for something to do, hopefully for profit.

They sat at a table away from everyone near one of the front windows. The sun streamed in and bounced off the tablecloth and floor, filling the room with a yellow glow. Dust from the two men swirled in the sunlight as they sat down.

"Well Ben, we're here about a murder," the Marshal said.

"Where was this?"

"Along a river a day's ride north of here," he said.

"It's near a small community on a lake in the

foothills," the Deputy said.

"I know of the trading post up there it's on a river at the foot of the hills, Ed someth'n-or-other, he comes by the general store now and again."

"Yeah, that's the area," the Deputy said.

"A woman and her little girl, by the name of Smith, were shot. I was contacted by the husband, name's Jersey, he was looking for the boy,"

"Boy?" The Sheriff said.

"Yeah, his son's missing. Tracks put him in the river and we're thinking he's under a rock in the deep water downstream. Anyway, no body. That's why we're still on it and come this far south."

Ben shook his head, "A mother and her daughter. It's savage."

"Also—I guess the woman stabbed the man. Have you seen any strangers come through with a bad leg or maybe a bandaged arm?"

"Truth is Jackson we been slow down here, ain't seen many new faces at all." He scratched his chin. "Not sure what's go'n on, town grew a lot over the past few years and then kinda slowed recent like."

"Looks like some building go'n on."

"Yeah, and the new church is a big deal but the towns numbers really haven't grown much in the past two years," he said.

"So you ain't seen noth'n?"

"Well—let's see, when did this happen?"

"A few days back."

"Been slow the last few days. Nah, we get a few new faces on the weekends, mostly at the Highlands and I make my rounds over there but no one stood out. I'll keep looking."

"Well, guess we'll just spend the night and head for

home tomorrow."

"Shoot Jackson, kick back a little, stick around for the weekend," the Sheriff said.

"How's the Highlands been on the weekends lately?" the Marshal asked.

"Great. Center park right out here gets going good too. All the girls and ladies that won't step in the Highlands come out for that, it's a fun gathering place."

The Deputy perked up. "Well, I'd like to rest a bit, lots of ride'n recently."

Ben and the Marshal looked at each other and smiled.

.

# Chapter 19

At the Highlands, Cane sat in his corner seat dealing a hand of poker. It was a regular thing with these men and always a friendly game, Cane made sure of that. He would entertain them with his card shuffling and if asked, a trick or two. The men were amazed how a man that could handle cards so well didn't seem to win very often. Of course a big pot to them, was small change to Cane and letting them win was a small price to pay for relationships of trust that would lead to a little help at some point and an alibi or two down the line.

Cane liked to spread the winning around between the players to keep them coming back. He could read them as easy and correctly as any players he'd ever known. He should, over three years of regular play with six to eight locals you get to know them and how they play. There was some card trickery involved, but when you're trying to help another man win it was more about knowing who to tip off and when. Many times no matter how good his hand was he would fold early just to watch, in fact he was more likely to fold on a good hand.

It had become fun for him to play a game of manipulating. If one hadn't won for a while he would do his best to help that man take home some cash. By doing so, each man felt they had a real friendship with him and never felt cheated. If one man felt he was told to fold by

Cane and it cost him the hand when confronted about it after the game Cane would buy him a drink, change the subject and talk to him for a while, real friendly like. The other big advantage of the regular game was that each man was an active member of the community. Cane heard all the goings on from every corner of town, gossip at the poker table was non-stop.

One of Cane's men from the compound, which they called the ranch came in through the back door. He walked past the table, glanced over, then went to the bar and stood waiting for Howard. Cane discreetly reached under and took his gun from a small shelf, put in his belt and covered it with his jacket.

"Men, I been ride'n cattle for a few weeks now and need to walk around a bit. B'side seems I'm on another losing streak."

Riding cattle and working on his father's ranch was the main excuse he used for all the times away; it's why they call the compound the ranch, people thought he was talking about his father's place. Cane pushed away from the table and walked to the bar as the men said okay and nodded at the same time.

"Well?" he said.

The man was taking his first sip but stopped and set the glass down. "Got a list of a few things needed from Clayton and Kaden."

He wiped his mouth with his sleeve and reached into his jacket, set a piece of paper on the bar and went back to drinking his beer.

Cane looked at the list. "I'll get this and head out in a little while. Is your horse out back?"

"Yeah," he said.

"Stop by the stable on your way out, tell them to get my ride ready, hitch him to my wagon."

Howard walked up to them, wiping a glass with a white towel.

"Get you another one Gord?" he asked.

Gordon looked at Cane and back at Howard, "No, just this one thanks."

Howard knew Cane didn't want men from the ranch in the Highlands.

"Haven't seen you in a while, how's things at the Gannon ranch?" he asked.

"Hmm? Oh—ah fine, just fine Howard."

Howard looked at Cane, seeing he'd interrupted them he stepped back, nodding to Cane.

"I got this one Howard," Cane said.

"Oh, well thank you mister Gannon sir, thank you," Gordon said.

"Sure Gord, no problem, see you next time."

Cane gave Howard an angry look, but when he saw his reflection in the mirror, he forced a smiled. Howard walked to the other end of the bar and looked out the front window. He held the glass up to the sunlight eyeing it close, he set it down and picked up another.

# Chapter 20

Cane drove his wagon behind the buildings east along the river, he pulled in between Fredrick's General store and a large house next to it. His horse was past the front porch sticking out onto Main Street. Fred the owner walked out and leaned on the railing of the side loading dock.

"Hey Cane, what can I do for you?"

Cane was looking across the street for the Widow Engilton then he turned to Fred.

"Ah Fred, got a list here."

Cane slipped a saddlebag over his shoulder, walked around the back of the wagon and reached up, handing Fred the list.

"Hmm, might be a bit short on the lard, have the rest for you next week."

"That's fine," Cane said.

"Give me a half hour?" Fred asked.

"Okay."

Fred called to a boy in the back to bring up three bales of hay. Cane walked between the wagon and the loading dock to the street. Ben and two men rounded the corner next door at the Sheriff's office. They stopped on the boardwalk out front when they saw Cane.

"Cane how are you?" the Sheriff asked.

"Oh, I'm fine Sheriff, just fine."

"This is Marshal Jackson and his deputy. Men this is Mr. Gannon, Cane Gannon, his family owns the large ranch south of town, his father is a great benefactor to this town," Ben said.

They shook hands and talked about the town and its growth.

"What brings you to Spring Valley?" Cane asked.

"Hunt'n down a murderer," the Deputy said.

"And we're looking for a missing boy, bout nine," the Marshal said.

Cane gave them his best look of concern. "Oh no, a murderer?"

"Killed a woman and her daughter,"

"How can anyone do something like that?"

"It's hard to figure, sir," said the Deputy.

The Sheriff noticed Cane's horse sticking out next to the store.

"Head'n out?" he asked.

"Hmm?" Cane look back at the horse. "Oh yeah, a little supply run," he said.

Rebecca walked up, smiled and went in the office.

"How's Rebecca Ben?"

"She's doing great, just gett'n back to her school'n," Ben said.

"Well okay, nice to meet you two and I'll keep my eyes open for any new boys in town," Cane said.

Cane touched the brim of his hat with his finger as he left. He heard the men talking as he walked away.

"Cane," Ben called. "Haven't seen you around for a while where you been?"

Cane stopped for a second, then turned around.

"Not think'n I'm this here murderer are you Sheriff?" he asked.

"Course not, but these are questions we have to ask everyone, you know."

Cane smiled, "I know just kid'n. I was, well I was on a cattle drive for three weeks just got back to town a few days ago, you can ask Howard at the Highlands."

# Chapter 21

Cane walked to the Sunny Side, had a cup of coffee and a pleasant chat with the people there. It was another place he counted on to get the latest talk around town, but more importantly he could rely on the ladies to spread bits of information he'd leave. Like three weeks ago when he told them he was leaving on a cattle drive with his father. Now that Kaden had lawmen in town looking for him, he hoped his advance deception would pay off. After all, the Sheriff spent more time in the Sunny Side than his office.

He left his change and winked at the girl working the floor as he left. He was thinking about Melissa Engilton and as he turned the corner onto Main street, she was there watering flowers in her front yard just across the street from his rig. She was looking beautiful, he thought. He stopped and leaned on the Sheriff's hitching post, rolling a smoke as he watched her.

Fred stepped out from his front door with a broom when he saw Cane. "All set Cane."

Cane walked up to Fred, opened his wallet handing him a hundred-dollar bill. "Will this catch me up?"

"Oh, oh yes, give you a credit it will."

"That's fine, is everything in there?

"All but a pound of lard."

Okay, thanks Fred," Cane said.

"Thank you, Mr. Gannon."

Cane sat on the bench of his wagon getting ready for the long ride. He picked up the reins but stayed there watching Melissa Engilton for a minute. Snapping the reins he turned out onto the street, he nodded to her and she smiled for a second before getting back to her garden. She was a difficult one to crack, he'd tried everything, but she wasn't interested. She'd said, 'it will never—ever happen'. He thought after getting her husband out of the way it would be a piece of cake, but when he made his move she pushed him out of the house. These strong-willed women had always been too much trouble, and in a town where he had already taken three women, and killed a few of the menfolk, he'd be pushing things to try anything more. Still, he thought of her often and wanted her badly. One day, he thought.

Taking the wagon always made it a slow and long ride to the compound, but it gave him time to think or plan, to work out details. He kept going over in his mind: when Kaden killed that woman at the river, what a waste it was and how the law was right now in his town looking for the man responsible, also there was the boy. He put that out of his thoughts for now as he went over a few planned jobs they'd been working on; they were coming up fast. They could still work out the details, but he needed to wait to see about this Marshal before moving forward with anything. He rode through the labyrinth of trees, boulders, and steep cliffs to the compound.

In his office, Cane knelt at a big safe behind his desk and rolled the tumbler until it unlocked. He placed stacks of money and a few papers from his saddlebag inside it. Susanne brought him a cup of coffee and set it on his desk and turned to leave, but he stopped her.

"What's been going on around here while I was gone?"

She turned, not wanting to look at him.

"It's the same as when you left, a nightmare," she said.

"What are you all up about?"

She said nothing.

"Come on out with it!"

She looked at him with a true hate.

"Why did you kill that little boy's family?"

"Yeah—that was Kaden," he looked away. "How is the boy?"

"How do think, he's heart-broken."

She started to leave, but he stood up. "Get back here."

She turned and walked back to the desk. Cane walked around the desk and pulled her close to him. She resisted, so he jerked her hard.

"The boy seems tough, he'll get over it," he said.

She shook her head and pulled her arm, but he squeezed tighter.

"I've missed you," he said.

"Missed me, you gave me to Albert when you left."

"You made me mad, now I think I'll take you back."

She pushed him and ran out, slamming the door.

# Chapter 22

Over the next two days, the compound was active with new arrivals that needed attending to. Everyone was expected to finish their normal duties as well. The men that came were, for the most part, wild and mean. They took their anger out on the slaves; some shots were fired, but none connected. Susanne voiced her concerns, but they were written off with, "they're just let'n off steam."

If this meeting was like any in the past, it was an hour or two long followed by a drunken party that could stretch on for two days. Being short handed, the preparation was strenuous for everyone and Cane's men stayed out of the way for fear that interfering would slow things down. In the kitchen the guards stood back, but still kept a very close watch at anything that was added to pot or pan. If anything was in doubt, a slave had to test it before they could continue.

The largest room in the house was cleared of furniture, and in its center two tables were placed together in a long rectangle. It was set for twenty but only fifteen were expected and that's how many showed up. When the clock struck seven, Jamie rang the dinner bell. The men filed into the big room and mingled as they picked a seat. After a few minutes Cane and his brother Clayton stood at the head of the table, Clayton tapped the butt of his gun down hard on it.

"Okay—everyone, this here meeting is commencing to start. First we eat, then we talk, so if'n you got someth'n to say, get it straight in your head while we eat. Now find a seat," Clayton said.

They devoured the food like a pack of wolves.

"Animals, filthy—animals," Jamie said.

He walked around the kitchen shaking his head and talking under his breath while two old cook women moved to the door peeking into the larger room.

"Oh—my," said one as she rushed back to shovel more green beans into serving bowls. "Well I'm glad I'm back here."

The other woman was shaking her head. "I think there's more on the floor than on the table."

They laughed out loud, and the guard jumped off the counter where he was sitting and yelled at them to get back to work. Jamie came back in followed by Susanne, both carrying empty bowls. They picked up full ones and hurried back out. Susanne winked at Martin, who was washing pots with an old man at a large sink made from a watering trough on a low stand.

When they finished eating the room was cleared of all signs of food, ashtrays and glasses were set out. Men grabbed at Susanne, but that stopped when it was passed along that she was Canes. Cigar boxes were passed around and Kentucky bourbon was poured, a few bottles were strewn about the table. The slaves were told to keep out. Only Jamie could be nearby in the kitchen to listen for a call in case something was needed. The talking and laughing was loud until Clayton hit the table again with his gun.

Cane raised his glass. "To a great year!"

They all raised their glasses. "A great year!"

He looked around the table full of marauders. The

gray smoke drifted and hung still at the ceiling above the glowing lamp lights.

"I consider all of you my friends and friends are honest with each other right?"

They agreed.

"If we stay honest, we will all make more money and we will all one day be very rich, that is, if you don't spend it all on women and whiskey."

They laughed.

"I'm thinking about you there, Hurley," Cane smiled and everyone laughed and some patted Hurley on the back.

"Well, let's start with you Hurley, how did the Ohio job go?" Cane asked.

Hurley nodded and reached beside him on the floor to a saddlebag and placed a stack of bills on the table. He smiled and said, "it went pretty good!" and laughed.

"Is that after payouts?" Clayton asked.

"Yeah, this is ready for us and the bankroll," Hurley said.

Cane looked around the table to make sure he had everyone's attention.

"This is just one of Hurley's jobs this year. We tried something a little different a few months back. It was before my trip to New Orleans, and some of you may not know about it yet. Now this is something we're gonna do more of. Hurley, why don't you tell everyone about that other Ohio job."

"Well, Cane had this idea bout sending a few men out look'n for work, you know, see if'n anyone was thinking about pull'n any jobs, so I did. Well, they come back kinda empty-handed but for this one fella. Now he heard of a train robbery planned and they was need'n an extra man or two so he joined up. Well, he comes back, and I goes over the plan with him and it was a good one. So we set up our own plan, and I sent a rider back to Cane tell'n him what's going on and that was that," Hurley said.

Everyone looked confused.

"You left out the best part Hurley," Clayton said.

"Hmm? Oh—well we did the job and went to the arranged place to divide up the money and Clayton and a few of our boys was there hide'n and took the money," Hurley said.

"They did all the work and we get all the money," Clayton said.

"Very little risk," Cane said.

"Won't they be a come'n after you now?" someone asked.

"They won't be come'n after anyone," Clayton said.

"So, Kaden and I and the Burton brothers took a shipment down to New Orleans, it was a profitable trip," Cane said.

He nodded to Kaden who picked up a heavy cloth bag with drawstrings and set it on the table, it made a loud thump; he slid it down the table to Albert. Everyone clapped and cheered.

"Where are the Burtons?" someone asked.

"We split up on the way back. You know those two—they's loners. We gave em their share and Clifford said they'd be up here at some point," Cane said.

"They's still a trifle wild, Cane?" Hurley asked.

Cane looked at Hurley and smiled. "Oh—they're still wild," he said.

"Too wild," Kaden said.

"If we could control them, even a little, they could be a big help up here," Cane said.

"Hey Cane, it looks like a few of the white women are gone too?"

"Yeah, there's a place near New Orleans where they handle that, it's very hush-hush, but we got even more than we thought we could. It was a very profitable trip."

"Are we sure we want to be sell'n white women Cane?"

One man spoke up, and a few seemed to agree. They looked down the long table to see Cane's reaction.

Cane looked around the room, "So it's okay to kill'm but we can't sell'm?"

"Well, I ain't never killed a woman before," one said.

"So," Clayton said.

"Look—I know a few of you may have a problem with this but it's just too much money to stop now. We won't be doing it for long, just a few more years and we'll all be rich," Cane looked around the table. "Can we agree that this is necessary?" he said.

Cane looked at the men nodding and took it as a yes.

"So no more about this, besides they'll be fine, they're going to some nice places," Cane said.

Kaden looked down at the table, avoiding eye contact.

They went around the table going over other jobs that had been done over the last few months and the money piled up. It was passed down to Albert, an old school friend of Cane and Claytons who was very good with numbers. He added everything up and made two large and uneven stacks. Cane went to his office and returned with a large box full of money and set it on edge, showing everyone its contents to a large round of yelps and clapping. He set it on the chair next to Albert, walked back to his seat, and lit a cigar. The men talked, told jokes, and did a few card tricks as they waited for Albert to finish counting. When he was done there was sixteen stacks of bills on the table, he took the largest stack and placed it in Cane's cash box. The attention shifted to Albert, "Well, there it is," he said.

"Tonight you can keep as much of this in the safe as you want, just wrap it up and put your name on it and we'll put it away together. When you leave I recommend you travel in groups to your banks, but if anyone wants to leave some of it here in a lockbox in the safe you're welcome to, it's a lot to carry around. In the morning, better make it eleven, we'll meet here to eat and we'll finish the plans for the next few jobs; tonight is time to have some fun," Cane said.

He looked at Clayton and smiled, Clayton yelled, "This meeting is adjourned," slamming his gun down on the table.

They cheered and talked as they took their share of the spoils. A few lined up at the safe the others went outside for fresh air, to stretch and play horseshoes. The last leg of beef was on a spit and an old man was sitting next to it, making an occasional turn on the crank. Its smell filled the air. A few men walked up to it almost standing in the fire cutting slices off and passed them around. One of them pulled out a fiddle, and they sang, drank, played checkers, and talked about how they would spend their money.

Clean up was moving quickly inside the house. The cooks went to bed; the rest set up for breakfast. Cane came in from the fire, stood in the kitchen talking with the guard. When it looked like things were wrapping up, he called Jamie over.

"Bring Susanne to my room," he said.

Clay walked through the compound to the gate, the guard saw him coming unlocking it as he got there. He walked down the path to the ladder and climbed up to the lookout ledge. He moved slowly along the dark narrow shelf to its end where it was wide enough for two men to stand, relieving the guard on duty.

"Go get some food and a drink before it's gone," he said.

He walked along the cliff path to its end and stood

looking out over the vast valley under the bright moon. When ancient glaciers cut through many regions of the country, this area held much of its vegetation and used it; the mountains were rounder, greener, and tree filled. The look-out perch was a shelf that overlooked the opening of the narrow last trail back to the compound. Clayton rolled a smoke and sat on the wide flat ledge. He leaned against a steep incline, watching the night sky. He enjoyed getting away from the uncontrollable men and the noise that followed them everywhere.

The Gannon brothers found this huge isolated clearing from above, while hunting in the hills. With the help of a few friends and a little gunpowder, they made it accessible. With a few more kegs of black powder the tall rock face was excavated to a point where no one could climb out on two sides. It was then that they—Cane, Clayton and a few school friends decided they needed help, or building the hideout would take forever. They hired a few tradesmen to help. At first it was just to help them out and they would take them back where they came from. It was decided it wouldn't be much of a hideout if people knew where it was. It was around that time that they became kidnappers, slave traders, and cold-blooded murderers. It took just a few short years to go from school boys to outlaws. Clayton blew smoke into the night air remembering the powder kegs. The thought of the massive explosions made him smile.

He thought about what to do with his share. It was too late to go home, Cane had wrecked the family. The old man was broken and wanted no part of him—which bled to Clayton as well. Maybe just leave, head east, get out from under Cane. But, he'd put so much into this place he wanted to get every penny out of it. He thought about what it could be worth? Well—even though it makes a lot of money, selling it was impossible. It was thieve'n and sell'n people, basically that was it. Who would buy a slave trade operation in the north.

You can't start a family here and he longed for a woman he could settle down with, a real beauty that didn't ask about his past. Yeah, a new life would be something. It may even be worth the sacrifice of the remaining years of greenbacks. He could make money anywhere—his father taught him all about that, before Cane drove them out of the family ranch. Clayton looked out on the dark valley at the shape of the distant hills across it, yearning for a woman he'd not yet met until he couldn't keep his eyes open. He was shaken awake by his relief and walked through the compound in the dark just as a few cooks were walking to the kitchen to start on breakfast.

# Chapter 23

Three years later

They'd made several trips to New Orleans to keep the number of captives at a manageable level with a small crew. They made hidden paths over the mountain to the valley on the other side and widened the secret entrance from the south. All new jobs were committed farther away, keeping the compound secure. Things had gone very well for Cane's gang, most jobs they pulled went off without a hitch, and it seemed each job brought in more than expected. Cane, Clayton, and Albert held large bank accounts in Pittsburgh. No one knew where or what Kaden did with his money.

In the summer of 52' an outlaw walked into the Highlands looking for someone. Howard pointed Cane out. The man came to the corner table, plopped down across from him, stretched his legs out, and gave him a smile. Cane looked at Howard and shook his head.

"Cane?" the man asked.

"Who's ask'n?"

"Never mind who I am, are you Cane?"

"Yeah, what do you want?" Cane said.

"Well, hear tell you got a good thing go'n up here," the man said.

He looked the room over, and Cane leaned forward with an elbow on the table.

"Keep it down, or I'll put you down," Cane said.

The young man leaned back in his chair and again looked around the room before looking back at Cane.

"You and who else?"

"Just me," Cane said as he pulled the hammer back on his new Colt, the sound from under the table was distinct and threatening. The man gave him a long hard look before easing up and smiling.

"Look, I just want to help out that's all," he said.

"Oh, just help out, so you're a giving kind of man are you?"

"Yeah—that's me, as long as I can get someth'n in return," he said.

"Put your gun on the table and we can talk," Cane said.

Cane didn't like him, not one bit. He looked like a killer—a reckless killer, the kind he didn't want around. He'd seen his type before, a loner entitled to whatever happened to cross his path. No sneaking around, just kill and take, no plan, run away fast and far. He could see no loyalty in those eyes. When this kind of man faces death, he will either cry like a little child or spit in the hangman's face. Cane was sure this was a crier.

"Hey, relax, I'm just here to talk."

The gunman pulled his gun out slowly with finger and thumb. As he set it on the table, the sound of a hammer easing up came from under the table. The gunman sat back again slumping, one arm over the chair's back, the mood had calmed. He didn't like having a gun pulled on him and wanted to kill Cane for it, but it was a long ride and it would have all been for nothing. Cane looked over and nodded to Howard who was standing behind the bar with a short barrel shotgun in his hands but out of view.

"Well, I'm listening," Cane said.

"I was look'n for work, I can shoot and ride and anything else you may need."

"What's your name?" Cane asked.

"Tommy."

"All right Tommy," Cane looked around the room, he leaned in and spoke low. "First I need to get you to my ranch and show you around. I think I got a job you can have some fun with. But, my number one rule is..."

Tommy smiled and looked away, thinking that was easy, I'm in—just like that. He rode in, sat down, and now he's in, with a job that he could have some fun with.

Cane looked at him and shook his head. "Hey? Are you listening to me?"

"Sure I am, now what were you say'n?"

Cane gave him a serious look. "My number one rule is stay out of Spring Valley, never ever come here again. Understand?"

Tommy nodded, Cane sat back in his chair with his gun in his lap.

"Okay—you need to ride out-of-town opposite the way you rode in, like you were just pass'n through. Circle back to the east of town and follow the river to where it cuts through the low hills and wait for me there. I have a few things to take care, I'll meet you there in a few hours. Now get up and say 'thank you Mr. Gannon, don't offer to shake my hand, have a beer at the bar on me, when you leave do it real normal like," Cane said.

Tommy stood smiled and put his gun in his holster as he said loudly. "Well thank you Mr. Gannon, you have a nice day."

"You too young man, and good luck."

Clay was playing cards at one of the front tables, watching the strange young man talking with Cane. He was losing so when the young man went to the bar he folded and walked to Cane's table.

"What was that about?"

"Not sure but we need to find out," Cane said.

"Oh?"

"This little shit comes in here asking for me by name and gets in my face and said he heard we had a good thing go'n up here,"

"So who's talking about us down south?" Clayton asked.

"Right, it must be one of our own," Cane said.

Clay took a deep breath and rubbed his chin, thinking for a good minute. "Which one of our contacts would say your name and tell about Spring Valley? I can see a slip-up or something, but to know the town and your name..."

"Well, who's working south of here? What if you were to take this young gun south, have him show you who said it," Cane said.

"No, no way I'm not going anywhere with him."

"Why?"

"Because one morning I'd wake up dead."

Cane shook his head and looked at the young gunman, he was smiling at himself in the back-bar mirror. "Fine."

They counted on their fingers a few men they trusted in West Virginia and farther south, but the list was very short.

"Well, I guess you need to take a few men and head down there, get to the bottom of it. We can't have this," Cane said.

"First let's get what we can out of this one, beat it outta him if he won't talk," Clay said, "Oh—besides we got that job coming up."

"What job?"

"The Payroll job, it's just south of the border."

"I don't like that job, the whole idea, I thought we cut that..."

"No," Clay interrupted. "No its Kaden's job, been

working on it for a month. Hey, maybe it's his guy down there that's got the big mouth."

Cane thought for a moment. "Let's have a talk with this young gun first then go back over the payroll job with Kaden."

"What should we do about this guy," Clayton asked.

He looked around, but the young man had gone.

"Hey,"

He turned back to a distracted Cane.

"He's gone," he said.

"Hmm? Yeah, I'm meeting him in the hills," Cane said.

"We gonna kill him, after we find out what he knows?"

"No—at least not yet, I'm think'n I'll take him to the ranch, be friendly and maybe get a lot more about who it was that sold us out. If it's not Kaden's man, we could send this young gun down to take care of it, like a test job to get our trust," Cane said.

"Then we kill him?"

"Probably, first we keep a close eye on him, keep hitting him for more information. I don't really like showing him the compound, but I want to know what he knows."

"Let's just beat it outta him."

"It may come to that, but let's act like he's part of us first. Let the guards know he's not to leave without our okay."

"Then we kill him?"

Cane rolled his eyes. "What is going on with you?"

"I don't like him, wears his gun too low and walks around all full of himself and smile'n," Clayton said.

Cane shook his head. "I reckon that's true, but you're sound'n a lot like Kaden."

"Mm."

"Is this because you might have to go down south?" Cane asked.

Clay lit a cigar, scratched his rough stubbled chin and mumbled. "I was just down there, it's time to kick back."

# Chapter 24

One of Blue's shoes split at a nail, so Jersey walked the last three miles into Spring Valley. They followed a river from the foothills, he mounted Blue to cross at a wide shallow section, only to slip off on the opposite bank. The clear, fast moving water led them to the east end of the little town. The morning sun crested the hilltop, rays of light coated the buildings, even the white structures were golden.

He was just coming up on the back of a large Church when its bells started ringing. Its dark roof and steeple stood stark against the pale morning sky. He could see in the distance down the river where it ran behind the town's buildings and a few scattered houses. People were crossing a small bridge that led down near the center of town. He walked along the back of the Church, turning onto the main street he walked next to the tall building. He saw people walking down the street in his direction. It was a one street town and he could see all the way to the other end. As he moved out into the open, he was face to face with what looked like the entire town talking and laughing in the low fenced yard of the Church. He'd hoped he could slip by unnoticed, but he looked like a wanderer. His two horses were over loaded with rope strapped bags and bundles. On top of cargo, on top of Number Three, Duke sat in his special riding box.

"We must be a sight to see, hey Blue," Jersey said.

He took his hat off and patted down his hair and beard, but he didn't look at the people. Everyone stopped and watched him pass, when he was up the street he heard them resume their morning chatter as they entered the Church. The street was wide and there were a few houses before he came upon the first business, the general store. The Sheriff's office was next to it, positioned on a corner where the main street split off and ran in a large loop around an open area with a few trees. Some tables were scattered and a large gazebo sat across from the Sheriff's office on the near end of the little park. The side street looped past a restaurant and a few small businesses before it reconnected with the main street. He continued pulling the two horses as Duke made a little whine, wanting down. Across Main Street from the park was the Highland's public house. He saw the sign for the blacksmith just a few buildings down and across.

The large thick rolling door was open, the inside was dirty but looked organized. He tied the horses up and helped Duke to the ground.

"Morning!" Jersey called out.

"Hmm?"

He heard shuffling and something fell.

"Come on in," a voice said from within.

Jersey walked in, and Duke followed. A large man emerged from the shadows. Jersey had his hand up to his eyes, trying to get used to the dark room. He was a black man with a friendly smile and a book under his arm.

"What can I do for you mister?" he said.

"Well friend, I'm in need of at least two shoes on one of those horses out there and would be mighty glad if you could check the rest, on both."

"Not today mister, it's the Sabbath."

He set his book down and looked past Jersey to the

horses and said, "I can do it first thing in the morning."

"That's fine, where's the stables?" Jersey asked.

The big man pointed west. "Next building is the barn, next to that is the stable."

"Thanks, you want me to bring them to you in the morning?" Jersey asked.

"Nah, I'll get um. What's your name mister?"

He turned a piece of paper around and slid it across the workbench, dipped a pen in an ink well, and held it out for Jersey. He took the pen and stepped up to the counter, looked at the paper, but wasn't sure what to write. He'd had so much time to come up with a name, but he didn't.

"I can write it for you if'n you need," the man said.

"Hmm, oh—no I'm just tired, long ride."

On the top of the paper were the words 'Bill of Sale'.

Jersey wrote Bill Smith on the form.

"Bill?" the man said, "I'm Otis."

Jersey extended his hand and with the firm shake he considered the name change formalized, he became Bill.

"Stop by after three tomorrow, unless you're in a rush. It'd be extra for a rush."

"No, three's fine, thanks," Bill said.

Otis picked up the pen and spoke each word as he wrote them. "Two shoes and more if'n needed."

Bill got to the door and turned. "I see your Bible there and you don't work on the Sabbath and I know it ain't my business but why not go to the Church?"

"Well Bill," Otis paused and put his pen away. "This here town has welcomed me pretty good, I'm not want'n to push my luck."

Bill nodded and walked back in. "Have you been here long?"

"Over two years," he said. "Are you planning on

staying long or just pass'n through?"

"Stay'n," Bill smiled. "I heard some good things about this area and wanted a change, spend some time with people again."

Otis looked at him and smiled. "It's a good little town," he said.

"What brought you here?" Bill asked.

Bill leaned an elbow on the workbench and showed real interest, Otis got serious and looked at the ground.

"Oh, hey—it's none of my business."

Bill stood up again.

"No, it was a time when it happened to more than just me," Otis said.

"What happened? Ah, if'n you don't mind me ask'n."

"I was ride'n with my wife head'n up to Pittsburgh, we stopped for the night just a days ride from here and she was get'n the fire going. I went to hunt for supper, on-a-count-a we ain't had anything good to eat for days. When I got back she was gone, just gone. After a few days of looking I stopped here and found out it happened here too, right around the same time."

"What happened?" Bill asked.

"Two women just vanished with no idea where, and they had a whole posse and didn't find'm. So I left and kept look'n but when I couldn't look no more I remembered how good these people were and see'ns how they had the same problem, I decided to try it here for a spell."

"So, no tracks to follow?" Bill asked.

"No—none to speak of," Otis said.

"Was it near a river?" Bill asked.

Otis nodded and said, "yes, like I said, we were not too far from here on the Youghiogheny river."

Bill shook his head and looked at the ground.

"So mister—I mean Bill, this town has been through a

bit and is stronger for it."

"Hmm, I should fit right in," Bill said.

He nodded, smiled, turned and on his way out said, "thanks Otis."

Otis said, "no problems Bill."

Bill found an empty stall at the stable and was bedding down the horses when a small boy came in.

"Hey mister, that's my job!"

"You're a bit small for pull'n a saddle down."

"Well—I can do bout anything else," he said.

"There was no one around, so I figured you were all in Church."

He was defiant, giving Bill a serious look. He climbed up the gate, leaned in looking at him up and down. After a moment, he broke a smile.

"They are, it's my Sunday to watch things, my names Dan—Dan Johnson."

He held out his little hand and shook Bills with as much strength as he could muster.

"I'm Bill. Tell me Dan do you mind if'n I continue bedding these two down?"

"No, that'd be fine Bill," he said,

"Dan, can you guard my things if I leave em here? Still looking for a room."

"Oh sure mister and be'n a Sunday and all, I can give you a discount."

Bill looked away and smiled, shaking his head. "So it's okay for you to work on the Sabbath?" he asked.

"No, that's just it, dad will think I'm play'n somewhere," Dan said.

He sat on the gate and didn't stop talking. Bill left there knowing all he would ever need to know about the Johnson family, all nine of them.

# Chapter 25

Bill walked to the general store and sat on a high loading dock on the side of the building, waiting for church to let out. He watched Duke walk down the alley where he could see the river and a few outbuildings, also part of a house across the water. When Church let out the streets filled with people chatting and slowly moving through town. Bill called Duke back and tried to look presentable. A pretty girl of sixteen or seventeen saw Bill and walked up to him.

"Can I pet your dog, mister?" she asked.

"Sure, his name is Duke."

"Well, hi fella."

She pet his head and rubbed behind his ears, he moaned and leaned against her.

"He's starve'n for attention," she said.

"We been on the trail for a few days..."

"My names Beck..."

Duke caused her to stop mid-name by letting out a howl and leaning his head against her Sunday dress.

"Well, how do you do Beck, I'm Bill."

The town Sheriff walked up. "Can I help you, mister?"

"Morning Sheriff, just wait'n for the store owner to show up," Bill said.

"Be a long wait, it's Sunday."

"Yeah, I was just hope'n he'd see me and stop," Bill said.

"Well, he cut across to his house it's just over there."

He pointed in an arc as if to say it's the other side of this here house. The Sheriff wanted to know more about this rough-looking man.

"Hey—I got a pot of coffee on the back burner, feel like a cup? I'm just next door."

"Yes. Yes, I could really use a cup right about now, it's been a long morning."

They walked across the wide general store front boardwalk, past a narrow alley and into the Sheriff's office.

"Rebecca, can you get us..."

The Sheriff looked over, Becky was already pouring the coffee. He nodded and smiled to Bill.

"I'm Ben Jenkins," he extended his hand.

"Yes, I've heard good things about you Sheriff," he shook his hand.

"Oh? Well, as long as it's good things," the Sheriff said.

"It was."

"Have a seat Bill, what brings you to Spring Valley?"

Becky set the coffee on Ben's desk and moved back to the potbelly stove. She added a few spoons of sugar to a third cup and sipped it with her back to the Sheriff.

"Now Rebecca, we've gone over this," the Sheriff said.

"Oh Ben, I'm seventeen now," she said.

"You're sixteen."

"Be seventeen soon."

"Not till Christmas—but let's just keep it to half a cup, okay?"

She smiled at Bill and called Duke to follow her outside. Bill could see through the side windows that the center park area was filling with people, a few were playing music in the large gazebo.

"So Bill, what is it you need from the store?" Ben said.

"I'm looking for work."

"Work? So you're not just pass'n through?"

"No—no, I'm planning to stay awhile," Bill said.

"Hmm, well what is it brought you here?"

"Been in the hills a while and it's time to, as a friend once said, 'join the human race, if'n they'll have me," Bill said.

"Yeah? Why here?"

"As I said I heard good things about you and about the general store owner."

Ben scratched his chin and looked out the window, took his coffee in hand and leaned back in his chair.

"Well, first Fred's got a young man that's work'n out just fine. Now they maybe could use some help up the street, I can ask around for you."

"That would be mighty kind, Sheriff," Bill said.

"You look a mite hungry, let's take a walk to center park they'll be bring'n out food any minute."

"They won't mind a stranger?" Bill asked.

"No. They're welcoming folks in these parts."

Bill sat on the grass eating chicken, and Duke watched the children play.

"Bill," a voice called out through the commotion, "Bill?"

Bill kept eating when Becky walked up to him. "Concentrating on that chicken?" she said.

"Hmm?"

"I was call'n to ya," she said.

"Oh, I'm sorry I'm just thinking."

"So Ben say's you're stay'n in Spring Valley."

"That's right, I need a place to settle. Say Beck, do you know if the young man that works at the general store is here?" Bill asked.

She looked around. "Ah, yes, that's him over there," she pointed.

The man was younger than he'd pictured.

"Bill, would you like some more chicken? I can ask

Corbin to come over too," Becky said.

He nodded. "Great, thanks."

She called to Duke, and they left together. Bill leaned against a tree and looked around. Most of the people were looking at him. He felt out of place and wanted a haircut and shave, but his plan was to leave Jersey behind—to start over as an unknown in a nice little town. He knew better than to think this place didn't have its share of demons, he just didn't want to be the one to chase them out, those days were behind him.

"Bill?"

He almost forgot his new name again as Becky approached with the young man.

"This is Corbin, he works at the store," she said.

Bill lifted his hand to the young man. "Have a seat," he said.

"Nice to meet you, sir," Corbin said.

"Here, you two enjoy this while I walk around with Duke," Becky said.

She put the plate on the ground and kind of pushed Corbin to sit down.

"So Corbin, you work at the general store. What else do you do around here, you know, for fun?" Bill asked.

"Oh, heck mister ain't noth'n go'n on round here."

"No?"

Corbin shook his head and said, "nah."

"Got family here?"

"Nah."

"Where's your family?"

"East, Boston mostly," he said. "Say have you tried this chicken?"

Corbin pointed to a few of the pieces Becky brought.

"No, not that kind, is it good?"

"It's great! I always look for Mrs. Engilton's chicken.

She lives across the street from the store." He leaned in. "Very pretty she is."

"Do you have a gathering like this every week?" Bill asked.

"I wish to geeminy we did! But nah, it's once a month, if'n the weather holds. You just showed up on the right Sunday."

"I truly did."

"Why are you here and your family's back east?" Bill asked.

"I wanted to get away, so I saved up and left. Money ran out in Cumberland and I didn't want to work in the mines so I made it up here."

"Hmm, would you like to go back home?"

"Yes sir, I surely would."

"Have you set aside any money for the trip?"

"A bit, but I can't go back empty-handed."

"That would be admit'n defeat?" Bill asked.

Corbin nodded. "I saved enough to get there and a little extra, but I need to have enough that if they don't want me to stay at home, I can find another place and not be begging. I can't look like a loser to them, you know?"

"Hmm," Bill nodded. "How much more do you need?"

"Goal is one fifty," he said, shaking his head as he took a bite of chicken. "It's take'n forever."

"One fifty more?"

"No—I need another seventy-five," Corbin said.

They sat eating the widow Engilton's chicken, watching the people. Corbin told Bill about everyone of importance in the little town. Otis nodded to Bill as he walked by carrying a dish. He set it on a long table of food and started filling a plate for himself.

"Corbin, what if you could do something, just one thing that would help you get the rest of the money?

Would you really take it and go back home?" Bill asked.

"Oh yes sir, I miss my parents someth'n fierce."

Bill reached into his coat pocket and pulled out a wide leather wallet. He looked around to make sure no one was watching. He set it just under his plate and thumbed through the bills. Corbin looked confused. When Bill got to the right number, he slid them out and set them on the ground next to his leg.

"That's eighty-five dollars, and it's yours if'n you pack and leave for home by tomorrow morning. All you have to do is not tell anyone where you got the money, understand?" Corbin stared at the money and nodded.

"You can leave a note on the door of the store for Fred, but again you can't say where you got the money, just say it's time to go back home or someth'n to that effect," Bill said.

"By Jingo, if this is a prank..."

"No Corbin it's not a prank, I just want your job and I have enough money set aside to help you out too."

"You must want my job mighty bad."

"Well, I heard good things about Fred and you just said the same. I just want my stay here to be a good one," Bill said.

"Well, how long are you planning on stay'n?"

"Forever—is it a deal?"

"Oh yes, yes—it's a deal. I can taste my mother's biscuits right now. I can take the north road then catch the train through the pass, I'll get there in no time," Corbin said.

"Remember—"

"I know, I promise I won't be tell'n nobody—not one whit."

Corbin looked around, pulled the money to his side, folded it, and stuffed it into his pocket. He got a little teary eyed and thought about home and couldn't believe his luck.

"Well, you must have a lot to do," Bill said.

"I do Bill, thank you. I hope to see you in Boston. Oh yeah, Fred's got my parents' numbers written down, come to see me, I owe you," Corbin said.

"I might just do that. My brother and sister live in Rhode Island, but you don't owe me anything, we're even."

Corbin left grinning and shaking his head, Bill leaned back listening to all the people as he finished his chicken. The beautiful day had just gotten better, and he was feeling pretty good.

# Chapter 26

Bill slept on a cot near his horses. He rose when the sun broke and walked to the little Inn which was a building or two past the Highlands common house. Yesterday he'd arranged a bath from a loud older woman at center park. He brought fresh clothes and asked if she could get the ones he was wearing washed.

"You're going to put these back on?"
She held them up and away.
"Until I get some new ones," he said.
"Okay," she said.
He sat in the tub and washed; it had been a while since he'd had a hot bath, he won't be missing the freezing mountain pools. He laid back in the hot water, his head leaning with a wet cloth over his face. He was thinking about an approach to take at the general store when the door swung open. He jumped up and covered his privates as the woman rushed up and poured another bucket of hot water in the tub.

"Heck ma'am! Give a guy a warning," Bill said.
"Where's the fun in that?"
Bill gave her a look. "Well give me a chance to cover up."
She reached for the door. "Oh, I seen um all honey." She turned at the door and smiled. "One of the perks."
Bill walked into the General Store acting like he was shopping. A tall man with dark hair and a slim mustache

was stocking shelves. When he heard the door's bell, he stopped and looked at the big man with long hair and beard.

"How can I help you, mister?"

"I'm looking for two things. First, I need a timepiece," Bill said.

"Oh, well we have one made nearby in Massachusetts by Mr. Dennison. It has interchangeable parts so it can be repaired right here in the USA."

Bill walked to the counter and looked through the glass.

"Hmm, not cheap is it."

"No, if you like you can look though the catalog and order one. Now, the more you spend the better the watch," Fred said.

"Can I see it?"

Fred took the watch from the display and handed it carefully to Bill.

"Does that chain come with it?" Bill asked.

"No, but if you take the watch today, I'll toss in that leather strap at no charge."

Bill looked it over close then set it on the counter and looked around the store.

"You said you were in need of two things?" Fred asked.

"Oh yes, I'm Bill Smith, Mr. Fredrick and I'm looking for a job."

Bill held out his hand and Fred shook it and got a funny look on his face.

"It's just Fred, not Mr. Fredrick, and as luck would have it Bill, I lost my assistant just this morning,"

"No! Well, this is a lucky day for both of us," Bill said.

"What qualifications have you got to do this type of work?"

"Ah—you can trust me to never steal or cheat. I haven't been sick in years so I'll be here when you need me."

"Have you ever done this work before?"

"Sure..."

Bill looked around the room then hung his head and said, "no I can't lie, I seen it done before though, at a trading post I frequented."

Fred rubbed his chin and thought for a minute. "You didn't have anything to do with Corbin's leav'n did you?"

Before Bill could be honest with him, Fred interrupted.

"Course not. Corbin left us a nice letter this morning, the boys just homesick. Can't blame him for that," Fred said.

Bill nodded and smiled.

"How long are you planning on staying here in our little town?" Fred asked.

"I plan on making this my home," Bill said.

"So the watch, was that just a conversation starter?"

"No, toss in the chain and you got a deal."

"You mean the leather strap?"

"Yes, the leather strap."

"Cash?"

"What else?"

Fred smiled. "The job comes with the upstairs apartment and I can pay you what I was pay'n Corbin, no more."

"When do I start?"

Bill extended his hand, and they shook.

"Oh ah, I have a dog..."

"Yeah, I saw him out there, I like dogs."

Bill reached into his waistcoat and counted out the money. He asked Fred to explain how to care for the timepiece, then Fred gave him the day to get settled in.

# Chapter 27

Bill loaded his possessions onto Number Three and walked them back to his new room. Fred was at the side door stairs with the key and showed him around. The entrance was from the alleyway between the store and the Sheriff's office. Both buildings were two stories tall and looked very similar. The steps hugged the wall on the outside of the building and it was identical on the Sheriff's building across the alley. There was a platform at the top long enough for the door and a double window where a weathered chair sat facing the street. The platform extended almost to the front of the building.

Bill hauled everything up to his new room. He unloaded bags and refolded his good clothes, placing them in cedar storage boxes under the bed. He hung coats and such in a tall cabinet. He lit a fire in his small stove and made a half pot of coffee. He opened the front curtains and windows, the main street of his new town was busy. Directly across the street he saw what must be the widow Engilton. Corbin was right, she was pretty. Her long dark hair was up loosely under a summer hat. Her house was back off the street more than the others, and she was working in her flower garden.

Bill's new front porch was the roof above the storefront's boardwalk. It was narrow, and the railing held the store's big sign. It looked safe to stand on, but to get out there you would have to climb out the window. He sat in an old chair on the small platform at the top of his stairs, smoked a cigar and drank a cup of coffee. Duke stretched out at his side with his paws between spindles high above the alley.

"What are you doing over there?"

Bill jumped. The voice was just next to his ear. He looked over, and Becky was leaning out of the window across the alley.

"This is my new place, I work downstairs at the store," he said.

"I guess we're neighbors then," she said smiling. "See you around town."

She lowered her head and disappeared into her room.

"Hey?" Bill said.

She returned smiling.

"Do you and the Sheriff live there?"

"No, Ben lives back there." She pointed back down the alley. "He built a house on the river a year ago, he wanted me to move in there but I'm seven..." she remembered Bill was there when that line was dispelled. "Almost, and it was time to have my own place."

"Oh—well how do you like it?"

"Ah." She looked around and then back at him. "I like it very much, it's all my own now."

She turned her head back and looked at the bottom of the stairs.

"Hey, is that your horse?"

"Yes."

"He's a beauty, what's his name?"

"Number Three," Bill said.

"What kind of name is that?"

"Well, his full name is 'Horse Number Three',"

She gave him a look.

"Me and a friend each had a horse, but we needed a pack horse, one that would be good in the hills so I ordered him special. She wasn't our first number three, she was replacing our second, which we gave to a friend for help'n out. Anyway, none of them were our main rides, they were a third horse so we just always called them number three."

She looked confused.

"We just call him horse number three, okay?"

"So, you had a number one number three, and a number two number three, is that right Bill?" she asked.

He looked out at the street and thought for a moment. "Hearing it out loud it sounds kinda stupid, but yes."

"Can I ride her sometime?"

"Yes, if you think you can handle him, we can go for a ride," Bill said.

"Do you have another horse?"

"Oh yes, my horse is called Blue."

She smiled and shook her head. "So let's see; your number two horse is called number three and your main horse is called Blue. Tell me is Blue actually blue?"

"Actually, he was kind of blue when I got him, they called him a Blue Roan now he's more of a gray," Bill said.

They smiled and nodded to each other then she pulled back inside.

"See you later Bill," she said from the dark window.

"Bye, Beck."

.

# Chapter 28

He enjoyed becoming Bill. Starting over was just the medicine he needed, and changing his name was the only way it could play out. He'd put a lot of time into grieving for his family. When the grieving had faded, when the thought of their fate didn't hit him hard every day, he saw how much it had changed him. He was a different man, a man he didn't recognize living in the hills. He never liked to analyze inner thoughts, she did enough of that for both of them; but being alone one's thoughts drift and one has a need for answers, and a desire for direction.

The bond he had with Catherine was based on a closeness of friendship—as kids running through the hills of their little town, or out on the cove, they spent all their days together. One day they'd grown up. Running through the forest had become buggies with basket lunches, and fishing boats on the cove became sailing on Block Island Sound.

He remembered that first kiss and how it changed everything, forever.

He'd never really been alone—then she was gone and loneliness bared down on him in ways he never imaged it could. He did have the company of Hamish, mornings, evenings, and the days he wasn't running through the hills. It probably prolonged his mourning, but it brought him back to ground level when his thoughts overcame him, when he wanted to give up. There was a time after the murders when he stood on a high ridge wanting to dive off. During the last year in the hills he stood on the same cliff, looking at the vast valley, the beauty of the distant hills, and he just wanted to move on. He wanted to be in the company of others, live around people again, the way it was before life got dark, gloomy and so awful it turned him into a different man.

He felt forced to leave to protect his friends, mainly Hamish. There was also a motivation of hope that he may regain a little of his old self. Even though he believed every time he killed a man it was justified, he'd still crossed a line and he could never go back to the man he was. What if, he thought, he'd lost that part of him that she loved? Was it now absolutely out of reach, gone forever? If she knew him now, would she love him? He knew the answer was no. Those bright eyes would look right through him, he'd seen it before, the way she looked at rough-looking men with questionable pasts.

Sometimes he tried to put her out of his mind. He could never live up to that standard. It was time to start over as best he could. The thing about starting over is meeting new people. Some of them become friends and after a while he felt that his dishonesty was the center of each new friendship. They were all founded on a lie; they thought he was someone he wasn't. Over time, that had an effect on him as it might with any honest man. Early on he decided to only lie about his name, if things were asked about his past he just wouldn't answer.

He also kept the circle of friends small, to pull back on contact with those friendships already made, but the latter became a promise impossible to keep. After six months he felt like Beck, Ben, Fred, and Fred's wife Milly had become close friends, almost family. No one understood his beard and long hair, but it didn't matter. With each one he let in, a strong relationship developed, the comfort of a family filled a void in him.

The rest of the town however, were starting to see Bill as the town bum. They saw him walking around unkempt with his dog. Occasionally he'd sit in front of different buildings just because Duke seemed to want to stop there; he'd whittle or even dose off. Once he woke to find two coins on the boardwalk next to him, after that he stuck closer to his room.

Bill worked out so well at the store that most days he left early. It seems Corbin had worked slowly, spreading the day out. Bill worked differently, if there was work to be done he did it, and did it right. Fred could see he was a smart man, he rarely used paper to cipher problems, it was natural to him. He counted back change so well the bank was always right on the money.

"Bill, where were you educated?"

"Home—for arithmetic we used Ray's, well it was the last one we used, and for read'n and spell'n and such we used 'Cobb's' then 'American Speller', 'Useful Knowledge', my parents did most of the teach'n," Bill said.

Bill noticed Fred was referring to the cash box and tally sheet.

"My brother was the arithmetic kid. Oh I learned it, but I had to make and mend all the quills and I usually did that during arithmetic because literature and the like was next and everyone needed a good pen."

"Must-a been a big family?"

Bill nodded. "No just the three kids, but we took in nearby children for school'n. I was the oldest and had to help out with the young ones, my little brother was the smart one he went on to a university."

"Where's he now?"

"Well, he left school and had a few adventures, he's back home in Anchor Bay."

"Anchor Bay, is that in Rhode Island?"

"Yes, you heard of it?"

"I been up that way before, beautiful country. You must miss your home and parents."

"I guess, they've been dead for a few years now."

"Oh sorry," Fred said.

"Not your fault Fred."

Bill was up before sunrise each day and rode Blue around the valley before work. After years in the hills, the local woods had become a part of him and he loved it. He felt he had the best of both worlds living in this little town. He kept Blue in a small pen and stall behind the store. When his workday was done he had different activities, like fishing and hunting or practice shooting. Sometimes he would sit on a high outcropping with a view of the valley and mountains and read a new book he'd ordered from one of Fred's catalogs. Once a week he would go for a ride with Becky. He gave her 'Horse Number Three', who she just called 'Three'.

Becky had been living on a little farm just outside of town when everything fell apart. Her father died, and a few months later her mother vanished.

"Some people say she ran off, but she didn't, she loved me. We had big plans for the farm," Becky said.

Two other women disappeared, and the whole town grieved. They were worried and worked together to protect each other, Becky told him they became a stronger community after that. Bill liked how the town took to and protected Becky. She was well adjusted, happy, and became a beautiful young woman full of life. They talked a lot while playing checkers or chess, or on their rides. Many evenings they would talk across the alley from their windows or the top of the stairways, and she would tell him how she really felt about things and he would do his best to offer advice. The kind of advice and insight he thought he'd be sharing with his own daughter had she'd lived.

# Chapter 29

An almost daily habit for Bill was to visit the Highlands for a beer. He couldn't bring the dog into the tavern, so he started the tradition of sitting at the window seat and watching Duke from there. He'd only have one beer, he'd sip it slowly and sometimes read a book and have a snack of bread and smoked fish or meat. Howard brewed ales out back. He wasn't precise in his brewing method, so the taste and strength varied. You knew it was a strong batch when the room was louder, and the crowd was rowdy. The thing he liked most about his stops at the Highlands was catching up on the town chatter. After a while it was like he wasn't there. To them he was the town bum and most of the men would say just about anything while he was sitting nearby.

During one of his first stops at the Highlands, Cane and Clayton made some comments out loud about him, everyone started laughing. When Bill stood up, most of the laughing stopped. He walked to the bar where a few men were still chuckling; when they saw how big he was, they looked anywhere but at him. He moved one of the men over and asked Howard for a bowl of water, which he took out to Duke. When he came back in he twisted his chair, sat down, and took a long sip of beer looking around the room from between his beer, hair, and hat brim just to see who was giving him looks. He put Cane and Clayton Gannon on his short list of possible problems in Spring Valley.

# Chapter 30

One afternoon Bill was standing on the bank of a creek
fishing when he saw Otis ride by. He waved, but Otis was in
a hurry and didn't see him. Bill walked back to the water's
edge until he heard more horses and moved to get a better
look. It was three men riding fast, and it looked like they
were after Otis. He called Blue over, left his new fishing rod
at the river, and they moved to higher ground. He heard a
gunshot but couldn't see anything and moved higher to see
over the trees. He saw them in the distance; he looked
through his spyglass. One man was down and another has
his hands up. The three men were getting off their horses
and arranged the rest of the people in a line. There was Otis
and four other black men and women, the one remaining
white man was separated from the rest at gunpoint.

Bill pulled his Sharps rifle and slipped off Blue in one
move, he grabbed the small leather covered box, his long
gloves, and ran to a ledge. He took another look with the
telescope; he set it down and slid opened the box. He
lifted the heavy rifle, pulling its lever down as the breach
block dropped which opened the cylinder. He quickly
pulled a paper cartridge bullet from the box put the lead
end in and pushed it until it stopped. Pulling the lever
back up it sheared off the end of the paper exposing
black powder to the inside chamber. He instinctively blew

the powder and scrap paper off as he reached for a small firing cap. He looked at them as he cocked the hammer halfway, setting the cap in place. He moved up on the flat stone, placing the gun in his lap while he put his gloves on. Eyeing them in the distance, he crawled onto the sandstone and lay flat.

Resting the end of the barrel on the ledge, he held his hand out at full length down the barrel. Matched the ink marks on the thumb of his glove with the height of the man holding a gun on his friend, he determined the shot was about a hundred and twenty yards away. He matched that with his new sight and clicked it a few times. He pulled it close to his cheek and looked down its long barrel and saw Otis and the other dark-skinned men and women being forced to their knees. The gunman was standing sideways, which made the target half as wide as if he was facing him. It was hard to gauge the wind as he was behind an outcropping of stone. He thought even if he missed it could get their attention off Otis and onto him. The distant man lifted his gun, aiming it at Otis. Bill made a quick sight adjustment and pulled the hammer back all the way.


Otis looked up at the ugly man. The sun was bright and shining off his sweat covered face. This was the situation on which his worst nightmares were built. When the man moved over to the others Otis felt for his knife, it was in his boot but his pants were too long to reach it without getting caught. The man walked back to him. When he lifted his gun Otis said a prayer, but the man lifted off the ground rushing sideways ten feet hitting the ground hard, a red mist followed him down. The other man looked at his friend in shock for a second. The sound of the distant gun passed by their ears and moved through the valley. Bill was already slipping another firing cap in place and re-aiming, his glove smoked from the burn of the combustion. Otis stood and pulled his knife, Bill cocked the hammer full setting his cheek on the wood stock, but Otis was in the way. The third rider was just turning from watching the only white captive—a covered wagon was between him and the others. The man he was watching lowered his hands and started looking for something to attack with. Bill couldn't wait, as the man twisted around it gave him a full on front shot, he took it.

Otis threw his knife and hit the last man in the shoulder, which gave him a second to rush at him. They landed off the trail on the grass and tall weeds. Otis didn't stop hitting him until he was pulled off. One of the women was crying into the arms of a man and everyone stood and watched as Bill came riding up fast, sliding off his moving horse.

"What the hey, Otis?" Bill asked.

"Bill?" Otis said.

"You know this man Otis?" asked the remaining white man.

"Yeah, he's a friend John, he's a friend."

"Thank you mister, these good people were done for," he said.

"You too, I think John," Bill said.

Bill looked at Otis, waiting for an explanation he could tell he didn't want to tell him.

"Hell Bill, this here is a secret, yah know," Otis said.

"You can trust me Otis,"

The other man spoke up. "We can't trust anyone mister," he said.

"Well Bill," Otis looked at Bill as if he was trusting him with his life. "These people are running to safety in the north and we help'n 'em.''

Bill walked around looking at the people, John slowly felt for the butt of his sidearm. Bill said something to one of the men, they conversed, he shook the man's hand. He turned back to Otis. "How can I help?"

Otis relaxed, John dropped his hand from his gun and blew out hard through his mouth. "Mister you already have."

John took the dead men away on their horses heading south and Bill and Otis drove the others in the wagon north a half day's ride to a farmhouse.

"That was some shoot'n Bill, what kind of gun is that?" Otis asked.

"It's a slant breach Sharps," Bill said. "It's 36 inch barrel makes it accurate at a good distance."

"I saw its smoke in the hills and mister that was a heck of a shot."

"So where are we going?" Bill asked.

"This is my run," Otis said.

"Your run?"

"Yeah, I pick up men and women that John or someone else brings up, back there near the river and take them north to a farmhouse, after that someone else takes 'em on from there. Probably Pittsburgh area, least wise til one place or another is found out. When that happens we meet and setup some-where's else to connect up, been lucky lately—till now."

"This is a free state, once across the line you'd think they'd be free," Bill said.

"Ain't no law around here, they been known to chase runners way up north."

"I don't see why he would kill them if he was to make money by bringing them back?"

"This is their third time escaped, could be a dead or alive out on 'em, side's I think he was just gonna kill me and scare them into submission," Otis said.

Bill shook his head. "All this happening right here under my nose. You know you read about it in the papers but..."

"Bill, you know how important this is, it's a secret you have to keep."

"That story you told me a while back that wasn't your wife that was taken was it?" Bill asked.

"No." Otis looked down shaking his head. "She was a woman I was help'n, and it was my fault. We got to like'n each other. If I'd just rode on through as usual, she'd be safe, living free right now. So you can see how you have to keep this secret, right?"

Bill thought for a minute. He looked at the ever present hills in the distance.

"Otis—I got a little secret for you too."

# Chapter 31

Becky had become a good friend. She thought Bill was a different kind of man, a kind she'd never known. Not boring like most of the town. She saw him through the window one night when he forgot to close the shade. He pulled his hair back and tied it, took his shirt off and stood at the wash bowl cleaning up, getting ready for bed. He looked different, not the oldish man but a strong, muscular younger man. It confirmed her suspicions that he was trying to fool people by wearing old baggy clothes, all that hair and the beard. He had scars around his sides and chest and arms. He leaned down to undo his pants; she jumped back, falling to the floor. He looked up, held his pants and walked to the window pulling the curtains closed.

Melissa Engilton had always been in Becky's life, but after her mother left they became much closer, over the years she looked at her as an older sister. They would read the same books, and Missy always had the newest magazines to read and talk about. Melissa would help her with her schoolwork, which as she got older became beyond Ben's knowledge. They would talk about everything, and lately much of the conversation drifted to Bill. At first because he was new in town and strange looking, but later because they could see he was not who he seemed to be. They sat at the table coming up with theories, they'd expound on them and laugh. Missy saw him walk out of the store with a broom. She stood watching him from her front window.

"You like him," Becky said.

"Like him? I can't even see what he looks like, I like his manner though, he holds himself well," she said.

"Well, what if I told you I saw him naked."

Missy turned to her quickly.

"What are you saying? He didn't?"

"What—no, I saw him through the window, not really naked, but I saw enough."

Missy was relieved. She sat down and leaned in.

"Well?"

"He's not the old man he acts like. He was washing up, his shirt was off and he pulled his hair back and he looked kind of handsome and he has a lot of scars all over, but he is very strong—you know with muscles,"

"Mm, yes, I know,"

Missy smiled, and they laughed.

"How much did he? Ah, well..."

"Disrobe?" Becky asked.

"Yes..."

"He started taking his trousers off and..."

Becky looked at her and smiled.

"No!" Missy said.

"No, that's when he remembered to close the curtains."

They laughed so loud Bill heard them from across the street.

# Chapter 32

Fred and his wife Milly noticed Bill would watch the widow Engilton when she was working in her garden. After a while, Milly brought in some food for Bill to take to her.

"Fred I don't have time to get this dish over to Mrs. Engilton." They watched Bill perk up. "Can you get it to her?"

"I'll take it over if you need," Bill said.

"Oh Bill, why that would be fine, thank you," Milly said.

"Thank you," Bill said.

He looked in the store mirror and decided to pull back his hair.

"I think no hat Bill what do you think?" Milly said.

He got halfway across the street when he had to return for the dish. Milly and Fred were conspicuous in their silence, smiling and looking around the room.

"I just forgot the..." Bill pointed to the casserole, picked it up and left.

He knew what was going on, but he'd been looking for any reason to say more than hello to the beauty across the street. She had filled his thoughts for a long time, and he was ready to take it to the next level—good or bad. He could stop thinking about her, or if everything could somehow fall into place, well that would be just fine.

"Hello Miss. or ah Misses? Um, here's a casserole Milly made for you," Bill said.

"Well hi Bill, how nice." She looked across the street

as Fred and Milly both moved away from the window, "Oh—I see," she said.

She stood and held out her hands, but they were dirty from the garden.

"Can you bring it into the house, please?"

Bill followed her in. She reached up and undid the ribbon to her hat with two fingers and flung it to a sofa. Her thin waist twisted around and her long brown hair fell softly on her pale blue dress. She smiled over her shoulder and her dark eyes lit up as she moved to the kitchen. She dipped her hands in a washing bowl and dried them on the cloth next to it. She smiled at him and reached for the casserole.

"Hi Bill," Becky said.

She was sitting at a dining table reading a magazine. Bill missed her because his eyes hadn't left Melissa and they wanted to get back to it.

"Oh, hey Beck, how are you today?"

"Oh, it's a pretty good day."

Melissa gave Becky a look, and she stood and walked by Bill and out.

"Guess I'll get back to school work," she said.

Bill looked around the room, it was full of light from a very large paned window which looked out onto a backyard of green bushes and scattered colorful flowers. The same flowers were in water on the table in front of him.

"What a nice home."

"Thank you, and thanks for bringing this over." She set the casserole on a counter and covered it with a towel. "You know we've never really had a chance to talk, do you have to get back or can you stay for a cup of coffee?"

Bill felt like he had all the time in the world. They talked for two cup's worth. She was full of questions, and Bill did his best to answer. He came up with a few good return questions. But her scent and face were as intoxicating as one of the strong ales brewed at the Highlands.

"I hear you're planning on staying here in our town."

"Yes," he said.

"Do you enjoy working at the store?"

"I do. They're the nicest people around," he said.

"Where did you come from?"

Bill smiled and said, "I'd like to know more about you too. Why don't we go for a ride and have lunch sometime soon? There's a nice meadow near the river just east of town, what do you think?"

"Well, I would like that. You know I could cut your hair for you and while I'm at it give you a nice close shave. I can see under all that is a good-looking man," she said.

"Someday I'd like that—but for now I just can't."

"Well, when you're ready."

"That's a date."

"That's not much of a date, but I'll take that lunch in the meadow. It will be nice to get away from here for a little while and enjoy the autumn colors," she said.


The next Saturday Bill had the Sunny Side make a lunch and borrowed Fred's wagon. He put on new clothes and pulled his hair back the way Roger used to have his, minus the feather, and trimmed his beard to about four inches. He pulled up in front of Melissa's house just as Cane rode up. Cane said something, Bill looked at him but they both turned to see Melissa exit the house. Bill jumped down and helped her in. As he walked back around, he noticed Cane was stopped in the street. He was looking at her but she was turned away looking at the front of her house. As Bill walked along the wagon, Cane turned his head and moved on.

Bill climbed up. "Is he bothering you?" he asked.

"He's always bothering me."

Bill turned to see Cane down the street, he slapped his hat hard against his leg and slowly rode to the Highlands. He'd seen Cane looking at her before, but all the men looked at her—best he could tell most of the women did too. But to stare at her like that was just rude. Cane was adding up to real trouble.

They talked and laughed; he had fun again. He felt something he hadn't felt for ages. The closeness of a woman, the excitement of the present enhanced by the possibility of a future. When he kissed her that day in the colorful meadow with the cool autumn breeze, she kissed him back.

They told each other about their past and how they ended up here in Spring Valley.

Her mother was from Boston, her father was Spanish and died on a ship off the Carolina coast. He was the captain. They were attacked and just a few men survived; it was said those that died were the lucky ones. Just a few years ago her husband died, he never returned from a hunting trip.

"Ben and a few men found him, and his friend at the bottom of a ravine, the ground must have been loose and fell from under them. They said it was a tall cliff and the..." she looked off at the tall mountains. "It wasn't far from here," she said.

"Horses too?"

"Hm?"

"Were the horses in the ravine as well?"

"No, that's how we knew something was up, the horses came back without the men."

"Mm. So they were off their horses up there, but didn't tie them off."

Bill saw her looking at him while he was thinking through the death of her husband. He had a few more questions, but now was not the time.

"I like your house, it suits you," he said.

"Oh, well—yes." She was glad to change the subject. "It took a while to build, he was a very good carpenter. We moved in as soon as we could and after working all day he'd come home and put in hours and hours on it. To him it wasn't ever really done—always something to do."

Bill told her about his place on the river and how beautiful it was, but he had to stop himself when he got to the children playing in the yard, and Catherine in the garden. Melissa knew something awful happened to them, but didn't want to push, she knew he'd tell her when the time was right. They laid back in silence for a while, looking up through a golden maple tree at the deepest of blue skies. It wasn't an uncomfortable silence—far from it.

She rolled over, leaning her cheek in her hand. "Are you running from something Bill, or someone? Are you an outlaw? Of course if you were an outlaw you wouldn't tell me," she said.

"I'm not an outlaw. You don't need to be afraid of me, I never hurt anyone that wasn't trying to hurt me or someone else."

"But, you are running from something."

He told her about the attack on Abby and that men were after him, anyone near him was in danger, so he left to keep them from harm.

# Chapter 33

Bill was playing chess with Ben in the Sheriff's office when Little Harry Johnson came in.

"Oh—hey Bill," Little Harry said.

"Harry."

"Ah Sheriff, some guy looks like trouble," Little Harry said.

Sheriff was concentrating on the chessboard. "Yeah, what guy?"

"Well, he was ask'n bout Jersey Smith and he's got two gun's on and, well he just looked kind'a crazy like."

Ben looked up at Little Harry and said, "Jersey Smith? Where is this guy now?"

"I saw him go into the Highlands," he said.

"Okay, he does sound like trouble, very good Harry, very good," Ben said.

Ben stood and put on his gun belt.

"What's go'n on Ben?" Bill said.

"Few years back a friend of mine came through town looking for a murderer."

He put more bullets in his holster belt.

"Well, he was looking for the killers of Jersey Smith's family, and I guess this Jersey Smith kind of moved into the mountains and went a little crazy, well you must'a heard the stories."

Ben looked at Bill.

"Ah, yeah, but they were good stories, right?"

"Most of em. I gotta get to the Highlands."

He walked out the door. Bill grabbed Little Harry by the arm before he could leave and pulled a coin from his pocket and put it in the boy's hand.

"Good job Harry."

The first thing Bill thought about was that he should have come up with a different last name. He had his usual little gun in his pocket and a knife in his boot sheath, but he ran up to his room and pulled the cedar box from under his bed. He strapped on his gun and knife belt; put on his longer coat to cover them and quickly walked to the Highlands.

Bill stood in the doorway of the Highlands. Ben confronted the man who said he was a bounty hunter looking for Jersey Smith.

"I know who's wanted by the law and Jersey Smith is not one of them, unless you got some new paperwork to prove other," Ben said.

"Oh, he's wanted Sheriff, and that's a fact."

Ben wanted to get him outta the Highlands and away from people. He asked him to come take a look at the current list of wanted descriptions, and the man reluctantly agreed. The last thing this stranger wanted was to go through warrants with a sheriff—his face would surely turn up. He'd hoped to avoid the law altogether in this little speck on the map. Bill backed out onto the front boardwalk, moving to the end post where he leaned. The two men walked out together and stepped down into the street; the young man stopped walking and put his hands on his guns.

One man in the doorway called to warn the Sheriff, but it was too late, the man's gun was half pulled. A large knife hit the man in the right shoulder. He froze in pain long enough for Ben to turn all the way around and pull his gun. The man looked at Bill, who gave him a little smile. He thought, that's Jersey Smith, and his eyes grew in surprise. Bill thought he could be the brother that the young deputy Jim mentioned. The marauder looked at Ben and raised his gun to shoot. Bill was afraid the Sheriff wouldn't shoot in time. He reached back for his gun, but Ben shot. The young man jerked backwards falling to the ground, fine sand plumed out from under him and drifted in the breeze.

"Someone get the doc," the Sheriff said.

Little Harry and his brother Dan ran at full speed up the street. Ben looked up from the man's body to thank Bill, but Bill was halfway to his room. Ben pulled the knife from the man's shoulder and wiped its blade on the man's pant leg. He stood up and watched Bill and Duke walking away. He looked over at the men standing on the boardwalk; they were looking at Bill and shaking their heads.

"Okay men, back inside, it's all over."

"That knife came from nowhere," and "Did you see that?" was heard from the crowd as they walked back inside. Ben watched them, he noticed Cane and Clayton watching from the window with serious looks on their faces. When they saw the Sheriff looking at them, they smiled, nodded, and moved back out of view.

# A letter to Bill from Hamish
To Bill of Fredrick's General Store
Spring Valley, Western Pennsylvania


Merry Christmas Jersey, good tidings of comfort and joy, I hope this letter finds you well.

Thank you for the letter, I was starting to worry about you, which is something I rarely do. You said you were called Bill now but I wasn't sure of the last name so I left it off.

Christmas here was a wonderful affair. The village was bursting with merriment. The celebration lasted two days until late this night. I sit here writing to you so excited I can't sleep. Singers walked the lantern filled street in the little village and the small Church was packed with people, of which many asked about you.

The food was most enjoyable and I brought some winter pie home. Speaking of great cooks remember Lars Koskinen's widow Betty, well we been getting along very well and I think I may ask her to tie the knot, hope'n she'll have me.

It's been a very good year here. The Marshal has settled in and is keeping things under control and everyone seems to like him. Ed Junior and Abby are married now and are (with the help of the whole village) building a home right down river from ours. It's been nice having some action out here during the day and seeing the pretty Abby hanging laundry out reminds me of our time here with Catherine and the children. Those were some of the best days of my life. It was a blessing to have that time with them.

I know this letter won't be in your hands until after Christmas but I hope the holiday touched you as it has me, we do have a lot to be thankful for.

For our Savior was born upon this day.
Come and visit (or stay) this year,
Oh Holy Night, Merry Christmas Jersey,
Hamish.

# Chapter 34

Kaden sat below high walls of sandstone and coal seams on a fallen tree near the path. He'd assembled a team of six men and was going over the job one last time. It was a bold plan that Cane was against, but Clayton convinced him to give Kaden a chance—and a few men.

"Everyone knows their part, right?" he asked.

One man spoke up. "Yeah—please don't go over it again Kaden."

They'd made their way around an open ridge so they could approach from above, but they weren't prepared for the weather. Spring held one last cold snap. Now though, they were protected by the big wall of stone and surrounded by trees up and down the hills. Occasional bits of snow danced in the breeze high on the hillside trail. They looked down at the mining camp. Beyond it in the distance was Cumberland, Maryland.

"That ledge don't look wide enough for me to walk the horses along." Kaden said.

A man reluctantly stood and looked down over the edge.

"No, it's just the angle, it's plenty wide, but you should go around the other way anyways. It's better—you won't be seen. Then you walk back from over there."

"When were you going to tell me that Reggy?" Kaden looked at the man who looked confused scratching his head. "Reggy, when we scouted this I was to walk the ledge, tie off the horses to the tree on the ledge."

"Well ya see, when I went down to get the tree stand ready it seemed... Ah."

"Ya?"

"Like you could get seen from the camp, they's a few openings in the treetops and with a pack horse clipp'n the mountainside along the path, well it might draw attention for em ta be look'n up, is all."

"Okay. So I go around and tie'm off in the forest on the other side of the cliff face."

"Right, that's near where you were gonna leave em anyway, at the edge of the woods over there."

Kaden looked the area over. The ledge was something he should have checked before, but never made time for it. Now he looked like he didn't even know his own operation, and he had another question for Reggy. He leaned close and said low. "Is that the tree there, the one that's touching the edge of the path?"

Reggy looked at Kaden and leaned back away from him, he turned his attention to the other cliff and looked down at it.

"No, it's next to that one. Not the big one that's against the ledge, it's the one this side of that one."

"Why don't I just use that one?"

"Once you get out on the other one you'll see. Much better view of the camp office. Now you be careful stepp'n out to it." Reggy saw the look of disgust as Kaden shook his head. "Yeah, you just lean on the thick branch near the trunk, and I cut a notch for your rifle on the other branch, you'll see it."

"Just step out, off the ledge to the tree?" Kaden said.

"Yep."

"How far down is the path below that?"

"The one where us is gonna be?"

"Ya—the one where you're gonna be."

"Oh, sixty-seventy feet."

"Mmm."

"It ain't hard to get to the tree, but you need both hands. You gotta strap for your gun?"

"Mmm."

Kaden left Reggy and walked back to his log and sat. He tried hard not to show his anger. He should have been on top of this—he'd spent too much time worrying about the others he neglected his own job. If it'd been a job with the brothers involved, this wouldn't be an issue, it would have been figured down to the smallest detail. They're the reason, well Cane was—that this had to go without a hitch. He wanted badly to see the look on Cane's face when he showed him the bags of money. That'd put him back in his place for a time.

The mid-day sky was an ominous gray and getting darker. Kaden looked at his pocket watch shaking his head.

"I hear someone come'n," Reggy said.

A lone rider came up the narrow tree-lined path, his horse huffing, its hooves dug in deep the last few yards up to level ground. He slipped off and walked to Kaden.

"Well?" Kaden asked.

"It's there," he said.

Everyone mumbled excitedly, Kaden smiled. "Good work Tim."

Two men mounted and edged up to Kaden. One of them said, "We'll be wait'n for you, on the other side of the hills."

Kaden nodded, giving them a grin. They left and Tim rode down soon after.

Kaden looked at his watch. "Okay this is it, we give

them thirty minutes, then we move in. Now let's get
into position."

The men mounted up, Kaden nodded for Reggy to
come to him.

"Yeah?"

"Look, don't be all excited in there. Once a shot is
fired you'll have a real hard time getting out."

"I got it Kaden, this ain't my first time," he said.

"I know, that's why you're in charge in there."

Kaden looked at the men who were looking at him.

"Okay, head down."

Reggy was an old friend, one of the few that was not
good enough of a friend to tell about the compound. He
was the closest of their southern connections, though like
a few others they kept him at a distance.

Kaden walked around the mountain wall into a cold
breeze, he took his ride to a lower path and rode to the
forest on the other side of the cliff to get into position.
He tied off his horse and the packhorse near a rock face
which went straight up, above the treetops of the forest.
He walked along the wall and across a narrow trail
where he edged up to the cliff facing the mining camp.
Trees blocked his view of the camp, he could see down
though it was seventy feet to the path below. He looked
the area over, the ledge he was on had been cut from the
mountain and the fallen rocks below had been pushed
off the path. Some stones down there were engulfed in
thick roots of tall trees and the path moved around the
larger rocks.

He made his way along the ledge, staying close to the
face of the mountain. A few tree tops were within reach,
he used them as cover and hunched over a few times
where they grew apart. Kaden stopped at the big tree that
rubbed the ledge and looked at the next closest tree, he

saw the groove Reggy had cut for his rifle. He looked off at the mining camp; it looked like it had been excavated years ago. The steep cut walls formed two sides of the camp, he was on one and the hill they just left was the other. He could just make out the actual mine entrance, it was on the other wall. It was a large hole cut in the stone framed in with logs.

Kaden walked a few feet to the tree stand, he edged out as far as he could, but had to step back. It was just a step to the nearest branch, but it would be quite a fall. He put the gun over his shoulder, looked at his watch and moved back to the edge. He had to take a big step to the branch then another step to the tree's trunk. He looked down and saw a few of his men looking up. He took the steps and tightly hugged the tree. The view was much better, Reggy had tied back a few branches. The camp spread out from a fence and tree line near the men below. There were rows of tents, and a few men were roaming, but most of them were supposed to be in the mine. The camp was windless in the mountain's shadow and the ground was wet with small mud puddles spotting the landscape.

Kaden sat on a branch and looked down at the zigzag path at the base of the steeply cut rock face. The tree he was in had been forced to grow out by the close wall, when it could grow unencumbered it turned back upright again. There was a lot of cover up there; trees, vines, even bushes, all clinging to the rugged rock wall. From the camp below it just looked like a steep wall with bits of gray-red rock behind a mass of green. He looked down at the main office with his spyglass. It was bigger than the little shelter tents, its lower half was of wood and the top was a dirty stained canvas. He kept his eye on the two guards who stood out front. They were probably the men that brought the payroll. They were talking and laughing when Kaden's men came up from behind. They made quick work of it, covering their mouths and dragging them across the small road and into a tent.

Kaden dropped a small rock to the lower path, a man came out looking up, Kaden gave him the okay. The man ran down to the rest of them near a back gate and they walked into the camp. Kaden watched as two of the men took the place of the taken guards and stood out front. The two men that took out the guards came back across the road with guns drawn—they entered the office.

Kaden readied himself on the tree's limb, resting the rifle's heavy barrel in the groove cut in the branch, aiming it down at the front door waiting. He wished at this crucial point that Clayton, or even Cane, was here. It was a big job in a tight place and although he'd worked with most of these men before, they weren't bound by years of friendship. He wondered how far any of them would go to help him in times of real trouble. He thought about the problem points in this plan and again went over the arranged backups for all of them; it seemed like everything would go fine. He wanted to be in there in the thick of it, but his place was outside perched with his rifle ready to help as needed. Besides, Cane insisted that he just oversee or he wouldn't free up the men he needed. Now that it was too late, he worried Reggy might not do as he'd been told.

After a few minutes he expected them to walk out with big bags and jump on the horses that Tim had arranged. He looked near the gate for the fresh horses, they must be behind the line of trees, he thought. He started to worry. He leaned up from the gun, propping it across branches as he looked around. He thought he saw some movement farther down the main road, but the swaying leaves in front of him played tricks, so he took out his pocket spyglass. Looking between leaves at the rows of tents, he saw nothing out of the ordinary. He scanned back to the men at the office door; they were nowhere in sight.

He looked up from the glass. "They must have gone in," he said.

Pulling the rifle back in place, he fully cocked it just as two men were tossed out. They laid still in the cold mud. He lifted his head and saw a few men were positioning themselves along the main road; they seemed to be converging on the front of the office.

"What the hell..."

He looked again to see if it was his men or theirs laying in the mud; it was his, one was Reggy.

Kaden pushed the rifle aside again and used the spyglass to get a closer look at the men sneaking up the road. A few of them were looking up at the wall in his direction. He saw Tim step from behind a tent onto the road and point up at the rock wall; the area exploded with gunfire.

Kaden fell out of the tree. His rifle dropped to the path below, on impact it fired. The men started shooting below him where the rifle smoke was. He held on to a thick vine on the steep wall behind leafy branches, with only a few feet to the upper path he frantically felt for a foothold. They started shooting farther up the wall, wood chips and branches started falling all around him. The sound of the gunfire and lead striking the trees and stone was deafening. He was hidden from view by dense branches of leaves and treetops, but they were falling away with every shot. Lead balls buzzed by, pounding into the wall across the path above him. He found a few small toeholds and edged up. He was pushed to the wall as blood and shattered rock hit his face, his shoulder burned with pain. He must have moved to an open area, if they could see him he had to move fast. When he got to the ledge, he was hit again, in the calf. He crawled quickly behind the trunk of the big tree that hugged the cliff's path; he took a breath. The gunfire slowed, then stopped—they had to be coming up the path after him. He looked at his leg; it was just a graze but was bleeding. Not wanting to leave a trail of blood, he took off his bandanna and dabbed at the wound. He opened his shirt, twisted the end of the bandanna, and pushed it into the exit hole on his shoulder.

Kaden leaned back on the tree and stretched his legs out by pushing his feet into a wide crack in the stone wall. Pulling his sidearm, he held its chamber on the leg wound, and fired a round. He screamed as it burned the wound. Quickly he slid the hot barrel over the area, pressing hard, sealing it closed. The tree again exploded with a spray of lead. Many bounced from the wall falling on him and the ground. They were burning hot. He put a glove on and picked a few up—cringing as he set them on his shoulder wound. When it looked like he'd stopped the bleeding, he started up the path along the cliff to the horses.

"There he goes." Came from below.

Lead pounded the wall and trees all around him. He hobbled faster.

When he made the turn he collapsed in relief, for the moment he was safe. Laying on the hard dirt catching his breath, he heard them on the path below yelling to each other. Kaden limped to his horse, but as he mounted he saw the powder kegs on the packhorse and dismounted. They were tied one on each side. He took the unopened keg and a few fuses and slapped the pack horse away. It ran down the curving trail between trees, around a stone outcropping and out of view.

If he could stop them here, he'd have a chance of getting away. He ran around the corner to the ledge with the keg under one arm. He moved down the path hunched over. The ledge was much brighter now, leaves and tree tops had been blown away. He looked down over the edge at the path below. A group of men were rushing up after him. He got to the big tree, its outside was battered and bare. Voices came from just down the path in front of him. Kaden pried out the keg's stopper and pushed a fuse in, then placed the powder keg sideways in the small crevice at the base of the tree. It was a slow-burning fuse, but it was short—once lit he'd have to hurry away. He struck a match and held it up as it caught fire.

"There he is!"

He drew without thinking, and two men fell in the path. One rolled over the edge and a third man yelled to the men below.

"He's put'n a match to someth'n, better run."

Kaden held his shoulder in pain, put his gun back and struck another match. He lit the fuse and backed away. He didn't want to chance that one of them would get to the fuse, so he waited. When a man came out, Kaden shot at him. The man ran back down the path screaming, "RUN! RUN!"

"Time to go," Kaden said.

He was on his horse and twenty yards into the forest when the explosion came; it was thunderous. He got another ten yards before the ground shook, and his horse lost its footing. They fell in the path and Kaden rolled off the trail but quickly crawled back up. His horse looked shaken, he was sitting in tall fern looking in every direction. Large rocks and boulders began falling from the sky, landing around them. Stones of all sizes cut through trees like cannon balls. The sound of cracking and breaking wood came from near and far. A few hit the scattered ground shale and burst apart as if shot from a gun. As he helped his ride up, he looked back—the massive wall was still crumbling in his direction. As soon as his horse was up it took off running. Kaden had his hand on the saddle horn with both legs dragging on the hard dirt path. His foot reached the stirrup, and he pulled himself up. His horse wanted out of there, all Kaden could do was hang on. The wall behind crumbled in his direction, a massive dust cloud overtook them.

# Chapter 35

Becky entered the back door of the Highlands with a basket full of food for the bar from the Sunny Side. She stood at the back of the room, set the basket on the end of the bar, and waited for Howard. She'd never been fully inside before, it was exciting. It was early on a Friday night, a man was playing the piano, everyone was happy and talking loud; she liked it. She scanned the room. When she looked to her side in a nearby corner, she saw Cane, who was looking at her dress. Cane was one of the men in town that gave her a bad feeling. She wasn't sure what it was, but something about him put her on edge.

"Well—well, Rebecca, you have really grown up into a fine young woman," Cane said.

She immediately looked away and stopped smiling; the room stopped being fun, and she was ready to leave. She side-stepped closer to the end of the bar where she could see down behind it and got Howard's attention. Howard grabbed a few dishes from under the bar and brought them. He took what was in her basket out and replaced it with the dirty dishes. He noticed she was perspiring and glancing toward Cane. Howard knew Cane had drank past his self-imposed limit.

"You okay Becky darl'n?" Howard asked.

"Ah, yes. Is there anything else you need?" she asked.

They both saw Cane stand up at his table through the corner of their eyes and Howard said, "Have Maggie send someone else tonight, now get!"

She left through the back door in a hurry. As she came out from between the buildings, she bumped into Bill.

"What's the hurry Beck?"

She was surprised then felt relief at seeing Bill. She quickly looked back up the alley to see if Cane was coming, when she saw he wasn't she settled down.

"Hey, Bill. I'm just running some food for the Sunny Side," she said.

Bill could see she was upset. "Well what happened in there?"

"Oh, I'm fine, but I'm not sure this new job is going to work out," she said.

"Tell me what happened," he insisted.

"Nothing, I gotta run Bill we'll talk later."

She left. Bill pointed to the porch of the Highlands, and Duke found his spot stretching out. He entered the public house looking for something different, something that might shed some light on Beck being so shaken. His window seat was taken as usual on a weekend evening, so he walked halfway down the bar, finding an open spot he stepped up. He heard something unusual—Cane being loud.

He ordered a beer.

The man that was always in control was getting drunk. It must have been Cane that upset Beck, he thought.

"Howard? Beck was just in here she seemed upset. What happened?"

Howard shook his head and shrugged his shoulders. "No idea, get you anything?" he said.

"Beer."

Howard walked to the other end of the bar and Harry

Johnson leaned over to Bill, "She was just stand'n in the back and Cane was looking at her all funny like, you know?"

"Yeah, I know. Was that all he did?" Bill asked.

"Yep, she left before he could get close to her."

"Thanks, Harry," Bill said.

He walked out to the porch where he leaned against a post sipping his beer, waiting for a window seat to open.

Cane wanted another drink but Howard sat him down, got close and said. "Remember when you told me to stop you from getting drunk because everything depended on it?"

Cane stopped smiling and Howard worried what his response was going to be, but Cane seem to get the focus back in his eyes.

"Yes—yes your right Howard thanks. Think I'll take a walk."

Cane stood, put his gun belt on, and walked surprisingly straight to the front door. Bill smiled and kind of raised his beer a bit. Cane stared at him for a moment as he stepped off the porch. He took a few steps and when he got alongside the dog he took some jerky from his pocket and handed it to Duke. Duke seemed not to want it. Cane pushed it close to his face—Duke growled and took a nip at Cane's hand. Cane jumped back and gave out a high-pitched yelp, Bill smiled.

"He's a mite picky about who feeds him," Bill said.

"You have to warn people, he's a dangerous dog!"

Bill smiled. "Consider yourself warned."

Cane looked at his hand and said, "hey, I'm bleed'n."

He walked back to the dog and kicked at him, but Duke was moving to the porch. The toe of Cane's boot hit the step edge between the dogs back legs. Cane let out a small moan as he limped in a little circle in the street. When he came back around he reached for his gun.

Bill was over the railing and hitting him in the face with his beer mug before the gun was full out. Beer washed up Cane's face and hat. As Cane fell back, Bill brought the heavy glass down on his thumb, wrist, and the gun's hammer—the gun fell. Cane twisted around holding his face looking at his gun on the ground, Bill kicked it farther away.

"That dog needs to be put down!" Cane said.

When he stood, he noticed the door and windows were full of people watching.

"This here dog bit me and I'm fix'n to put it down,"

A man said, "come on Cane that dogs harmless."

The gathering crowd seemed to agree. Cane walked bent over to his gun but when he stood up Bill was there. When he lifted his gun, Bill stopped it, holding it low as he swung with his other fist. The contact was hard—very hard, and the bystanders now spilling out onto the porch let out sounds of displeasure. Cane's head flipped back, causing a stumble backwards. He tried to keep from falling, and by the time he fell he was in the center of Main street. He squirmed for a minute before stopping and laying still. A few men went to help, but he was out cold.

"Better get the Doc," one man said.

Bill picked up the broken handle of his beer glass, shook his head. "That was almost full."

He handed it to one of the men standing there. Slowly he walked away making a clicking sound for Duke to follow. One of the Johnson boys quickly walked along his side.

"Ain't you afered he's gonna get you back?"

"Not today," Bill said.

# Chapter 36

Ben sat in the shade on the porch of his office reading the paper. It was a few days old, and he was enjoying it. Cane slowly rode by, looking over his gear as he headed out of town.

"Head'n to the ranch?" Ben asked.

"Yeah, time to check in," Cane said.

"Well, have a good ride."

"Yeah, thanks Ben."

Cane rode east out of town, when he passed the church out of view Ben went inside. He grabbed a few things, hung his 'Went Fishing, if problem see Stan' sign on the door and left out the back. He tossed his saddle on and rode off to see where Cane was heading. By the time he got outside of town he'd lost sight of him, but he'd followed him before and had an idea which way he was heading, he was sure it wasn't to his father's ranch. The terrain became hilly and tree filled, and he had to slow down. When he got to a ridge, he spotted Cane below where the trail opened up. The Hills were in the distance, the trail ran straight for a mile. This is where he'd lost him the last time. If he continued following, all Cane had to do was look back. The last time he circled around from the south, so this time he tried going north heading for a high ridge where he should be able to see down on a large section of the foothills where hopefully he'd see where Cane was heading. It was a used trail but a rough one and it looked like someone had ridden it recently so he needed to keep alert.

Bill was on an outcropping of shale scanning the low land at the rim of the hills miles east of town. He spotted Cane in the distance, riding into a dense section of trees, but he never came out. He started scanning the hillside, but it was tree filled, he saw nothing. He stood leaning against a tall pine tree as he cleaned the glass in his telescope; he spotted Ben riding in the distance. Ben was on the same path he'd taken an hour earlier. He sat on the ledge with his feet hanging twenty feet above Blue, waiting.

Ben was startled to see a horse. He pulled his gun.

"Looking for someone?" Bill asked.

Ben lowered his gun and joined Bill on the high rocks.

"Nice spot," he said.

"I lost him in the rough, I think he's up in the hills somewhere, but he could have gone farther south," Bill said.

Ben was looking through the telescope.

"Who?"

"Really?" Bill said.

Ben felt Bill staring at him.

"Fine. Fine, but how did you get ahead of me?

"I was in the Highlands, heard Cane say he was heading to the ranch for a few days, so I was on the trail before he was. I turned off there at the clearing and came up here to see where he was heading," Bill said.

"Is this what you do on your afternoon rides?"

"What follow people? No. what about you?" Bill asked.

"I know he's not going to his father's ranch and, well I would like to know where he is going and why he lies about it."

"This is a difficult area to follow someone without being seen," Bill said.

"Yeah, last time I lost him by heading south, I thought I'd try up here this time," Ben said.

Ben kept looking through the spyglass, Bill leaned against the tree.

"Why are you following after Cane?"

Ben sat on a fallen tree and slowly pumped Bill's telescope in and out.

"I need a glass like this," he said.

He looked at Bill. "It's just a hunch, ya know," he said.

"Yeah I know, so tell me your hunch."

"Well, as Sheriff, when bad things happen a Marshal or another Sheriff will come to pay me a visit, that's if it happens close by. Or, I'll get a detail sheet in the mail. One day I was talking to Cane's dad at Fredricks when he was in town gett'n supplies and he tells me Cane wasn't with him on a cattle drive, now this was a drive that Cane told me he was on. I could see the old man thought he'd said too much. So, the whole thing got me to thinking. I started keeping track of the times Cane was out of town for more than a few days. I also tried to remember back at all the times, he'd been gone in the past," Ben said.

He smiled at Bill.

"And..." Bill said.

"Ah—well, I got out my notes of crimes and a few of them matched up. Not enough to do anything and now he's been around a lot more and, well anyway that's where I am. What about you, why are you following him?"

"I don't like him and I know he's hiding something and I think it's something big."

They mounted up and started back down the narrow trail, Ben looked around and said, "where's Duke?"

"Wandered off," Bill said.

"Well, like I was saying—there have been some big

robberies and Cane's been here in town so it's hard to do or say anything."

"Well, the man can't commit every crime, can't you check up on the ones where the dates match up? Anyway, I know he's bad. I watch him in his environment, but he's also very smart, he plays with the people of Spring Valley like it's a game, and it's a game he's good at," Bill said.

# Chapter 37

The compound gate was opened from within. Cane rode through looking everything over as he went. He stopped at the main bunkhouse where a young black woman was sweeping the porch.

"Is Susanne here?" he asked.

"She at the kitchen, Sir."

He rode to the house, handing his horse off to Jamie.

"Is Susanne inside?"

"I think she's in the kitchen, Sir," Jamie said.

Cane nodded.

"Ah, there was nothing I could do to stop it Sir," Jamie said.

Day-to-day events at the compound were not something Cane cared much about, so things were kept from him. They had to be very important for him to get involved, but he asked anyway.

"Well, did you try to stop it?" Cane asked.

"Ah—well, didn't know it was happening, when it was happening, Sir," Jamie said,

Cane was tired, he walked to the door scratching his head. "Well, whatever," he mumbled.

Martin was washing potatoes and putting them in a bowl next to Susanne, who was peeling. They were talking and laughing. Like everyone there, they knew Cane was

back and that what little fun they were having was about
to end. She enjoyed Martin being there. Someone she
could be a mother to, plus the boy was smart and funny.

"What the hell!" Cane's voice came from another
room, "Susanne!"

"He must have seen the office. You keep working."

Susanne left, Martin looked at the cook lady.

"Can I peel now?" he asked.

"No you can not."

The guard smiled, Martin gave him an angry look.

Susanne walked into Cane's office in fear, she never
knew how he was going to be on the first day back and for
him to walk into this had to send him over the edge.

"Yes?" she said.

He was standing in the center of the room with papers
in his hand and he looked up and at her.

"What the hell is going on?"

"You need to talk to Clayton—I think someone stole
something from in here but he didn't tell me anything. He
was angry and slapped Jamie around," she said.

"Where is Clayton?"

"Hunting with Dirty Frank."

"Do you have any idea who did this?"

"I got the idea that it might be the young outlaw
Tommy, because Clayton said his name and spit and
called him a few names," she said.

"Did he get into the safe?"

She shook her head. "Don't know."

"Why is this cash box sitting out and empty?"

She shook her head again. "Don't know."

"Well, get the hell outta here," he said.

When Clayton returned, they spent an hour in the
office with the door closed. During dinner they didn't
talk much, but yelled at everyone else. Cane seemed to

calm down as he watched Susanne clear the table. She felt him stare at her; she thought the night could take a bad turn. Jamie and Susanne tried to piece together what little they'd heard but couldn't come up with much. They had wiped down the last kitchen counter and the guard had left, taking with him the box of knives and such to lock up. Martin had gone to bed two hours earlier.

Dirty Frank left the table, Cane and Clayton sat talking low, drinking and smoking. Susanne was upset, pacing, worried what could happen next.

"I'll go see if we can leave," Jamie said.

She clinched her fingers tightly together and nodded as he turned and walked out.

"We're all done sir, is there anything else I can get for you before I turn in?" Jamie said.

Cane looked up from his talk with Clayton. "Is Susanne back there?"

"Oh, I think she went to bed," Jamie said.

"Went to bed without my permission?"

"I can go check."

"Yeah, you do that."

Jamie left and Cane looked at Clayton. "He just lied to me," he said.

"Can you blame him?" Clayton said.

"I reckon not."

Cane poured another drink for each of them.

"We need to hunt that bastard down and make an example of him," Cane said.

"He has to have gone to the hills cause I looked all around today and found no trace."

Susanne interrupted by walking into the room.

"Well, where were you?"

'Take'n the garbage out," she said.

Clay stood. "We can finish this in the morning."

Clay left and Cane told Susanne to sit at the table where Clayton had been sitting. She was reluctant, he insisted. He disgusted her, his face, his voice, and most of all his hands—the hands that touched her and held her down. This night she was finding it hard to hold back her feelings and he could tell. He was drunk again; she thought, one more drink he may pass out. Slowly she poured him another. She felt him looking at her. She put the cork back in and set the bottle to the side. He wanted her, but she was giving him a bad feeling and he needed her more submissive. He took another drink, this time slowly sipping as he eyed her over the glass.

"Can I go now?" She asked.

He slammed his fist down hard.

"No! No you can't go anywhere," he said.

She looked down at the table and cringed, thinking of what he might do to her tonight. She stopped listening to him and played the game she often played when he was back; it was called what could I use to kill him with right now. Martin confessed to playing it, but she told him not to for fear he might actually try something. She envisioned dousing him with his whiskey and striking one of those matches, it's right there she thought. What about the whiskey bottle, if she could get him to look the other way she could break it over his head. She liked the idea, he'd fall to the floor and I could take his gun and shoot him, she thought. Oh, to see the look on that smug, ugly face. She could have enough time to stomp on his hands before the guard comes. To jump up and down on his hands, the hands that touch her—Satan's hands. When the others come in, she could shoot them until the gun was empty.

He poured himself another drink. His slurring was at a point where she knew he'd have to tell her to leave before he passed out. When he looked at his drink, she glanced at the front window to see if the night guard was there. She saw him sitting in the window looking out at the yard. Cane slurred his words, but he was looking right at her and his eyes seemed to reveal a man still in control.

"You know—I saw Becky yesterday," he said.

Everything stopped. Her complete attention was focused on the monster in front of her and what he'd say next. She squeezed her folded fingers tight together on her lap. 'So this is how he will make me suffer even more, with Rebecca,' she thought. She waited, and he looked around the room taking his time, knowing he was upsetting her.

"She's turning into quite the young woman," he said.

Susanne gripped the seat on her chair, leaning toward Cane.

"Don't," she said.

"Yeah, I mean looking good," he smiled. "Real good."

She thought of his hands again, touching her. The first time—when she woke in her own bed with him on top of her, holding her down, beating her. When she woke again she was here, his slave. He smiled at her as he took a sip from his little shot glass. She looked at his hand on the glass and thought of that hand on her little girl.

Susanne lunged for Cane they both fell to the floor, he was pushing her away when he realized she was going for his gun; it was in her hand. The door swung open as the guard stepped in, but he didn't see them behind the big table. Cane hit her, she flew sideways out in the open. The man at the door was moving around the table. He saw Cane on the other side. Over the table he saw her getting to her knees, she was holding a gun; he raised his own gun, but she shot first. The lead ball cut through the table, then it put the guard into the corner. Cane was on his knees getting ready to jump when she turned to him. He stopped and raised his hands.

"Wait," he said.

Susanne smiled and pulled the trigger. Cane felt it pass his ear, he jumped at her and she pulled the trigger again but he was on her; it's combustion burned his arm. He took the gun, slapped her a few times, raising his fist high he hit her hard, and she was out.

Susanne woke in the shed. It was a very small building used for punishment. It was dark, but streams of sunlight came in through a few thin cracks and spaces in the wood. Once her eyes adjusted, she ripped off a part of her dress and wrapped it around her hand and killed every spider and bug she saw. She sat on the wood floor and thought of Becky, what could she do to keep him away from her. Maybe she could promise him she would never runaway; do as he says and act like she liked it. Yes, she thought, acting like she liked it, he would go for that. It's worth a try. She remembered shooting the guard and felt sick, there was only one punishment for that.

She jumped as a voice came from behind the shed, "Susanne?"

"Martin?"

"Yes."

"Honey, you have to go. You can't get caught back there."

"Hey? See this knot in the board?"

"What?"

"It's a knot in the board, if we could get one of them out we can talk and put it back after I go," he said.

She heard him counting.

"Here let's try this one, it's a tad loose, it's four boards up and right in the center. Can you push on it," he said.

They each took turns pushing at it until it came out, Martin scrapped it with a stone to make it come out easier the next time. Susanne felt a cool breeze from the mountain behind and put her face up to it and took a big breath.

"I'll be right back," Martin said.

"What?" she said.

She put her eye to the knothole, but he was gone. The hole also added more light. She started looking near the front for another knot. If she could get air moving through it would cool the room down a little.

The shed was near the front corner of the house and on its other side was a fenced in garden of tall corn and like every other location in the compound its back edge had a path so they could patrol along the perimeter.

"Here," Martin said as he pushed a large thin strip of jerky through.

"Thank you, but you have to go," she said.

"Not til I'm done, here's some water put your mouth up to the knothole," he said.

Martin stepped back, looking the area over. He saw the shed was built up off the ground a few inches. He got on his knees and brushed out the sandy ground to make room to roll under if he needed to hide quickly. He walked down the stone wall path a few feet and pulled a cornstalk up, broke a few feet off, and brought it to the shed. He brushed the loose sand into the rubble at the cliff edge and rolled under the little building to see if it would work. He could only get a foot or so under, but if he laid on his side with his elbow in the joist it worked. He reached out and pulled the cornstalk under; he pushed it up under the floorboards where it stayed.

"What are you doing?" she asked.

"Nothing," he said.

They talked through the knot hole for a while. Once Martin understood her punishment he cried, and she cheered him up by changing the subject. She talked about finding her daughter and his father. Martin mentioned his dad's name, Susanne had heard it before. Recently Cane and Clayton were talking about a man called Jersey. She almost told him, but thought better of it. Martin started to leave but remembered he had a few things in his pocket from the girl at the bunkhouse. He handed through socks and a candle and flint. He heard someone walking along the garden and looked around the corner he saw a man through the cornstalks. Martin took a big breath, the man heard him and stopped; he looked around. Martin rolled under the shed. He took the cornstalk and swept it across the ground to clean his footprints away. Susanne saw one of the tiny streams of light break along the side of the shed and heard a noise there. The man walked between the shed and the corn garden. Cautiously he looked down the stone wall in both directions but saw nothing. He stepped around the back of the little shed and stood looking at the small corral between the tall stone wall and the house, and up at the waterfall pouring from the corner beyond. Everything looked fine. He stood there for a moment. He looked at the ground at the back of the shed; the area was too narrow for anyone to hide under, so he rounded the corner and walked along the front porch of the house.

Martin lay there for a few minutes. He thought about what was going to happen to Susanne and how he could get her out of this. He needed to get to Cane and beg him not to hurt her. She heard him crawl out. "I'll be back in a while," he said.

Minutes later she heard knocking at the door of the house. She pressed her ear to the thin wall. Jamie answered the door, she heard Martin's voice asking about Cane.

"No, Martin!" Susanne said.

Jamie let Martin in, he heard Susanne as he closed the door.

Susanne stood and stretched and started looking for the best place to relieve her bladder when she heard someone come up and open the door. She squinted as the sunlight poured in.

"Outhouse break," he said.

"Thank God," she said.

She hurried to the outhouse while the man waited nearby. When she came out Cane and Clayton were standing in the center of the open area near the front of the pond, his men were all around, even the lookouts were on the distant ledge looking down. The slaves were gathered in front of the cornfield in a line. She looked at the ground and started to tear up, 'at least Martin wasn't here', she thought. The man next to her tied her hands behind her back and gave her a push farther into the big open area. In a way she was glad it was over, all the abuse, the fear of setting one of them off by saying something wrong or looking at them in the wrong way. Once more she looked up to make sure Martin wasn't around. Cane waved to the man to bring her over, he pushed her to Cane. She stood tall and defiant. Cane slapped her across the face, she looked back at him through a mass of hair.

"You are all here to see what happens when one of you goes after one of my men," Cane said.

He pushed her to the ground and pulled his gun, aimed it up at the sky.

"Anything you want to say?"

"Eternity is a long time," she looked up at him. "That's how long you'll burn in hell."

Cane lowered his gun, pulled the hammer back, aimed, but Martin came running around from the back of the house.

"No!" he yelled.

"How did he get away?" Cane said.

Clay shrugged. "Don't know."

Martin ran up to Cane and hugged his waist. Cane looked up and shook his head while Martin took the knife from his belt, sliding it up his sleeve.

"Please Cane please, she's my mommy."

Cane pushed him away and raised his gun again, but Martin got up and jumped back to his waist.

"She's my mommy," he said.

Martin looked up at Cane. "And you're like my daddy now."

Susanne saw the look in Cane's eye as he patted the boy on the head. The boy had seen his sister and mother killed, and now this. Martin was sobbing and Cane looked over at Clayton, who shrugged again and said, "I don't know."

"Okay! Okay—I'm giving you a week in the shed! Now everyone get back to work," Cane said.

"Wow, get'n soft," Clayton said.

"The boy watched Kaden kill his mother and sister I figure I'll spare him this, take care of her next week, make it look like an accident," he said.

Cane looked up, many were still standing around.

"You heard me, now get!"

Martin ran to Susanne and hugged her. "Mommy, mommy," he said.

He slipped the knife in her sock; she was pulled up and pushed to the shed. Jamie came walking up to Cane and Clayton holding his head. "Sorry he hit me with a frying pan."

"Just get him away from her," Clayton said.

Jamie took Martin by the arm, forcing him away, almost dragging him at times. Martin put up a good fight, but when they got closer to the bunkhouse he fought less.

"How did I do?" Martin asked.

"You did great, just great boy," Jamie said.

As they walked into the bunkhouse Jamie mumbled, "Daddy," and shook his head smiling. "That was very smart Martin, very smart," he said.

# Chapter 38

Clay walked out and stood on the porch while Cane mounted up.

"I should be back in a few days," Cane said.

"The men from the Cumberland job should'a been back by now, also from Ohio. I think we'll have a full house by the weekend," Clayton said.

"How's the food?"

"I'll get Jamie to check but I'm sure we'll need at least a side of beef,"

"See if we can get one from dad, but with Jimmy gone make sure the place is secure before you leave and send a man to me with a list for the rest."

"Hey, ease off on the drinking, you need to keep up the act," Clayton said.

"Don't," Cane slowly shook his head. "Don't tell me what to do Clayton."

"We got a few big jobs going on, ya can't let these other things get to you, we'll get that bastard."

"Yeah, better make it before he spends all the money."

"He didn't get it all, just one cash box."

"It was the big one," Cane said.

Clay nodded. "Well, keep things together, we don't want everything to fall apart just because we couldn't keep up the act, or some stupid little mistake. I'll get after Tommy and the money as soon as a few more men get here."

"Yeah well you need to get Tommy before he tells anyone about this place—then all hell's gonna break loose," Cane said.

"I spec."

"By the way the Sheriff was behind me yesterday," Cane said.

"Following you?"

"Not sure, could'a been, he pulled away at the big clearing."

"Hmm. Well, that ain't good."

# Chapter 39

Bill was stocking shelves when a young man walked in the store. He walked up to the counter and read from a list as Fred retrieved items. He looked like he'd been riding a while. Bill looked out the front window to see his setup. There were two horses, a strange man sat reading a book on one, they also had a pack mule with a light load. The strange man looked up from his book to the sky smiling, there was something familiar about him. As he watched a few people on the street, his horse turned slightly revealing crutches held in a leather sheath and a stump where his lower leg should have been.

It was the outlaw he'd shot at the common house in Milford. Bill remembered him shouting from behind a building, something about finding and killing him. He was the only one of that bunch that showed some talent with a gun, and now he's here. Bill turned from the window and started moving items around that were closer to the counter as he listened to the man place his order. He waited to hear the young man ask about Jersey Smith, but he didn't. He did ask where he could find a room, and Frank told him about the bathhouse near the Highlands. Bill watched them ride down the street up to the bathhouse. The other man dismounted and stood with the outlaw's crutches as he pulled himself down with a little effort.

Bill took a few tools and keys from the locksmith box and put them in his pocket. He went to his room, grabbed his old hat, its wide flopping brim would hide his face better. He checked his boot-gun and put the bedside gun in his belt. He stood leaning over the end of his balcony, looking down the street at the bathhouse. The two men came out and walked across in the direction of center park. Bill hurried down the street.

"Well hello Bill, can I get a bath ready for you?"

"Ah—no. Those men that came in? They, um, forgot something at the store. Did they get a room?"

"Yes honey, they did."

"How long are they plan'n to stay?"

"Don't know that, only one night here though."

"What room is it?"

"Three, but they went to the Sunny Side."

"Good," Bill said.

He walked up the stairs as the woman shrugged and went into a backroom.

The hallway was empty, so Bill fiddled with the lock. He reasoned with himself; only one night booked, he hasn't seen me yet and if he does he probably won't recognize me. The lock wouldn't open. He knelt and looked into the keyhole and tried a different tool. I should just leave, lay low, and let this play out. He could be gone tomorrow. The lock turned, and he opened the door. Well, I got a half an hour, take a little look around, maybe find something that tells why he's here, he thought. He was only in the room for a few minutes when the door opened. Bill jumped around bent over with his gun drawn. The one legged man stood there tall and surprised in the doorway, he was unarmed. Bill relaxed and stood up.

"Well, you must be the town thief?" the one

legged man said.

The outlaw looked at the table next to the door, "I came back for this," he said.

He picked up a small pouch. "You're not a very good thief," he tossed the bag up and caught it as it jingled. He leaned on the doorjamb, one crutch under his arm and opened the little bag. "Here, take this and go." He pulled out two coins, he looked at Bill and took out two more, "and get a new hat."

Bill was confused, this has to be the most courteous outlaw he'd ever met, not the angry man he'd known from the Tom Monrow days.

"I don't want your money."

"At least buy a hat—really."

Bill just looked at the man.

"Well, if it's not about money why are you here?" the outlaw asked.

"I thought I recognized you."

"And did you?" he asked.

"Not sure," Bill scratched his chin. "How'd ya lose that leg?"

"Well," the man stepped in the room.

"My names Joss," he dropped the cash bag back on the table, closed the door and hobbled to the bed where he sat.

"I got it shot off. Well, not really, before I bled to death a old man living in the middle of nowhere found me and cut it off. He said he learned how to cut off appendages in the war. At first I hated him for it and thought when I get my strength back I'm gonna kill him."

"Doesn't sound like you did."

"No," the outlaw looked at the floor thinking for a moment. "No, he saved my life in more ways than one. He was an interesting old boy, he read to me from boxes of books until I could get around, some amazing stories and even a few poems."

"What's your name?" the outlaw asked.

"Bill."

"You ever read poems, Bill?"

"I have, only liked a few though," Bill said.

"After a while I realized what he was doing—he saw that I was enjoying the books, and he thought it was a way to keep me around. You see he was sick and didn't want to die alone. So I made sure he didn't. Once I saw how hard it was gonna be with only one leg, I started to see what he was teaching me and the books he read to me were for a reason. I guess the old boy saw the bad in me from the beginning and he made it his mission to teach me and give me a way out, and I took it."

Bill sat in a chair and listened to the man tell his story of redemption, of climbing out from an ash heap of a life. The old man never asked about his past but showed him that whatever he'd done, there was a way to put it behind him. Anyone could change, could be forgiven, a new fresh start was there to be had. He found his brother and together they were going to get their mother, then head up to Detroit to start over.

"What about you, Bill?" he asked.

Bill was engrossed in the man's story. He didn't want to lie after so much honesty, so he was vague. He told him about his job and how he hoped to stay here in this little town. When he ran out of things to say, he left in a hurry.

At the door Bill looked back at the ex-outlaw and nodded. "It was good to meet you, Joss."

The man nodded, but when Bill turned away he said, "it was good to see you again, Jersey Smith."

Bill turned and looked at him.

"We all have secrets, Jersey, if I can call you that. You

know another good thing that old man taught me was about the past. We've both done things—well, I know I did. Anyway—he said that regrets are best buried in the past, and the past is no place to live. Wouldn't you agree?"

"I do, it's a very hard thing, but I truly do."

The next day Bill saw them ride through town to the Church. He saw Joss talk with Pastor Dale on a bench in the churchyard. As they rode back through, Bill was out front sweeping the boardwalk.

"It was good to see you—Bill."

Bill leaned on his broomstick and nodded. "You too Joss," he said.

As they moved away Joss turned in his saddle and smiled. "Seriously though, get a new hat."

# Chapter 40

Cane was sitting at his table in the Highlands, drinking. He'd been back in town for two days and had controlled himself fairly well, he thought, considering so much was falling apart. After seeing Bill with Melissa again, he started drinking. 'Why get so pissed off about that?' he asked himself, 'the guys a bum.'

Clayton came in through the front door, walked to the table and plopped in the seat across from Cane. He looked at him for a moment, then twisted to Howard at the bar holding up two fingers.

"Did you want another one?" he asked.

Cane knew something was up. "Should I?"

Clay looked back at Howard and held up three fingers.

"Well?" Cane said.

Clay sat back and scratched his chin. He looked for Howard and the drinks to arrive. It looked to Cane like he was avoiding telling him something.

"Let me guess, no Tommy."

"That's not it. "

"Worse?"

Clay nodded. "Yeah."

"Well, come-on out with it," Cane said.

Clay sat up, leaned on the table and talked low. "The Cumberland job went bad," he said.

Cane looked up at the ceiling and put his fingertips on the edge of the table. He breathed out through his mouth and shook his head.

"How bad?" he said.

"No one came back. I just heard there was some powder kegs used and a lot of men were killed," Clayton said.

"Wait—Kaden didn't come back?" Cane asked.

"No, no one came back."

"Remember what I said about this job? I bet he even went in with them—didn't he?"

"No, I don't think so. The guy I talked to said the explosion came from the hills next to the camp," Clayton said.

"How... How many are dead?"

"Not sure, at least fifteen."

"No."

"And, there were a lot of men hurt, some very bad, so this guy said the number will go up."

"Oh, this—this is great, just..." He looked at Clayton. "Anything else?"

Clay looked at the table.

"No, really? There's more?"

"The explosion caused a cave-in at the mine and thirty men are trapped inside."

Cane slammed his fist down hard, then put his elbows on the table as his face fell to his hands.

After a minute Clayton said, "What do you want to do? If it gets out that it was us," he looked around, then spoke even lower, "I'm not sure where we could hide."

Clay kept talking but Cane couldn't hear him, his own thoughts had his full attention. It was hard to imagine worse news. With this many people dead the law won't stop until they catch who was responsible, this little payroll job will now be in every newspaper.

After a few minutes Cane said, "We have to be calm

while we arrange to leave."

"Leave?" Clayton said.

"Clay, we've been over this before. We've got forged papers, we can disappear, course they were made a while back but they'll be fine," Cane said.

"So—leave and never come back."

"Yeah, leave and never come back. We've gone over this," Cane said.

"But that was years ago, and that job went fine."

Clay saw the look on Cane's face. "Okay, I know what you mean, it's just hard to throw everything away," Clayton said.

"Well, we can leave and be free or stay and go to jail, or worse."

Howard brought two more glasses, Clayton looked at them, then at Cane.

"You need to get to the ranch and check the papers, hell just bring them here and we can both look them over and..." Cane was interrupted.

"If we get caught with them, they won't believe anything we say," Clayton said.

"Yeah, I'll come out tomorrow, we'll go over everything. You know we have to destroy the compound too?" Cane said.

"What?"

"What can we do, just let them all go? Take them with us? Well?" Cane asked.

Clay sat back in his chair and slumped down.

"Oh."

Cane saw Bill walk in. He wanted to shoot him—just pull out his gun, aim it at his chest and fire away. Instead, he quickly drank another shot of whiskey as Clayton gave him another look.

"I know, I know, I'll slow down," he looked at

Clayton. *"If you do,"* he said.

"You need to keep your head brother," Clayton said.

"The only way we can be linked to this," Cane stopped and looked around, he leaned close. "Is if someone lived to tell about it, so let's get ready to leave and see what happens in the next day or two. Is there someone we could trust to send down there and ask around?"

"I could go," Clayton said.

"No, at this point we need to stay close, what about Dirty Frank?"

"I think we need someone we can trust at the compound," Clayton said.

"Well, when are the men showing up from the Ohio job? We'll send one or two of them. Has to be a quick run there and back or we'll be gone."

"Ya know Kaden took a few kegs of gun-powder, if it was him that blew up that mountain it's hard to believe he died in it. Maybe he's just taking the long way back," Clayton said.

Cane nodded. "Let's hope so. We need to know what the law knows. You head to the compound. I'll get someone over to the Sheriff's office, find out what he knows. I'll see you tomorrow." Cane looked past Clay. "It might be the next day, I got something I want to do."

Clayton turned to see Cane was looking at Bill. "Don't be stupid, too much going on to waste time on him."

# Chapter 41

The next day Melissa asked Bill to lunch at the Sunny Side. They sat at the window near the door; it was just past noon, and the sun was overhead and bright. Bill was looking over Missy's shoulder watching Cane from between curtains, he was on the other side of the town park hitching his horse and yelling at a passerby. Cane walked through the park angrily, shaking his head. He crossed the street, then walked up to the little restaurant.

"This could get interesting," Bill said.

She looked up as Cane walked in, but Cane didn't see them. He walked to a table facing the back with a view of the waitress area.

"He didn't see us, do you want to leave?" she asked.

"Leave, why? We haven't got our food yet? You're scared—has he bothered you again?"

Bill started to stand, but she touched his arm.

"Please," she said.

He sat back down.

"Has he?"

She leaned close. "No. Lately he just looks, he's just very bothersome, I get an awful feeling when he's around," she said.

"I won't let anything happen to you."

"If you weren't here I would have left," she said.

Bill changed seats with Melissa, watching Cane as they ate. He was reading a few papers or letters from his coat pocket and trying to hide his anger. He rested his forehead in his hand, rubbed his temple as he sipped coffee. Looking at the table he slammed his fist down hard, everything on it bounced. He looked around the room with a fake smile, which disappeared when he saw Bill and Melissa. He went back to what he was doing, but Bill could tell he was acting different.

Cane could tell Bill had been watching him, he knew he still was. He could feel it, and it was eating at him. The feeling that he was back there staring at him caused him to lose his train of thought, and right now he needed to think clearly. After a few minutes he put the papers in his coat, stood and walked out, not looking at the two in the window seat.

Ben walked in, spotted them and walked up to their table. "Hey you two mind if I sit?" he asked.

They nodded, and he sat down.

"What's going on, Ben?" Bill asked.

"Payroll robbery down in Cumberland," he said.

"Oh no," Missy said.

Bill leaned back near the window ledge and listened.

"About twenty men were killed."

"Oh my," she said.

"I guess the last man set off some kind of explosion to keep them off his trail, but it took out half the mountain," Ben said.

"Bill, can you believe this?" Melissa asked.

"That's not all Missy, the mine is caved in and lots more men are still down there and last we heard men were try'n to dig them out."

Ben looked at Bill and said, "I need to ask a favor."

"Sure," Bill said.

"A Marshal just rode through, they's pretty sure one of them got away, they think he could be head'n north, maybe north-west."

"From Cumberland that could put him in Pennsylvania," Bill said.

"Yeah, well, the Marshal came from the north and is following the rail line through the pass, he'll be looking south to where it happened. He asked if I'd take a few men south on this side of the mountains, as far as the border, and have a look around. Kind of make a wide sweep down and back," Ben said,

"Yeah, I'll come along," Bill said.

"No Bill, I was hoping you'd stay and keep an eye on Becky," Ben said.

"Ben, this could be a dangerous trip, you need help," Bill said.

"I'll get help. I worry about Becky though. It would help me a lot to know you were looking after her. I wouldn't have to think about it."

Bill looked at Melissa, she smiled.

"Fine, you won't have to worry about her," Bill said.

Ben looked relieved. He sat back for a moment. "Well, I have to tell Becky and pack," he said.

"Are you leaving now?"

"No, first thing in the morning, I need to get the men together and get some rest."

# Chapter 42

As usual Bill woke early, but instead of taking a ride he went to see Ben off. The night sky glowed to the east as the sun made its way back around. He could see down his stairs and up the alley without a lantern. Through the front window he could see Stan sleeping at the desk, no one else was in sight. Bill looked up and down the street. He sat on one of Ben's porch chairs. He got a strange feeling about something he'd just seen in the shadows and looked back up the dark street. Something was hanging from the tree next to the gazebo, it was still dark under there but it was something large.

He squinted, stood, and walked down the stairs. It was Duke; he was hanging out over the street. He walked up to him and patted him. He was only a few feet off the ground, hanging from a thick low branch, the one the kids always sat on. Bill put his arm around Duke, cut the rope and felt his full weight. He set him near the grass at the street's edge, where the fence opened at the big tree. He sat next to him scratched between his shoulder blades where he liked it. He saw the hole in his side and looked around to see if there was any blood in the area. It didn't look like he was killed there in the center of town; he didn't want to leave him to look farther. He pulled Duke to the grass and sat leaning against the ancient tree.

"Duke, we had some good times, didn't we boy. You were a dam good dog."

Bill looked up, two men were standing there looking at Duke. They were dark and back lit in the early morning sky. Ben stepped on the office porch yawning, he saw a few men down the street. He stretched as he slowly turned, looking things over; he saw people silently gathered across the side street at the old tree.

"Stan, better get out here."

He ran, and Stan followed. Becky woke when she heard Ben from her town side window. She saw Duke under the big tree with Bill sitting next to him and men standing around; she started crying and ran down.

Bill didn't want to be there. All the people gathering were getting on his nerves. He felt sluggish, like everything was moving slow now. Everyone shook their heads not understanding how someone could hang Duke up like that. Ben looked the area over and walked back to Bill. Becky came running around the building up to Bill and his dog. She knelt there close; she saw the wound and put her hand on Duke's head.

"Let's get outta the street Ben," Bill said.

"Stan can you get Duke to the office?" Ben said.

"I'll help you," Becky said.

They walked back to the Sheriff's office, Ben carried the rope.

"Hey Stan, is the coffee on?"

"Yeah, full pot,"

"You know who did this," Bill said.

"Yeah, I got a good idea, but what can I do? Unless we got a witness or we can prove this is his rope," Ben said.

He saw the look in Bill's eyes.

"I'll be asking around and talking with Cane. If there's anything I can do I will, but—well heck, everyone liked old Duke but still he was a dog and you can't put a man away for very long for kill'n a dog. Although hanging old Duke in the center of town, well that's a matter I'll have to look into," Ben said.

He looked at Bill and saw his anger was building.

"I'll be gone for two days. I want you to promise me you won't do anything until I get back and then we'll both get to the bottom of this, okay?" Ben said.

Bill said nothing. He was looking out the door at Stan as he carried Duke in setting him on the floor. Fred came over from next door, he looked down at Duke, then at Bill.

"Bill, I'm so sorry, can I help you at all?" he asked.

Bill looked up. "Can I use your wagon?"

"Promise me Bill," Ben said.

Bill looked at him for a minute then nodded. "Two days."


He buried Duke near the river a half a mile outside of town, marking it with a pile of smooth river stones. He remembered the kid's faces when he brought the puppy home, the hours they played together. He was mostly Martin's dog, in fact it was probably just after Martin was gone that Duke started wandering off, maybe he was looking for Martin. After the murders he put in the time needed to train him better. Old Duke helped him out of a few tight spots over the years. On the ride back he thought about retribution. This can't look like revenge. He thought about how becoming Bill had changed him into a better man, but now he seemed to be right back where he was when he walked into town. He had people he cared about again, and trouble was starting up again. It was two things he just couldn't shake.

Cane was sending a message. He didn't just kill the

dog; he hung him out in the center of town. He's calling me out, he thought, or at least trying to see how far I can be pushed. He could have poisoned Duke or done it any other way. But he wanted to make sure I knew it was him, and that he got away with it. Jersey would have sought revenge and gotten it. How can Bill be any different, isn't it normal to seek revenge, after-all 'an eye for an eye'. But, Bill is supposed to be a changed man, a New Testament man, a turn the other cheek man. I'm just not that good, he thought. I can't turn the other cheek when someone does something so overtly offensive as to murder an innocent dog as a message. I guess I haven't really changed at all, he thought.

Jersey was getting tired of being Bill. Though it was a good thing, Melissa and Beck had brought out a side of him he felt was gone forever. He thought—wasn't that why you did this in the first place? To help people, but also to get back a bit of who you once were. He liked this new life, but was it really him? Right now he wanted to walk in the Highlands and beat Cane into a crying heap in the corner behind his little card table. Show his friends how a coward takes a beating. Was that something Bill would do? Yes, I think it is, he thought. He killed my dog.

This is because of Missy, and if that's so, does he really think this would scare me or stop me from seeing her? Maybe I could get him thrown in jail. Wow, that sounds too much like Bill. Jersey would catch him and kill him, it'd be fair, but—still kill him. He's not a stupid man, but he does seem to be very angry lately. Maybe I'll give Ben the two days and see if Cane makes any more mistakes—justice could serve as revenge.

A man like Cane has an unusual desire for money, maybe that's where he's having problems, surely it can't just be Missy, having money problems makes sense. He doesn't seem to work; I guess his dad could give him money, but he's not that kind of man. More like the kind of guy that might set up an accident for his old man and take over the ranch for himself. But, that would be a lot of actual work, it was obvious Cane was not fond of real work, hell most of the time he sits on his butt chatting up the locals. He has a big share in the Highlands, that's obvious, but how much, why not be upfront about that? Upfront, that was it, a front; the whole thing seems like an act to mask something else. Nothing about Cane was right. I need to keep digging, he thought, and see what's out there east of town—whatever he's got going on can't be good.

Becky rode out to meet him. She tied Three to the back of the wagon so they could ride home together.

"Where did you bury Duke?" she asked.

"Oh, it's a nice spot across the river from the clearing. It reminds me of..."

She noticed the look on his face when he couldn't keep talking.

"Can we go there sometime?" she asked.

"Sure," he said.

"Do you think it was Cane?"

"Mm hmm," he nodded.

"Well, that's the talk, you know after he kicked Old Duke, or tried to, people started looking at him different. Well some people, maybe not the men at the Highlands but most everyone else," she said.

"Don't kill him Bill, if you do you'll go to jail."

"Now why would you think I would kill him?"

She looked around at the fields, the trees and the unusually deep blue of the sky gathering her thoughts.

"Because you're not who you say you are."

He looked over at her. She was beautiful, and he thought of Catherine when they were young, innocent and honest. And like Catherine, nothing got by her.

"You do a good job of hiding it, but all of us close to you know for some reason you're hiding your past," she said.

He was done lying to her, but if he didn't say anything he wouldn't be lying.

"It's okay Bill, we know you're good, whatever you did before. Ben wouldn't trust you with me if he didn't know you were a good man."

Becky put her arm through his and leaned her head on his shoulder.

"Duke was the best dog I ever knew. Wait for Ben to get back before you do anything, please."

# Chapter 43

Old Duke

It was cold and late in the day when Jersey constructed a lean-to. When it was good enough to sleep in, he laid back on leaves and pine branches to test it out. It was next to the little clearing in the hills near the river, the same river he'd built his house on a few miles out into the valley. The sound of the rushing water could play tricks on you, so he decided to build the lodge a little ways from it. The lean-to was positioned where he could look the area over as he constructed it in his head. He started to doze off when an unusual sound had him sit up. It was a dogs frantic bark, but also a screaming sound he'd never heard before. He put his rifle back in the saddle sheath and went to see what was going on.

He found the poor dog just off the lower trail, she'd been torn apart, her litter of pups were bloody and motionless laying huddled near her. It was a strange scene, there was no shelter in sight, maybe she was bringing her pups down, they were very young but could walk. Each one had been bitten but not eaten, just killed. The mother had been killed but also not for food; she was savagely raked repeatedly by sharp claws. He'd never seen one, but this had to be a mountain lion attack. He looked closer and saw the tracks, 'he's huge,' he thought.

He stayed on his horse looking around, there were still some in the hills but they'd mostly been killed off. He'd heard that if hungry they'd stalk a man, you wouldn't hear them coming. They'd jump you from behind, hold the back of your neck in their jaws and rake your back out with their hind claws until you were done screaming. It was something of nightmares, but it came horribly true for this poor dog.

Why would it not eat what it killed? When he realized he'd possibly interrupted its meal, he started looking in the nearby rough. His horse's ears turned to the rear, and he kind of shifted in the path.

"Something nearby, boy?" he said.

Jersey's coat was heavy and cumbersome, he undid a few buttons and reached inside for his gun. He saw something move at his side. He ducked down, but it surprised him how big it was and how hard it hit.

Before he knew it he was on the ground. His horse was trying to get away, he'd shifted around, his hind was off the trail, hooves stomping and digging. Its big head was bent down, Jersey was laying on his reins. He'd landed on his back and it took a moment to catch his breath. The horse was trying to pull away. He got to one elbow, his gun—like the cat, was nowhere in sight. Jersey pulled the leather rein out and unloosed a few extra feet, which he had on for walking. The horse lifted its head, its front hooves repeatedly bounced together on the hard path. He tried to moved away, pulling Jersey up a little, up just enough to see the big cat slowly moving towards the path from the rough below. It was huge, its head low to the ground in stalking mode, edging closer and growling, its teeth white and sharp.

Jersey pulled on the reins to keep the horse from

running away and dragging him with it. He knew it couldn't outrun this cat, and it would be on him in no time. He scooted backwards, fumbling for the knife in his boot. The horse was frantic, dancing around the narrow path just missing his feet. The giant cat jumped, taking Jersey's boot in his jaws and pulling at him, trying to get him off the path away from the horse's pounding hooves. He could feel its teeth pierce his foot, he kicked him with his other boot. His horse came down hard on its tail. The cat hunched down low, looking up growling at the horse. Jersey took that moment to bring his foot close, he slipped the knife out and leaned up. The lion saw him rise; it forgot about the horse and jumped for Jersey's head. He swung his knife from under as hard and fast as he could. It pierced its neck at the throat; he pushed up into its head, stopping when it connected with bone. It fell limp, its big claws stretched out over his shoulders. Jersey pushed it off his chest and lay back resting until his horse started pulling at him again.

While he was getting the animal ready to haul, he heard a faint noise and looked around. He moved the dead puppies and found one still alive. He dragged the cat to the trading post on a makeshift travois, holding Duke inside his big coat.

From that day he was always prepared for a cougar attack, which meant he was prepared for any attack. He packed a loaded handgun on his saddle, he always carried a gun and a knife on him and within reach, not in his boot. He tried his gun on his side or on a leg, but he couldn't work like that, it was always in the way. He wanted free movement. He remembered how he did it when he was a kid so his father couldn't see it. He fastened the holster sideways on the back of his belt. Its butt was easily reachable, yet out of the way for working and walking. He fastened his knife sheath under the holster so the handle could be reached with his other hand, and it solved all his problems. He just had to get used to pulling them out quickly when needed. He started wearing a waistcoat because they were above his belt. When winter came and big coats were a must, he sewed pockets just inside, high across his chest for easy reach. In the winter his knife and sheath could be out in the weather, so it was kept on his back just over his shoulder.

He never saw another cougar. In fact the only one any man in the area had seen was the hide and head hanging on the wall at the trading post, where someone wrote with a piece of coal under it, 'Jersey got me with a knife.'

Duke grew up in the valley and foothills. He came and went as he pleased, but he always remembered what he'd been taught. When he was with Jersey his obedience was dependable, and his attention was absolute. He was a good dog.

# Chapter 44

Bill gave Ben his two days, after that he took a walk to the Highlands, it was the first time without Duke and it felt strange. When he entered everyone looked at him. Cane and Clayton were at the usual table, together they took up the corner, Clayton on the left, his back to the side wall. When Bill got to the table's edge, Clayton quickly stood pulling his gun.

Bill was looking at Cane as he reached his left hand to stop Clayton from lifting his gun too high. For a second things stopped, Jersey released the gun hand as he back handed Clayton in the throat. Clayton dropped the gun, and it fell to the table. Grabbing his neck he leaned way back, his head almost hitting the wall. He looked like he might fall over backwards until Bill stomped on the toe of his boot. Clayton swung over forward, face hovering above the table. Bill kept eye contact with Cane, his right thumb in his belt near his gun waiting for him to reach under the table. He slammed Clayton's head down, his face connecting hard with the table. Cane reached for the gun under the table, as quick as that Bill's gun was out a few inches from his forehead. As Clayton's head bounced up from the table he was almost standing, Bill punched him hard with his left fist on the side of his head. Clayton hit the corner wall before he dropped to the floor.

"I know about the gun you keep under the table there Cane,"

Cane sat back then looked across the table at his brother's empty seat, never in his life had he seen anyone get the better of Clayton, but this bum made it look easy.

"What do you want Bill?"

"I just came over to ask if you saw anything three nights ago when someone killed my dog, but now I'm wondering why would Clayton pull his gun on me?" he paused. "Say," Bill nudged his hat up as he scratched his head. "You boys didn't have anything to do with the murder of my dog—did you?"

Bill put his gun back then picked up Clayton's gun from the table, he proceeded to take it apart setting each piece on the table as he waited for Cane's response. He hoped Cane would reach for his gun and put an end to it.

"No, course not," Cane said. "I guess Clayton just thought you were going to hit me or something, he is my brother, he protects me. I guess sometimes he gets a little carried away."

"Well, if he keeps acting like that—he really will get carried away, by a few of these good men at the bar," Bill said.

"What do you want, Bill?" Cane asked.

"My dog was killed and I'm asking around to see if anyone saw anything."

"Well, we haven't seen anything."

Clayton crawled back into his chair, he held his head with both hands, Bill could tell he might be getting his breath back so he kept his hand low and ready.

"Well, if you hear anything," Bill turned taking a few steps before turning back. "Ya know Old Duke was killed real cowardly like, defenseless, shot and hung from a tree, as like to be an example or someth'n. Ya know, I don't think I'm alone hope'n the coward that did this gets similar treatment," Bill paused making sure Cane understood what he was saying. "Don't ya hope the killer gets it like that in the end?"

Bill kept looking at Cane waiting for a response, finally Cane said, "yes, yes—fine."

Bill looked at Clayton then turned, the men at the bar looked away as he walked by and out the front door.

# Chapter 45

Ben and his men were near the state line on the national highway, stopping travelers, stage coaches, and big Conestoga wagons hauling freight west. After finding nothing, they moved along the border west to the other side of the valley where they turned back north again, riding the trail near the foothills. They looked around carefully, stopping at every camp, house, or settlement.

Following the trail north, they saw smoke from a chimney to the west near the foothills, and recent tracks leading down a side path. Hidden in a cove of trees was a small shack of a house. But for the chimney smoke—it looked abandoned. They rode up to the front as an old man walked out with a long flintlock rifle, aiming it at Ben.

"Now hold on mister, we're the law."

Ben pointed to his badge.

"Oh, sorry my sight ain't what it were."

They relaxed and started a conversation. The other two rode around the sides of the little house. Ben talked with the old man.

"Seen any strangers here-abouts?"

"Nah, we're alone out here mister or um, Sheriff."

"Mind if we take a look inside?" Ben asked.

The man got visibly upset.

"I don't think you should, my wife is might sick

throwing up with blood and all. Unless you think you can get in and out without get'n yourself sick," the old man said.

The two rode back, waiting at the path.

"Ah Ben lets go, I can't get sick, at least not like that, I got a big family," Harry Johnson said.

Ben looked at Wayne, and he nodded to leave.

"Well, good luck, sir."

They rode down the narrow path, turning north on to the main trail.



The old man went back in his little shack, shut the door and looked down at Kaden—who was tied to a bed, gagged, unconscious and naked. His body had poultice patches on a few wounds but a fresh set of whip marks, bruises and hot poker burn holes were distributed from his feet to his head. An old woman with a mass of kinky gray hair came out from behind a stove, hunched over carrying an ax.

"Well, that was too close, let's just kill him before they come back," she said.

"I ain't done with him yet," he said.

She shook her head and thought for a minute.

"Well, at least go dig the hole, get that outt'a the way,"

He nodded and walked out to the back of the house where there were seven graves with crosses and three more without. He walked to the nearest grave and started digging next to it.



"I'm glad we didn't go in there Ben, there were seven graves behind that house," Harry said. "Whatever they have it can't be good."

They were walking to give the horses a rest.

"Seven graves, there's no way they raised seven kids in that place. How old were the gravestones?"

"Hard to tell, they were just sticks tied as crosses."

"Well, was the rope new or old?" Ben asked.

"Rope? You mean that tied the sticks?"

"Yeah—was it old or new?"

"Ah, not new but not too old either," Harry said.

"Harry you gotta tell me about anything strange as soon as you see it."

"Oh—heck Ben I'm sorry but when he said they was sick, I put two and two together," he said.

"Well—probably noth'n. Anything else strange about the place?" Ben asked.

"Ah, one thing was, they had a very nice horse."

"Yeah?"

"Yeah, he was back in a large lean-to, a Appaloosa he was," Harry said.

Wayne perked up.

"What? An Appaloosa?"

"Ah yeah."

"What color was he?"

"Dark brown with white," Harry said.

"Oh wait Ben, we gotta go back there," Wayne said.

"Well, it does sound like a better horse than they would have, but..."

"No, I think it's Kaden's horse, he's been missing for a few days now, they been talking about it at the Highlands."

"Anything else you want to tell us about Harry?"

"No, that covers it."

# Chapter 46

The old man dug a shallow grave near the others out back. When he returned, he poured a cup of coffee as they talked about their good fortune.

"Well, I won't have to hunt for a few weeks now," he said.

She pulled out the money they'd gotten from Kaden's pockets.

"Look at all this, plus sell'n the horse and his guns, let's get more chickens and another goat."

Kaden woke, his eyes opened to see the dark ceiling boards with two large dead crows hanging by their claws. He felt the gag in his mouth as he remembered. He yelled as best he could. His wrists and ankles were tied apart to each bedpost, and he felt cold all over. He saw the ugly old woman standing at his feet, staring at him. She sipped her hot coffee as she walked along the side of the bed, her dirty finger tracing his body. She poured hot coffee on his chest; he jerked around, but he was tied so tight he could only squirm. He moaned and looked around for something, anything to help him get out of this. She leaned over him, looking close into his eyes.

"I'm think'n this one's a outlaw."

"Yeah?" The old man said.

"Um—hmm. Dark soul he has."

She put her aged face inches from his, one of her eyes was out of line and gray. "You a bad egg, mister?"

She slapped him, and the old man chuckled. She leaned back down, her cheek rubbed against his, he jerked away as far as possible. "Gonna make you pay for dem past sins—you ain't gonna like it."

"Hey, it's my turn," the old man said.

"Well," she said. "That's fine, make it a jiffy I want at him."

Kaden looked past the old woman's head through her smelly gray hair as the old man stood pulling a long rod from the little stove, held its glowing end up, then he smiled.

The door burst open, and Ben stepped in with a shotgun. Not believing his eyes, he pulled his gun tight across his chest as he stepped back against the open door in disbelief. Kaden, wide eyed and naked, tied to a bed with a witch of an old woman standing over him. The old man scrambled at him with the hot poker high overhead. Ben pulled the trigger. The man flew across the room, hitting the wall.

Wayne pushed in past Ben. He too was shocked at the sight. "Kaden?" he said.

Ben stared the old woman down as he walked to Kaden. She stood frozen at the side of the bed.

"Keep a gun on that witch," he said.

Wayne stepped to the foot of the bed, pointing his gun at her chest. Ben leaned the shotgun against the wall and cut the ropes from Kaden's closest hand. Kaden twisted up and swung at the woman, she jumped back with a scream which turned into a crazed laugh.

"You can't hurt me, this here's a lawman and I'm a given up."

"This here's a evil place, Ben," Wayne said.

The bed shook as Kaden jerked at her, she stood an

inch from his reach. He pulled the gag from his mouth. "You old witch," he yelled.

"Okay, Kaden let's get you outta here. Now I'm gonna cut you loose, but you have to promise me you won't attack her. She's gonna get hers, I'll see to it," Ben said.

Ben looked at Kaden until he looked away from the old woman and nodded okay. He laid his head back down so Ben could reach across to cut his other hand free. Kaden saw Ben's holstered gun. He took it, swinging it around with speed. She lost her smile. The old woman backed away screaming. Kaden fired away, her cup of coffee blew apart, the woman flew back. Ben jumped away, powder burns on his arm, his ears ringing. Kaden put four shots into her, then two in the old man's corpse. He kept pulling the trigger until Ben took the gun.

Wayne handed him his clothes, Kaden didn't make eye contact or talk as he dressed.

The men looked at each other when they saw Kaden's back was in worse shape than his front. The bed was blood soaked. Ben walked behind the house and went through Kaden's saddle bags but found nothing to link him with the Cumberland job. Just the fact that he was down here was enough to put him on the list. He walked back in the little shack. Kaden was dressed and moving slowly around the bed. He went to the old man and kicked him a few times and did the same to the old witch.

"Let's collect anything of value and burn this place down," Ben said.

Kaden looked at Ben for the first time and nodded in agreement. He walked outside where Harry was saddling the Appaloosa. Ben found a large box of odds and ends, and some papers that must have been from other people they'd held captive. Ben hoped he could use some of it to find out a few of their names.

The shack burned fast, and they waited until it was just smoking before they got back on the trail. Kaden didn't talk, no one asked him to. It was the middle of the night when they rode up to Spring Valley. Kaden stopped, Ben rode a few yards before he noticed and turned in his saddle.

"Now I want you men to promise me you'll never say a word about me and that hell hole down in the south valley," Kaden said.

"I'll be write'n a report Kaden, have to. But I won't be tell'n anyone here abouts."

Kaden looked at the others, they nodded. Then Kaden yelled. "Say it!"

They promised him.

As they rode into town Wayne and Harry peeled off heading home. Ben and Kaden went to the doctors where Ben stayed until the doctor told him Kaden would be out for hours, probably until mid-day and he should go home. After four hours of sleep, Ben walked to the doctor's office, but on the way he noticed Kaden's horse was missing from behind the jail where he'd left it. He went to the doctor's office where he found out Cane had been there two hours earlier. The doctor looked in on Kaden an hour ago, and he was sleeping.

"But now he's gone?" Ben asked.

"Was I, ah I mean did you want me to keep him here? Is Kaden in trouble for something?"

"I'm not sure Doc, but yeah, I had a few questions for him. I would like to know how long he was at... Ah," he stopped himself from revealing his promise. "How long he's been outta town," Ben said.

"Well, he wasn't in very good shape, I can't believe he even got out of bed, but if he comes back, I'll come get you," Doc said.

"Did Cane say how he found out Kadin was here?"

"No, he didn't say much really," the Doc said.

"Well, I'll check with Cane myself," Ben said.

# Chapter 47

A faint sound stirred her from a dream. It brought her back but not all the way, she felt cheated and tried to go to where she was, but she couldn't. She couldn't even remember where it was, and why she wanted to get back there.

The second sound was a floorboard at the foot of her bed. It was familiar because she made that sound daily. Becky pictured the board in question it was near the wall, she saw her bare foot standing on it in front of the wash table. She'd rock back and forth on the loose plank, trying to make the noise into something funny or make it talk. She imagined a man's boot standing on it and opened her eyes. Her unconsciousness peeled away, her hearing slipped back from the void. She saw only the oblique pattern of the window panes from the moonlight across her bed—everything was still and dark. She slowly looked sideways, the latch on the door—it looked like it was still fastened.

She felt like she imagined or dreamed the noise and started to drift back to sleep; she heard the sound again and realized she was not alone in her room. She couldn't move—frozen in fear, she tried to control the sound of her breathing, to make it sound like she was still asleep. She needed time to think. Her mind was racing, her body was starting to sweat, she knew her face was in the shadows so she looked around as best she could. She scanned the room without moving her head. As her eyes were getting used to the dark, she looked at the wall at the foot of her bed, ever so slightly a shadow moved. Every hair on her body rose, she wanted to scream but couldn't get anything out.

From the darkness clear and loud, came Cane's voice. "I know you're awake, Rebecca."

She jumped for the door, but the latch was fastened. He took her by her waist, throwing her back on the bed. In an instant he was on top of her, his big hand covering her mouth. The bed bounced, she fought hard pushing him back. He flipped her over putting his knee in her back; he pulled a cloth from his pocket, gagging her. While on her stomach, she reached under the pillow for the knife Bill had given her, pulling it from its sheath. He rolled her over slapping her hard twice and grabbed her by her night shirt under the chin pulling her up face to face; she smelled sweat and whiskey.

"We're going to have some fun, then I'll take you for a ride, you can see..."

She swung the knife fast and hard into his side; he became still. It went in too easy; she knew she missed the mark. He moaned in pain as he reached for the knife. She pulled it out and stabbed at his reaching arm, trying to hit his chest. Cane moved off her and she pushed with her heels moving back to the headboard, she reached for the gag, but he hit her hard in the face and she was out.

Cane stood up and looked around the dark room, scratching his chin he hunched over in pain. He pulled a flask from his coat, taking a few big drinks he cringed. In the moonlight he saw blood dripping from his arm. He ripped a strip of cloth from her nightshirt and wrapped it. Reaching his hand inside his shirt he felt the side wound, he lowered his bloody hand to the dim rays of light from the window. He couldn't leave a trail, so he took his shirt off, falling into the wall. He ripped a long narrow strip from the bedding and tried to wrap it around his side but kept falling sideways. Leaning against the wall, he was able to wrap the wound tightly. He put his shirt back on and sat on the bed drinking the rest of the flask.

"I may have to kill you now—you know your mother just tried to do the same thing. Just when I was arranging a reunion," he said.

He tightened her gag, picked up the knife from the floor, and brushed the hair from her face. Cane moaned, holding his side; every time he felt the pain he wanted to hit her. He stood next to the bed loosely holding the knife at her throat he ran it around her face, down to her chest, cutting a few buttons off. He wanted her to wake up; it was taking too long. He felt like he had to kill her now. His wound made it hard to lift his arm, let alone carry her down the stairs without waking Bill the bum across the alley.

He touched her leg and felt his way up to see if she was faking it. She moaned, opened her eyes, and looked up into Cane's dark face. She slapped the knife from his hand and quickly reached for the gag. He jumped at her, picking her up by the throat. Her heels knocked against the wall as she kicked at him. He slapped her face a few times, then tossed her across the bed to the floor near the door. She reached for the gag, but he slapped her hands away. Cane picked her up moaning with pain and punched her so hard he felt he may have killed her. She went limp, and he tossed her across the bed. She hit the wall headfirst, dropping to the floor taking the corner table with her, she laid still.

Cane stepped to the window and looked across the

alley at Bill's place. He pulled his gun hoping Bill would look out. He looked down at the street and felt dizzy and drunk. If he shot his gun he'd never get away. Seeing no movement at Bill's, Cane walked around the bed to make sure the girl was dead. She was packed into the corner with her head twisted around; it looked like she'd broken her neck. It was tight between the wall and the bed. He felt her neck for a pulse. He couldn't find one. He almost passed out from bending over, standing up fast he got dizzy, he had to lean against the wall for a full minute. He was tired and drunk; the pain was not a problem now. He shook his head a few times trying to think straight; he stumbled around the foot of the bed to the door. He started to leave but looked back inside to see if he'd forgot anything, but the room looked darker now. He thought about what he'd done and mumbled, "that little shit stabbed me."

# Chapter 48

Cane walked out, closed the door, and looked around to make sure he hadn't been seen. The moon was full, and everything had a bit of a glow. He looked across the alley at Bill's, but his eyes automatically drifted across the street to Melissa's house. He walked down the stairs talking himself into taking the beautiful Mrs. Engilton.

"If I can't have the one, I'll have the other."

He shushed himself as he looked up at Bill's window. Cane stagger to the center of the street, he stood out front of the store looking around and saw no one. He continued through her garden gate, zigzagging and bumping his way down the short stone path. His toe hit a rock, and he stumbled forward. Melissa woke to the sound of Cane's head slamming hard into her front door.

He tried to open the door but quickly became frustrated. She rolled out of bed, creeping to the front room where she saw Cane in the moonlight trying to get in. He was talking to himself; he stopped and stepped away. She felt relief, but then the door crashed open as he fell into the house moaning. He slowly stood from behind the sofa holding his side. He looked around but couldn't see, so he lit a match and held it high. Pulling his gun out, and holding the match, he slowly moved into the room. "Missy," he called out low. He slowly moved the lit match around, looking into the room. He started for the other room, but the match burned his finger and he threw it to the floor. He turned to see which end of a new match to strike in the faint moonlight.

It's first glow lit the room revealing Melissa standing with a Colt Navy aiming at his head. She held the gun with confidence in one hand the other was on her hip.

"If I see your gun move at all I will shoot," she said.

"Woo, Missy..."

"If you call me Missy again, I will shoot you in your privates." She lowered her aim, "Now drop the gun," she said, "then take that match and light the candle, and if the match goes out I will shoot, I have to—you'd do the same."

Cane dropped his gun on the couch and very slowly he lowered the match to a candle on a table next to him.

"Be very careful with that gun, Missy—lissa,"

"Oh—I know, this trigger is so touchy I almost shot Bill when he was teaching me how to shoot."

Cane thought how much he hated Bill. She looked at him expressionless.

"Well—get!"

He turned rushing for the door but ran into the wall next to it. Rubbing his forehead he continued out to the street, stopping for a moment he looked back at the little house—what a mistake he'd made. Hell, he thought, I killed Becky tonight, I can never come back here again. He looked up the street at the Highlands and at the Sheriff's office, then with disdain he looked at Bill's room above the store. Cane held his side as he ran up main street for the last time.


The gun became heavy in her hand; she started shaking and fought the impulse to cry. Keeping her eyes on the street, Melissa fell back in a chair. She heard him ride away. After a few minutes, she lit a lantern and slowly walked out into the street. She turned around to see in all directions, no sign of him. She crossed the street for the Sheriff's office, but instead turned down the alley to Bill's room, running up the stairs. Bill was out of the bed when he heard someone coming up.

Melissa knocked, "Bill! Bill help!"

He swung the door open. She fell in his arms as he took the gun from her, easing the hammer back down he tossed it on the bed.

"What is it?" he asked.

"It was Cane, he broke my door down and..."

She choked up. He pulled her away by her arm, holding her lantern high he looked her over up and down.

"Are you okay," he said.

"Yes, I had the gun and chased him away."

He set the lantern on a table, put on a shirt and sat on the bed, pulling his boots on.

"That man is going crazy right before our eyes, was he drunk?"

"Yes, and he held his side in pain a few times, he was bleeding," she said.

"Bleeding? Did it happen when he broke your door?"

"I don't think so, I got the feeling he was already hurt," she said.

Bill strapped his gun and knife on and cautiously looked out the door. Waving for her, she followed. When they got to the street, Bill stopped and walked back a few steps.

"That's blood here."

He held the lantern high, looking back down the alley.

"Did he come this way?" he asked.

"No, it sounded like he went down the street towards the church."

"Stay here."

He walked down the alley following the blood, it stopped before the end of the buildings, he turned looking back at her. He took a look at his steps, then walked to Becky's where he saw blood.

"Beck!" he yelled.

He ran up the stairs four steps at a time, Melissa ran after him. Bill swung the door open, rushing in he held the lantern high. He didn't see her. The room was a mess; he ran to a back room calling for her but nothing. He walked back out. Melissa was at the window in the moonlight. He saw Becky in the corner behind the bed and ran to her.

"Beck."

He knelt in the tight space and touched her hand. "She's not cold," he said.

"Put her on the bed," Melissa said.

Bill lifted her carefully, Melissa held the lamp up as she felt for a pulse.

"Oh—no, I can't feel one," she cried.

She was crying as she felt for a better place to check.

Bill walked in a small circle at the foot of the bed rubbing his temples trying to keep from exploding. Why couldn't I protect her? He stopped and looked at Melissa—he almost lost both of the most important women in his life—again. Melissa set the lamp on the night table and bent over, closer this time, trying her neck again.

"Bill?"

He clinched his fists, stretched his arms high, looked at the ceiling and screamed out a yell he'd only done once before in his life. Melissa jumped.

"Bill?" she said,

"My name is Jersey."

"I think I'm getting a faint pulse here." She looked up. "We need..."

He was already out the door jumping down the stairs

running for the doctor. Melissa brought the washbowl to the bed and started to clean Becky's face. She thought about what Bill had said, there was only one man she ever heard of called Jersey. She put it out of her mind while getting Becky ready for the doctor. It wasn't long before they entered the room, both were out of breath.

"I need more light," the doctor said.

Jersey lit two more lamps.

"Bill you better leave, Melissa you stay and give me a hand?"

Melissa looked at Jersey. "You need to go tell Ben," she said.

The morning sky was cresting the mountain tops with pink and blue but still dark over head as Jersey hurried down the stairs. He turned when he saw movement out near the street; it was Stan, the night shift deputy crawling off the porch.

Jersey ran to him. "What happened to you?"

"Someone must-a hit me from behind," Stan said.

The back of his shirt was covered in blood. Jersey helped him to his feet.

"Can you walk?"

"Think so," he said.

"Doc is upstairs in Beck's room, head on up there. I'm going for Ben," Jersey said.

He ran down the alley towards the river and the Sheriff's house.

"Why's the doctor upstairs," Stan yelled.

He cringed, holding his head in pain.

Jersey yelled from over his shoulder. "Beck's hurt bad, he's with her."

"Becky? Oh—no! No, this can't be."

Stan dropped to his knees crying. He laid down and rolled over. Alone in the alley he lay looking up at the fading stars, "I should'a been there."

# Jersey Smith

## Part Three

# Chapter 49

Melissa found Jersey in his room leaning back on the headboard. He'd roughly cut his hair, it was wet and combed back, his beard was chopped off close to his face. He was wearing clothes that were not his usual, they actually fit. He noticed her looking at him with surprise.

"Ah—I washed up in the river," he said.
She nodded. "Sounds cold."
"How is she?" he asked.
Melissa shook her head. "He beat her something awful, doc's not sure if she'll make it."
She moved next to him at the bed, sat down, and started to cry. He opened his arms, and she filled them. They laid silent for some time with her head on his chest. He was thinking about his next move, she was thinking how bad it could have been. It was like he saw this coming, the gift of the gun and teaching her how to use it properly. But it's not Bill, she thought, he's been lying to me, to everyone, for all this time.
"So, you're Jersey Smith."
He said nothing. His shirt was soft to her touch and his strong arm around her gave her the safe feeling she'd wanted for so long. She'd acted tough for so many years that she became the strong woman she needed to be. It wasn't that hard. It was acting, at least at first it was, but

at some point it took. She got stronger. Although her confidence had always been there, she'd gained an independence, took control of her life. She was happy with things the way she'd made them. Sure she wanted a man, but not to take over her life, as before. What if this man was really as different as he seemed, someone that wanted to share her life, not lead it. Well, she thought, that could be something.

The narrow alley had filled with people spilling into the street. Outside the window they heard Ben step out of Becky's room, he had the crowd's full attention. He'd been crying and his voice cracked a few times. "She's alive."

A feeling of relief spread through the crowd.

"She's in bad shape and hasn't woke up yet," he said. "I have to be honest with you, Doc says she might not make it."

Someone in the crowd yelled up to Ben. "Who did it?"

He didn't want to say yet. In the heat of anger a few men might run off to the Gannon ranch and Ben knew Cane wasn't going there.

"I need a few men to meet me at the Highlands in three hours, we're going after him."

The crowd became loud, and the sheriff raised his hands.

"Now let's break this up and go home. As soon as we know someth'n, we'll send someone around with the news."

"Pastor Dale, this is a good time for you to be up here. And Justin Hecht, can you meet me in my office in a few minutes? Now everyone else go on home."

They were slow to move.

"I mean it, go on," he said.

Ben walked to his office, Justin was waiting.

"Now Justin I know you probably want to go after this

guy but you have two young ones at home, so I have another way you can help."

Ben sat at his desk writing.

"I need you to ride to the rail line and send off a few notices."

"Okay Ben," he said.

Ben handed him the first note. "Wait for a reply on this one," he said.

Ben looked over at Becky's desk and let out a little moan.

"You okay sheriff?"

"Hmm? Oh, ah-yeah, I'll be fine. Hey, take someone with you to keep watch," he said. "I know it's a long ride but I need you to get there as fast as you can. When you get back check in with Stanley, give him the reply."

Ben handed him the rest of the notes, "I know you did this before, but you gotta follow the dots and dashes close. A wrong dot can change a word. The code book is in the box, make sure they're right before you send 'em."

"I will."

Justin walked to the door, Ben called to him. "Justin you better take the telegraph sounder." He pointed to the black box and a spool of wire sitting on his desk.

"Oh, right."

"You remember how to hook it up?"

"Yeah, I'll get it done and fast too."


Melissa leaned up on Jersey's chest. Her thin finger drew a line along his jaw, making a scratching sound.

"You have three hours, why don't I give you that haircut and finish your beard with a nice hot shave," she said.

"Missy that would feel so good, a clean shave again—I really hated that beard."

"You heat some water, I'll run for my kit."

She made quick work of his hair, but she was out of practice with a straight razor. Not wanting to cut him she was slow and precise. She was close and concentrating. He was enjoying her closeness—her smell, her smooth skin, the big eyes, and the odd strand of hair that kept falling in her face. When she finished she wiped his face with a hot wet cloth, he pulled her onto his lap and looked into her dark eyes.

"When this is over Missy..."

"First you need to come back," she said.

He looked in a mirror she held up.

"That's fine," he said.

"Oh my, I can't believe you're the same man, I like the new you."

"Better than the old one?"

"Which one is the real one?"

"Bill was me trying to go back to the way I was before," he said.

"Before?"

"Before things got dark and out of control."

"Did you have a beard and long hair before?"

"No."

"So tell me Jersey Smith—are you an outlaw?"

"No. I never shot anyone that wasn't going to shoot me or someone else."

"Well, I..." she thought for a moment. "I think you're a kind man and I'm quite sure I'm in love with you."

He smiled at her, then noticed the look on her face.

"But?" he asked.

"Well, there were a few stories."

"Believe the good ones and forget the bad ones. When I get back I'll tell you my side to everything. Also, don't say anything about the real me—yet."

"Okay. What about Becky when she wakes?"

"That'd be fine."

"Don't go getting killed on me just when things are..."

In the best way he knew Jersey stopped her from talking.

# Chapter 50

Jersey's desire to do this alone was strong, but he'd lost Cane in those foothills before. Besides, Ben and the rest deserved some satisfaction. Jersey filled his large saddle bags with everything he might need, picked up his good bedroll, put two canteens over his shoulder, and walked behind the store to saddled up. He led Blue from the stall a few steps to the river and filled the canteens while Blue drank.

"I got a special mix for dinner Blue, with oats, also I brought a few apples."

He always emphasized the words oats and apples because Blue knew them. He usually raised his head and blew out through his snout. Often he'd nudge at Jersey like he wanted them now.

Jersey thought of Beck and Melissa and how he'd moved here to keep people he cared about safe. Once more events closed in. He felt like himself again, not just because he was wearing his old clothes and had his face back, or that his Colt and knife were again strapped across his back just below his waistcoat. It was much more than that, it was something inside him; it had defined him, and it was back stronger than ever. An unmistakable aching, the haunting feeling that kept his senses sharp and his drive focused.

It was a hatred fueled desire to get even that created the Jersey Smith of local stories. He knew an evil man's deed changed him into something he didn't recognize. Often his thoughts went to Catherine and Marie by the river. Lately, nightmares of Martin being dragged off by wolves woke him in a sweat. He had a responsibility to them and he failed. The need for revenge was unfulfilled, and for so long it burned a hole in his heart.

With atonement abandoned, what horrors had others gone through at the hands of that man? What of the living left in his wake? A deed so evil was beyond revenge—restitution was impossible to reach when the damage done could never be undone. Getting even would never be enough. He knew one thing for certain—if he ever found the man that killed his family, the Jersey Smith he didn't recognize, the one that murderer created—he would be the one exacting vengeance, and then some.

He had a little time before the meeting so he walked Blue slowly along the river west behind the Sunny Side and the other buildings. They turned in, walking down the Blacksmith shop's alley. He stepped out onto the street as Otis was rolling the big door shut. Otis turned and saw a tall man standing there with Bill's horse.

"Hey that's not your..."

Jersey smiled, and Otis recognized him.

"Bill?"

"Jersey."

Otis smiled, he looked down and shook his head. "Oh boy—this is gonna get interesting isn't it. You still keep'n it a secret?"

Jersey nodded. "For a bit still."

They walked down the center of the street leading their horses up to the Highlands.

Jersey and Otis walked in, looked around the crowded

room, then sat with Ben near the front door. Ben was going over a few maps, they were spread out.

He looked up at Otis. "Hey Otis."

He looked at the man next to him. When Jersey smiled, Ben could see it was Bill.

"What the... Oh. Well you look different."

Jersey smiled and nodded. "What's the holdup?" he said.

"Just waiting on a few more, said they'd be here soon. I sent Justin off to send a few telegraphs, try'n to get a tracker to meet us on the trail."

Otis stood and said, "Jer..., ah—Bill, you want some coffee?"

"Yes, thanks Otis."

Jersey looked back at Ben. "Do you think we need to wait around for a tracker?"

"You've been there, neither of us found out where he was going, a tracker could give us the edge we need. Cane takes wagons of supplies out there, he could have an army, we need all the help we can get," Ben said.

"I spec so, with a tracker we may even surprise him."

Otis poured coffee from a large pot on the center stove. He noticed Wayne gave him a strange look. The men were talking about hunting stories and were having a pretty good time considering. Wayne was finishing up his adventurous story as Otis sat back down.

One man spoke up. "Hey, that's a Jersey Smith story! It's not about you."

Otis perked up and nudged Jersey.

"Well, I'm not surprised you'd say that, a few of those stories have been falsely attributed to Jersey Smith," Wayne said.

"What?" one man spoke up.

"Well, I encountered Jersey Smith a few years back, little man really, not like they say in the stories."

Otis looked at Jersey and smiled. "I heard he was about your size, Bill," Otis said.

Jersey gave him a look, then he saw that Ben was looking at them, so he smiled and shrugged it off.

"Yeah, he was just an average outlaw," Wayne said.

One of the men stood leaning on the table. "He weren't such!"

"Was—was indeed. Wanted back east he was, and I was sent to track him down and that's what I did."

Jersey said nothing but sipped his coffee and watched the man closely. He'd known Wayne from the first day he came to Spring Valley. There were things about him, things he did, that put him on the short list of problem men in town. In fact, he was going to insist that both Wayne and Howard not go with the posse.

"I felt sorry for him in the end," Wayne said. "He kept begging—so I let him go. I kicked the hell out of him first."

Jersey spit coffee across the table. Otis had a hard time suppressing laughter as Ben reached over, patting Jersey on the back.

"I don't know what's got into you two this morning. Down the wrong pipe there Bill?"

"Yeah, wrong pipe."

Otis straightened up. They listened for a bit longer.

"Ya know, I made a map of the area, I'll run out and get it from my saddlebag," Jersey said.

Jersey left and Otis moved around to the other side of the table to have a better view of the men talking. He was having a good time; he was in on a secret, and it was a doozie. He was looking forward to the trail when Wayne and the others find out that Bill is really Jersey. Then Wayne said something that stopped everything, something that made his blood boil.

"I don't think we should be taking that negro along on

this important run. Anybody with me on that?" Wayne said.

The men were silent for a moment. Ben started to stand up, but Otis touched his wrist.

"Let's see how this plays out Ben, if'n you don't mind," Otis said.

Ben sat back down, twisted his chair around and watched the room change.

A few of the men stood up talking to each other, then they turned to Wayne.

"This here's Pennsylvania mister—we don't say or do that kind of thing up here."

"Otis is one of us," another man said.

"In the north every man's a free man," Fred said.

Otis felt the closeness and friendship that he remembered from the first few weeks in town. Ben was glad Otis had stopped him from interrupting. The group of standing men turned to Wayne and said, "look here Wayne, we don't want you come'n along."

A few more men agreed.

"What? Are you crazy, you're gonna take that ni—"

"Wayne." Fred interrupted. "We think you should just leave now."

"You don't speak for everyone! Who wants me to stay and Otis here to leave?" Wayne asked.

The room was silent. Four of the men led him to the door and pushed him out. Two of the men patted Otis on the shoulder as they walked back by.

Jersey came in and sat back at the table with his map spreading it out. Things were different in the room. He looked at Ben now standing at the bar, he was looking back at him.

"What's going on Ben?" Jersey asked.

"Wayne's not going," Ben said.

The men mumbled in agreement.

"Well, hell—Wayne wasn't go'n anyway," Jersey said.

Ben looked puzzled.

"What do you mean by that?" he asked.

"He works for Cane! You weren't really going to let him ride with us, were you? I mean, that's as bad as taking Howard here along," Jersey said.

"What?" Ben said.

Jersey looked past Ben to Howard, who had stopped wiping a glass and looked up.

"Howard, how much of this place does Cane own now, has to be over half, right? Is it more?" Jersey asked.

Ben turned to Howard. "Is this true?"

The men at the bar looked at Howard. When Ben turned to look back at Jersey, the men turned as well.

"Oh hell, I couldn't believe we were meeting here in the first place," Jersey said, he leaned back in his chair. "Now's a good time to come clean Howard."

Everyone turned back to Howard.

"I'm sorry everyone, it just kinda happened. At first I needed some money, and he used things over me and well, it's all his now. This whole place is Cane's, has been for almost a year."

"Tell'm about Wayne," Jersey said.

"Wayne," he felt shame looking around at his friends. "He's a slaver, not sure if that's what you call it, but he takes black folk back to the south," Howard said.

Even Jersey was surprised to hear that. He looked over at Otis who was holding back rage, his fists tightly gripping nothing, then he got up hurrying for the door looking for Wayne.

Jersey followed. "Otis, one minute," he said.

Otis stopped in the doorway, then he turned back in.

"What about Otis?" Jersey asked.

Howard looked around at the men across the bar. Otis

stepped back in the room.

"Well," Howard took a big swallow. "Wayne wanted to take him away but Cane made sure he stayed on-a-count-a he's such a dam good Smithy."

"But I'm a free man—I got papers," Otis said.

Howard shook his head. "That don't matter to them. Once you're south, Wayne say's you're a slave even if you never was, they have a place that makes phony papers in case they get stopped and to use at the auctions."

Ben looked concerned.

"When you say them, do you mean Cane was in on this?" he asked.

Again Howard looked like he didn't want to say. A few men started over the bar, and Howard put his hands out.

"Yes," he said.

He tossed his towel to the floor and leaned on the back bar. "Cane is also selling men, and women, I heard even children."

The crowd started talking and yelling. A few men jumped over the bar.

Ben yelled to stop then called to Stan. "Stan get Howard to the jail and stick close by till I get back."

"I didn't do anything," Howard said.

"We'll sort this out when we get back," Ben said.

Jersey called to Ben. "We'll be waiting where you're meeting the tracker."

"That will be at the first rise overlooking the clearing, where are you going?"

"We gotta stop Wayne before he gets to Cane."

Otis and Jersey stepped outside.

"He's not far, his horse was tied off at the land office a few minutes ago," Jersey said.

# Chapter 51

Cane stopped outside of town when the sky gave him enough light to check his wounds. His bleeding had slowed from his side, it wasn't as bad as he'd thought; the knife pierced the skin and ran along the back muscle. Once wrapped, it laid flat and quickly clotted. His arm was sliced in a few places. One wound would not stop bleeding. He wrapped it with a cloth, then twisted three layers of leather straps as tight as he could get them. When he was sure he wouldn't leave a blood trail, he continued. It was cold and seemed to take forever. When he finally arrived the guard fumbled to open the gate. He rode slowly through the compound, stumbled through the house and climbed in bed. He called out for anyone to help, when no one came he fell asleep.

Susanne stood up when she heard someone unlocking the door of the shed. The guard took her to the outhouse, then to the kitchen, and told her to wash up. Martin came running in and the guard looked at him and yelled. "Hey, get outta here!" Martin looked at him, but ran to Susanne hugging her. The guard shook his head and went to his chair in the corner. Martin ran around getting food for her, and the guard gave up trying to stop him. When she looked presentable, the guard stood up.

"Okay, you need to give Jamie a hand in Cane's room,

he's been hurt," he said.

"And he trusts me to help with that?" she said.

He shrugged. "I know, sounds crazy, but you better get along."

Martin held on to the back of her dress as they walked down the hallway. Not knowing what to expect, they opened the door slowly. Cane was sitting up in his bed with a white cloth wrapped around his chest and arm. He was talking with Clayton, and Kaden was sitting in a chair in the corner looking angry.

"Susanne, how nice of you to come visit with me,"

"I was told you needed help," she said.

"All done now, but you can get in the kitchen and get dinner going. Martin, how are you today?"

"I'm fine sir, thank you," Martin said.

"Well—kitchen."

He pointed, they left.

"Does this mean you don't have to go back in the shed?" Martin asked.

"No—I'll be back in there before the nights over," she looked at him. "But we can have a little fun while I'm out, right?"

Martin knew she meant they could have fun while working very hard in the kitchen, but that was okay, they were together and maybe something would happen tonight. He often thought of how maybe something would happen, like all the bad guys would just die. He smiled at the thought of that. He came up with a few more thoughts that would be agreeable, none played out well for Cane.


"Clayton, did you get the powder kegs set?" Cane asked.

"No, I'm setting the tunnel charge soon, but wait'n till after dark for the rest."

Kaden sat up in his chair. "Wait—what?" he said.

They both looked at him.

"We have to leave, tomorrow," Cane said.

"What happened in Spring Valley yesterday? You're all cut up, who's after you?" Kaden asked.

"Things did come to a head."

"Is it the law?" Clayton asked.

Cane looked at Clayton, then away.

"So, we got the law bearing down on us?" Kaden said.

Cane rubbed his chin thinking for a minute. "Probably," he said.

"All this work, all the money—think about how much money we spent on this place," Kaden said.

"We got it all back and made a lot more, we're taking a small fortune with us. Hell, I'm looking forward to something new and smaller, this is too big now," Cane said.

Clayton nodded. "I'm all for something smaller, this place got way outta hand."

"What about Powder Kegs? Are we blowing this place up?" Kaden looked at the ceiling. "With everyone in it?"

"You're no one to talk about blowing people up, Kaden. What happened at the mining camp anyway? You came back a different man," Clayton said.

Kaden saw a flash of the insane old couple, their faces up close. A cold sweat covered his body the hairs on his neck rose, he felt like he might get sick right there on the floor. He sat back in his chair quietly while the brothers planned out how the next day should play out.

"The guest bunkhouse is half full," Clayton said.

"I don't think we'll see too many more show up," Cane said.

"Why's that?"

"I'm think'n they won't get passed Ben and probably a few locals."

"What?"

"By now their assemble'n men, could be in the valley already."

Clayton looked at Kaden and shook his head, he looked back at Cane. "What happen in town yesterday?"

"Like I said, things kinda flared up," Cane said.

"This is really someth'n Cane."

"Well, we could see a few more of our men show up if they come from the south."

Kaden spoke up. "Just more to split the money with."

"No—more to fight 'em off while we leave with the money," Cane said.

"Well, the Burton brothers are here, if they get wind of this no tell'n what they might do," Clayton said.

"Mm, who else knows?"

"Just Frank."

"Let's keep it that way until morning we could use the Burton boys with us," Cane said.

"If we got men after us, why don't we leave now?" Clayton asked.

"If they get past the ambush point, they still have to find the place and I know they can't do that in the dark. Only one way in for them. In the morning we head out the back way. We'll be riding north through the valley when they..."

Clayton interrupted. "North? that's where they're come'n from."

"By morning they'll be in the hills, if they're early enough they'll be blown up and slide down the mountain. If they come later, they'll be searching through the rubble for survivors."

# Chapter 52

Jersey and Otis trotted through town looking between buildings and houses. They stopped at the Church where the pastor was sitting on a bench in the yard reading.

"Dale, did you see Wayne ride by?" Jersey asked.

"Bill? Is that you?"

Jersey nodded, the pastor pointed past the church east towards the mountains.

"Maybe ten minutes ago," he said. "Well Bill you look ah—different, a bit more organized. You know, not so untidy," Pastor Dale said.

"Um, thanks."

Once out of town they turned on the speed, talking loud to each other when they could ride side by side.

"We have to stop before we get to the clearing, if he's going to ambush us that would be the place," Jersey said.

They had to slow down, twisting through the heavy trees.

"Why not here, around a turn?"

"He could, but with all these trees we'd be close, have to use a handgun, he'd have a mess on his hands. He's yellow. He's gonna want some distance between us and him, he'll lay in wait with a rifle."

When they came up on a ridge just before the clearing they stopped. Jersey got his telescope out.

"Hold my belt so I can stand," he said.

Otis edged his horse over grabbing Jersey's belt while he stood on his saddle. He slowly stood looking over the crest in the trail at each new tree and rock as he moved up. He ducked back down quickly.

"I think I see him."

Jersey slipped off Blue and ran to a bush next to the trail at the high point. He slid the telescope open and lifted his head, looking through the bush.

"Yep, in a tree, maybe fifty yards up just off the path on the south side. He's got the tree trunk for cover, tough shot from here."

They both looked south.

Otis pointed. "This ridge here runs a good ways, why don't I take a rifle and come up from behind him."

Jersey nodded, he looked around the immediate area.

"I'll get his attention along here. Otis dismounted and pulled his new rifle out.

"Loaded?" Jersey asked.

"Yeah,"

"Sighted?"

"No, not yet," Otis said.

"Take mine, you'll only get one clean shot."

He nodded and put his gun back. Jersey handed him his Sharps. He took a sight out of the little box and held it up. He read the little lines and started clicking the sight hole down from the last time he'd used it.

"Here, it's set for thirty yards,"

Otis put four extra paper shell cartridges in his shirt pocket, then put the long gloves on.

"If you get closer than thirty, take the dam thing off," Jersey said.

They both knew Jersey was the wise choice for this attack, but they also knew this slave trader needed to be taken by Otis.

"Should I kill him Jersey?"

Jersey was surprised, compassion had been in short supply and coming from an ex-slave who was hunting down a slave trader, mercy seemed strange.

"I'm not the man to ask such a question." Compassion or not he thought. "If he's shoot'n at me, take him out. You know he's the worst kind of man, he would be at the top of any law man's list."

Otis nodded a few times.

"Wait till I get him shooting, you can get closer when he's distracted," Jersey said.

Otis nodded, he moved hunched over off the trail into the rough and along the little hill.

Jersey grabbed his saddle Colt putting it in his belt, then he took his rope, moving low and cautiously along the little ridge that crossed the trail. He laid on the ground tied the rope to the base of a bush as high as he could reach without being seen. He did the same to a bush on the other side of the trail; he knelt near a large rock with both ends of the rope.

Otis found enough cover to sneak up close, so he took the sight off. Wayne was sitting sideways on a thick branch in a large old tree, but he was on the other side of the trunk. Otis didn't have a clean shot and felt like he could only move east to keep from being seen.

Jersey pulled the ropes and the bushes moved, he held his hat up edging it to the ridge on the trail. Wayne saw the movement and started shooting, lead skipped off the ground and buzzed off in the distance. Otis moved through the brush, found a spot, took a knee and aimed the gun at Wayne's back. He thought if he keeps firing I could walk right up to him and take him without a shot, but he looked down the barrel and pulled the trigger. Otis shot the branch near the tree's trunk. Wayne, the branch and his gun fell with speed fifteen feet, hitting a thick branch on the way. Otis was already running as Jersey walked over the ridge cautiously with both guns out.

Jersey called to Blue, who was tied to Otis's horse, they both came over the hill. Otis was kneeling at Wayne's body. He'd fallen shoulder and head first onto a large rock and was out cold. Jersey looked at the branch on the ground and saw it had been shot off.

"Oh, well that was expert Otis, just perfect."

Otis looked up at him and smiled with satisfaction. "A public trial will be a good way to get the names of those he sold," he said.

"We gotta load him up and head to the ridge, set up camp," Jersey said.

"We got something to cook-up? I'm hungry," Otis said.

"You're always hungry."

# Chapter 53

They made their way to the meeting place and set up camp. They didn't know where this tracker fellow was coming from, but they knew they were at least a days ride from anywhere, so they got comfortable. Wayne was tied to the base of a tree and after a long grilling from Otis, he fell asleep.

"We can get two of the men out of the way by having them take Wayne back to Stan," Jersey said.

"What do you mean out of the way? You don't want to ride with some of them?"

"No, I don't want to see these guys get hurt. Some of them don't know how to hold a gun, they're just here for Beck and revenge," he said.

"Right, yeah a few are farmers and shop owners."

After another hour the posse showed up, and the place was chaos for a while. The gap between men that knew what to do, and those that didn't was wide, so Jersey took the first watch. His view from high on a nearby outcropping was almost 360°. He waited for the men to get organized and calm down. They kept the fire low, eating dried meat, fish, and bread for dinner. They decided the tracker wouldn't get there until early in the morning.

"By the way," Ben said. "Could be damp in the morning so cover your guns and keep your powder dry, you're going to need 'em tomorrow."

They set up two-man shifts to keep watch. There was enough men to keep the shifts down to three hours each.

"We can't let anyone ride by us. You have to run down here and get us if you see anyone out there," Ben said.

Ben, Fred, Jersey, Harry and Otis slept in a small group on one side of the fire. After a few hours they couldn't sleep and sat up talking the rest of the night. The sun was still below the horizon, but the dome overhead lit the ground enough to see. The lookout yelled something and everyone saw him pointing as the tracker, and another man, rode into camp.

Jersey was a bit angry they'd had to wait so long, he just wanted to get on the trail. This man had better be worth the wait. What if Cane had just lit out? He didn't want to lose him because they waited. Jersey stood stretching then strapped on his gun and knife, he started putting his things away. Most of the men saw him and did the same. Ben walked to the tracker and shook his hand. Everyone was moving around in the dim light. Jersey stood at the dying fire shaking out his bedroll, as he rolled it up the tracker yelled across the camp. "By jingo, is—is that you Jersey?"

Jersey smiled when he recognized Trapper Earl's voice.

"Earl?"

He turned looking across the fire and saw the looks on all the men's faces.

"Well, I guess the wait was worth it after all," Jersey said.

They greeted each other as the long-lost friends they were, with a hug, some backslapping, and lots of laughing. They walked to the edge of the camp where the terrain dropped, and the view was vast. They stood talking for a while as the sky lit from the sun behind the Highland hills. When they turned around, the whole camp was standing with their horses staring at them.

"What?" Earl asked.

"Have you got a plan?" Ben asked.

"Yeah," Jersey said. "Let's get back down to the trail and leave it to trap—ah Tracker Earl here."

"Let's mount up," Ben yelled. "We need to have a little talk Jersey," he said.

Earl and Jersey, Ben and Otis, rode two wide up front. The rest followed, talking low about the times they should have seen Bill was really Jersey Smith.

"When were you gonna tell your little secret?" Ben asked.

"I wasn't, not really. I'd planned on being Bill for the rest of my life if I had to, or at least as long as I stayed here. I did feel bad about lie'n, but I couldn't say anything. I had this reputation that got outta control so a few men were after me. Heck, you helped with that one outlaw out front of the Highlands." Jersey looked at Earl. "Remember when Abby got attacked in the hills? And remember the one man was left alive? Well his brother, I was told, was come'n for me—cut me into little pieces he was."

"And did he?" Earl asked, he was looking around intently.

Jersey smiled. "Several did come. The last time almost got me for good. After that I left before some friend or Hamish was hurt or worse."

Everyone kept looking around as they talked. Jersey could see Ben was a bit offended being lied to, so he kept explaining.

"Well anyway, another one showed up here in Spring Valley looking for me, and Ben here put him in his place."

"No. Really?" Earl said.

"Yeah, the guy was going to shoot him in the back," Jersey said.

"Okay—okay." Ben turned to Earl. "We all know why I didn't get shot in the back."

Earl glanced over to see Ben nodding to Jersey.

Earl broke off mid conversation. He rode to the side of the trail as everyone stopped.

"Got someth'n?" Ben asked.

"Somethin's different," Earl said.

They were in the deep trees at the foothills past where Jersey lost Cane the last time, only this time they were down in the thick of it.

"Sheriff, you can have everyone take a break, I need to look around," Earl said.

Ben yelled it along and Otis walked back a way's with Earl checking the side of the trail, Jersey walked ahead. After a while the trail became far more rugged. Earl and Otis came back walking along the other side.

Jersey returned shaking his head. "Trail dries up out there," he said.

We got two options and both go south. One is right close by it goes over to that out cropping of shale there," he pointed through the tree tops.

"And the other?" Ben asked.

"Well it's a ways back maybe quarter mile, I saw it and was planning on heading back there if we happened on a place like this," Earl said. "I think it's a hidden turnoff, you have to look real hard to see it. Look on the south side, well beyond the line of trees. It looked like a trail was over there. And when we got to higher ground I looked back and could see a well traveled path and a clearing to the south."

"But—if it's an ambush they could be up on that shale ridge right now," Jersey said.

"Right, that's why we came on this far, I could see that long stretch of rock there," Earl said.

"Well, if there's an ambush right there then they know we're here, we ain't been too quiet," Ben said.

He looked up at the rock and how it ran out of view.

"It looks like a good place for an ambush, I think we need to check both out. Let's send a couple to check the ledge while the rest of us head to the hidden trail, fire off a shot if it's clear."

Earl and Otis took the nearby path, walking their rides slowly along the bottom of the tall shale walls. The rest headed back looking for Earl's hidden trail. It was hard to find. Jersey was surprised Earl had seen it at all. It was an area of dense trees where the rider could step off the trail around a few tall bushes. They would brush their tracks, then move on through the trees. Once back there it was a well worn winding path. It ran parallel with the mountains and led to an open area and a road heading south. In just a few short years Earl had become a very good tracker, Jersey thought.

They'd traveled another hundred yards where the trees cleared and the land became open. Jersey yelled for the men up front to hold-up, they didn't hear him. When he got to the opening he leaned up in his stirrups and cupped his hands at his mouth to yell again. One of the men flew off his horse. The gun blast echoed through the valley as more lead ripped through the thin line of trees they'd been behind. Most of the men jumped to the ground—it was an open expanse, and they were sitting ducks.

"Get behind something! Get out of the open!" Ben yelled.

Another man was hit and spun to the ground. Most everyone ran east to a line of rocks and bushes. Large blocks of shale were scattered and sticking up a few feet out of the ground. They were pinned down. Jersey looked around for Blue, he spotted him under a few trees with some other horses looking in Jersey's direction.

Fred leaned away from a large stone with a spyglass in his hand and yelled, "they're up on the high ledge, back where we were. Must be a quarter mile away. I think they only got two up there, maybe three."

"Yeah?" Ben said.

"Judging by the amount of fire, that sounds right," Jersey said to Ben.

He moved around peeking over the big stones until he found a spot he felt had good cover, where a bush also hid his face. One of the men out on the open ground laying flat behind a log moved, and a gunshot hit the ground next to his head.

"Play dead man, don't move, we'll get you when we can," Ben yelled.

Jersey looked around the nearby area to make sure he had extra room and waited. Another lead ball hit a rock somewhere down the line. Jersey made a low whistle and waved to Blue, who came running. Jersey took his reins, made two snap sounds with his fingers then pulled down on his reins and said "Get DOWN!" Blue sat down then lowered himself the rest of the way.

"Shit Bill, I mean Jersey, how..."

"Oh—be ready he doesn't like this, could jump up at any time so keep back."

He talked to Blue saying how great he was as he undid the extra ten feet of leash on his reins tying them low to the base of a bush. Jersey reached for the Sharps and the rest of his gear, also an apple.

"You got a fix on um?" Ben asked.

Jersey was getting the rifle ready to shoot. "Yeah, tough spot though, it's like a castle parapet that they can run behind all the way along the ridge," he said. "Yell to Joe out there to get ready to run."

Jersey slipped on his gloves, and took aim as Ben yelled to Joe.

# Chapter 54

Earl and Otis jumped back against the layered stone wall when they heard the first gunshot. They looked up; it had to be close-by, almost above them. A few more shots exploded, they saw smoke blow out over the ledge above. The wall was long, they'd come a ways, but they decided to split up. Earl went ahead, Otis backtracked to a crevice they'd passed, it lead to higher ground, though it looked to be treacherous.

"Once up there you may have to go into the trees a little to come out behind them," Earl said.

Otis walked his horse back quickly. He found the crack in the rockwall and left his horse. He looked up at the vertical path, and down at his new rifle, he needed both hands to get up there. He leaned it on the rock, checked his sidearm and started climbing. It was difficult as he made his way up through fallen stones and rubble, nearly falling a few times. Another shot was heard as he got to the top. It was a perfect place to stage an ambush, in fact it looked designed for it. A line of large squared stones had been moved to the edge of the cliff where they sat apart enough for a man to shoot from. A man with a long rifle came out from between rocks, he stood reloading then moved back taking another shot. Otis moved from rock to bush, he'd need to be closer to get an accurate shot off.

Earl got to a place where the tall cliff was ramping down to level ground. He stepped away from the wall and looked it over; it was the only way up. He tied his horse off and ran along the wall to the low corner. He looked up as he rounded the base. It was like a walkway of wide stone, he ran up it with two guns out. He made it to the top without being seen and stood at the edge some fifty feet up looking down at his horse. He was hidden from the outlaws behind a boulder at the edge. Looking out at the vast valley he knew Jersey was out there somewhere aiming his Sharps. He took off his red bandanna and waved it before tying it to his hat. He took a deep breath as he edged around the large rock and into the open. Another shot exploded and echoed off the mountain. He jumped back between the next set of tall stones, hitting his heels on a low wedge of shale, he almost fell over the cliff.

Jersey saw Earl wave a red flag. He quickly pulled his telescope and took a look.

"Don't shoot the man up there with the red on his hat, it's Earl."

Most of the men had found safety behind the rocks, some with telescopes called out the shooter's changing positions on the cliffs.

Otis decided not to let the man take another shot. He moved quickly to the base of a tall tree, directly behind the man. He was reloading. Otis didn't want to shoot him in the back—he didn't have to.

Jersey finally had a decent shot, the gunman was leaning on a rock down between two tall upended chunks of shale. He leveled his rifle and took a distance measurement with the marks on his gloved thumb. It was harder to gauge not seeing the full height of his target. He made a few clicks on his sight and said. "Hold on there Blue,"

Otis stepped on an acorn, and the gunman glanced around. He sat up, reaching for his sidearm, that's when Jersey had a clean shot and took it. The combustion was enormous. Flames blew out and down his gloved hand—the tip of the barrel lifted.

Fred looked away from his spyglass. "Oh my... Did you see that?"

The man flew through a red mist next to Otis, where the ancient oak stopped him. Otis didn't want to look at the mess that was the outlaw, so he looked away, but he couldn't avoid the man's arm on the ground at his feet.

Jersey looked at Ben. "I think I see Otis up there too," he said.

"Yeah," Fred said. "Otis is chase'n after the other one now,"

Jersey had put his gun away and was stashing the rest in the saddlebag. "We need to get that guy before he can run to Cane."

"Cane probably heard all this and knows we're here anyway," Ben said.

Jersey put a leg across Blue and pulled the slipknot from the bush. "Maybe," he said. He whispered something to Blue, and they both rose. He nodded to the men. "Cover me," he yelled.

Blue made a tight turn away kicking up loose dirt, Jersey pulled the rein back at the rock and Blue knew they were jumping. He finished the turn and took a moment to dig in. They both saw the lowest point over the rock and bushes, Blue timed a few short strides and sprung over. He hit the soft ground running between bushes, when the field was clear he turned on the speed.

Jersey yelled back. "Stay here, wait till we get back."

The men opened fire at the cliffs.

Otis stood behind a rock as he heard a mass of

gunfire in the distance, a few lead balls pinged off the stones and cliff's face. He heard the other gunman call to his friend. He looked down the line of massive rocks as the outlaw stepped out to see what had happened. Seeing Otis the man pulled his rifle up but remembering he needed to reload he dropped it and ran. Otis shot, hitting him in the leg. The man was limping but still managed to run. Otis followed but had to stop to take careful aim before shooting again.

Earl heard the shooter running in his direction, then a gunshot. He stepped out from behind the tall rocks with guns ready. The surprised man sidestepped at the last second, stumbling to the ground. Earl heard the sound of a bullet hiss by his head. He jumped backwards between the tall rocks, shuffling through loose pebbles his foot clipped a bump in the stone underfoot. His gun-filled hands scrapped the large rocks on both sides, falling backwards he couldn't get a grip. Jersey was riding low in the saddle and briefly saw Earl swinging his arms above his head at the high cliff edge, then he fell over.

Earl landed on his back hard. He felt the air leave his lungs and he couldn't fill them back up; he took small breaths, but they still wouldn't fill. He looked up at the blue sky trying to concentrate. Feeling dizzy he looked sideways at the green trees of the valley; everything washed of color as he closed his eyes.

The outlaw somersaulted back to his feet as he continued running. Otis took another shot but stopped when he got to where he saw Earl step out of sight. He wasn't there. Otis felt mistaken, he stepped backwards to see if it was the right place, it was. Thinking the worst, he stepped between the tall stones and up to the cliff's edge. He knew how far down it had to be. He leaned out over the edge and saw a small ledge five feet down, Earl was sprawled out across it.

Jersey got to the stone wall where he thought Earl would have fallen. He saw his gun there, picked it up and raced down the path. He grabbed the reins of Earl's horse pulling it to the shale ramp up to his friends. He rounded the wall's low end and rode up the large slanted shelf until he found where he thought Earl went over. He saw Otis' head as he was climbing down; he ran to help.

"Push him over to one side and slap his back a few times," Jersey said.

Earl coughed, then started breathing better.

"Help me stand up."

Earl twisted and stretched. "Guess nothin's broke." He glanced over the edge. "Well that could'a been worse."

Jersey reached for his hands, pulling him up while Otis pushed.

"Otis, take Earl's horse and go get yours. Hey, I saw some blood, how bad is he hit?"

"I hit his leg for sure. I took two more shots, but he kept run'n, I'm not sure if one connected," Otis said.

"We need to stop him before he gets to Cane."

Otis mounted and looked behind them up into the hills. "Do you think we're close?"

"I hope not, if so we lost our surprise," Jersey said.

Otis rode off while Jersey got his canteen for Earl.

"I thought I was done for Jersey, ya know—just be dead there at the base of this here wall."

"I did too," Jersey said. "Lose this?" he held out a gun.

Earl nodded. "Thanks that's a new one, what do ya think?"

"She's a beaut. When we're done here I'd like to give it a try. Feeling better?"

"Yeah—I do, let's walk down there, wait for Otis. You know he nearly shot my ear off."

# Chapter 55

Fred turned away from the line of boulders with his telescope calling out. "They just rode into the hills after the gunman."

"All three went?" Ben asked.

"Yeah."

A few men were standing around their friend's body talking and praying. Two men came out of the woods to the west dragging a few thick saplings and branches.

"Okay, those that know how to make a travois give them a hand," Ben said.

The man that had been shot was laying on a flat rock being attended to. "I can ride Ben," he said.

"You sure?" Ben asked.

Ben looked at the man that was seeing to his wound, he shook his head—no.

"Look everyone, this is camp for a few hours so let's get lookouts posted and a fire behind that rock—get some coffee on. We need to keep watch behind as well. More of Cane's men could pass through here to get—well, wherever he's at. Harry, can you arrange that? Two men, short shifts?" Ben said.

Ben saw that a few of the men were sickened by the sight of a friend dead on the ground and another hurt.

"Everyone, everyone!"

He waited until they were all looking at him.

"It's been a rough day, and it's not going to get any easier; these are very dangerous men we're after. Now some of you were not made to do this kind of thing, and no one will hold it against you if you want to leave. In fact, Bill—I mean Jersey, told me not to bring all of you for fear of what just happened—friends getting killed. Now I want volunteers to take these two men back to Spring Valley," Ben said.

"Yeah, what about Bill? I mean lots of stories have been going around about Jersey Smith, which ones do we believe?" one of the men said.

"Like I said it's been a rough day, but finding out Bill is Jersey Smith was a high point in my book," Ben said.

Most of the men agreed, they started talking about it.

"We know who he is deep down. After all this time he's one of us and not because he lives with us, but because he dove in and helped us. Hell, he's got me out of more than one pickle. When he gets back we can ask him a few questions, but don't be surprised if he doesn't answer them. I'll tell you what he told me," Ben looked around at the men's faces as they stopped and listened.

"He came to our town because he had men after him and he worried that people close to him were going to getting caught in the middle. He said stories were going around that were exaggerated or not true, and that bothered him too. I think he just wanted to start over. Can't blame him for that," Ben said.

# Chapter 56

Otis and Jersey rode behind Earl. Every few minutes Earl would say, "more blood," and the two would examine the red dots in the dirt as they rode by. Jersey and Otis were talking so much that Earl turned in his saddle.

"Now, you two know I'm looking down, right? And that means you need to be a look'n up, and around, right?"

"Oh sure, course—that's what we's do'n," Otis said.

"Mm."

They became more attentive. After two hours they found the shooter dead on the ground holding the reins of his horse. They went through his things but found nothing to help find Cane.

"Well, at least we're far enough away from the ambush that we still might have surprise on our side," Earl said.

They agreed, and mounted up, riding another half hour when the trail seemed to end at the face of the mountain. The shale was high and ran at an angle into a thick section of trees so close together no trail had ever been there. Past that, they saw the mountain above.

"Just like before," Otis said.

"No, this is different," Earl got down and looked around so the others followed. "This is much different. Let's fan out, walk off the path a ways see if you can't see another side trail or anything."

In five minutes Jersey was waist deep in fern standing in an untouched forest when he heard Earl's whistle.

Otis was standing in the path as Jersey walked up. They stood looking around for Earl; they heard him talking, but couldn't see him.

He appeared from behind a large bush just past the dead end. The bush was covering a hole in the stone wall that was wide enough to drive a wagon through. Earl walked around the bush and came out shaking his head. He looked up at the wall. Part of it ran behind him and reached back connecting to the base of the mountain.

"Well, this is really someth'n. Well hidden. What looks like the base of the mountain isn't," Earl said.

"No?"

"No, there's another side to this high ridge here and you get to it from behind that heavy thicket. That big bush is hiding a tunnel that leads to a big clearing."

"Looks like that-there logs in the way," Otis said.

"No—it's hollow, you just lift the end and swing it out of the way, it's easy to swing it back."

After a few minutes on the other side, they heard the distant sound of hammering, like a blacksmith pounding down on an anvil. They left their horses and walked between steep cliffs; the path took a long turn. At the end of the turn Earl stopped and held up his hand, they backed up.

"I see a lookout up on a high ledge," he said.

They looked for a way to get by. Jersey peeked around the corner at the man.

"He looks a mite familiar, hey—he's walking in the other direction."

Jersey took off running for the cover of trees in the center of an open area, Earl and Otis followed shortly after.

"Jersey can I see your spy glass?" Otis asked.

He pulled the telescope open and looked up through trees at the man.

"Well hell, that's Dirty Frank," Otis said.

"Dirty who?" Earl asked.

"Comes to my Smith shop. Dam, that means I been shoe'n for Cane's men too."

"You a Smithy Otis?"

"Yeah," he said.

"Any good?"

"Very good."

"Oh, that's great I need a hook made that I can—"

Jersey stopped him. "Look, let's get out of here first then have a chat about hooks and such."

"Just be'n friendly JS," Earl said.

"He's guarding this here path, we're very close," Jersey said.

The hammering came echoing through the pass louder now.

"Sounds like they got their own Smithy—maybe that's why I haven't seen him for a while," Otis said.

They stood under the only trees at the bottom of a deep ravine. The ground at their feet was dirt and pine needles; everything else was rock and sand. The tall shale walls closed in ahead and the path was only a wagon wide. Excavated rubble lined the edges at the base as far as they could see.

"We need to get a closer look, get the lay of the land so we can plan an attack for the men. We need to find the best way in, but we can't go any farther down this path," Jersey said.

"Yeah, but this has to be the main way in—maybe the only way," Earl said.

They decided to go back the way they came and look for other ways in. Jersey was to go around and up—coming out above the lookout. Earl would go down and around along the wall in the valley, approaching from below. Otis was to head back to tell the others before they came looking.

# Chapter 57

Otis watched them as they walked back to the horses. They talked like it was something they'd done often; they knew just what they were getting ready for. As they came around a new bend, they would look over the areas each was going to head to. Jersey looked up and Earl looked down.

"You may have a spot there where Dirty Frank has a view," Jersey said.

"Yeah, I see that open area down there."

They got to the horses and walked them out of the little dead end pocket and stood on the open trail in the sunlight. As they got ready, they looked to where they were heading, checking for footholds and branches. Otis sat on a log on the trail's edge watching and listening.

"Take'n your saddle Colt?" Earl asked.

"Nah, too much climbing and probably on my stomach a bit, but I got this now," he showed off his new Colt 49.

"Oh—very nice," Earl said.

"Six shot 31 caliber; it's small but not too small," Jersey said.

"So—you like my new Colt?" Earl asked.

"Very much, looks expensive."

"Yeah, but worth it. Hey, how should I..." Earl held the new gun at his stomach. Jersey looked at Earl's new setup, then down the steep hill he was descending. "Well,

I'd put it on and twist it around back till you need it. If you got a hammer latch on that holster use it."

Earl put two knives in his boot sheaths. Jersey spooled his rope out down the hill and brought it back in big loops, he tied it off and slipped it over his head and one shoulder. Earl tossed both ends of his rope down from around a tree in the path. This way he could retrieve it at the bottom by pulling one end. They kept glancing at the areas they each had to traverse. Jersey put another small gun in his boot-holder.

"When did you start carrying a baby gun?" Earl asked.

"Oh, first summer in town I had to hide a gun somewhere."

"Did you need it?"

"I wanted to be ready if Ben needed any help."

"Did he?"

"A bit."

"Well that thing's a mite small-ish, is it a two shooter?"

"Yeah, accurate up to three feet," they laughed.

They kept strapping things on and unloading other things, Otis finally stood up.

"I guess you boy's done this before," he said.

They looked at each other and back at Otis, then said at the same time. "Once or twice."

Jersey pulled out his watch and said to Earl. "Let's be back no later than—"

"What the hey... Jersey Smith with a timepiece? What's the world coming to."

"And I got a job too, times change, now can we get going? Don't be longer than three hours."

"Okay."

Otis mounted. "Good luck, see you in a few hours."

He rode away down the path.

# Chapter 58

Jersey walked around the huge rock face they'd been standing in front of and found a steep rugged path. It took him into the forest before coming out above the lookout. Beyond the guard was a clearing—Jersey edged out as far as he dared. All he could see was the very top of a stockade like fence of upended pine logs. He decided to take a wide sweep back into the woods, up the hill, and come out on the other side of the lookout and above the log fence.

He emerged from the trees and walked out onto the stone cliff top. It was a huge, mostly flat, weathered surface riddled with ins and outs and a few loose stones. The whole top was a slab that slanted downward towards the edge. He stopped and knelt before it got too steep; the angle was getting dangerous. He saw the top of the tall log fence below. He laid on his stomach edging forward a little more with his elbows, a few small pebbles rolled down and over the edge. He thought he saw movement next to him; it was a large snake. It was curled up next to a smooth pocket of run-off water. It was laying in the warm sun and didn't like being interrupted.

The snake started in his direction. Jersey reached for his boot knife by rolling over on his left side, but moving seemed to encourage it. Springing—it bit at him. He rolled more to stay out of its reach. It coiled, only to spool out again after him. Jersey kept rolling away. The next time he stopped he came up with a knife in each hand and as it lunged again, he sliced it's head off at the jaw. It's body coiled, rolling onto itself, but it's head bounced down the smooth surface then over the edge.

Jersey moved as close to the edge as he could. The place looked like a prison; people were being forced to work in gardens. He couldn't see a lot of the operation, but he felt he saw all he could from up there. He crawled back off the big ledge and made his way back down.

# Chapter 59

Once down, Earl pulled on one end of the rope, when it passed the tree it fell freely. He wound it up large, placing it over his head and arm. The ground was level and thick with brush and trees as he made his way along the hillside. When he got to the open area he could see the guard high on the cliff. The path they'd been on was below the guard, and Earl was now one hundred feet below that. He had to cross a treeless area of a couple hundred feet before the safety of cover at a massive stone wall. He planned out a few bushes to stop at, then Dirty Frank turned away, he was looking in the other direction. Earl ran for it, almost falling several times for looking up at the guard and not down at his path.

Once across, he stood at the base of the wall. It was a high rugged vertical face of shale and the pieces that had fallen over time were strewn out in front of him. The fallen stones were also piled along the base, curving out of view. There had to be a plateau up there, everything he needed to know was on the top of that cliff. The stone face would be an hour to climb, if he made it he'd have to find a way back down. He looked around the corner to see if Dirty Frank had seen him, but he'd been replaced by a new lookout.

Earl walked along the wall looking for a way up. It

was rough going through loose gravel and stone, which was deep enough to keep anything from growing. He stood on a tall outcropping and saw an old road down the hill, it seemed to follow the cliff face then turned out of view. He moved down through a thicket and took the road. Water was falling from above, and he had to cross a fast moving stream. The little road became steeper, and it turned as did the wall, which wasn't as high now. The road ended abruptly at the side of the mountain just ahead. Why would a road lead straight into a mountainside, he thought.

As he approached the place where the mountain and wall connected, the little road seemed to turn back out of view in a massive dark corner. The area was full of large squared chunks of stone that had fallen and were strewn about. Some were trapped above in a large break in the mountain. Many were on the ground filling the dark recess. They were protruding from piles of gravel and leaning in every direction. It spooked Earl. He'd never seen anything like it, eerie monoliths jutting up from deep gravel and debris.

He heard the faint sound of splashing water as he continued into the dark corner. The sound grew louder which led him to a cave, part of which looked man made, chiseled into a tunnel wide enough to drive a wagon through. He walked in and it slanted up for thirty feet or so, then it leveled off. He saw light inside dancing off the walls. Rounding a corner he saw the back of a waterfall, it glowed from daylight on the other side. He walked up to it, the area opened a bit—the ground was wet, a thick wooden gate was fastened to the wall just inside. It was well constructed, the frame was tight into cut rock on all edges and the gate was locked shut with a chain on the other side. There were two wagons parked in a tight recess. He couldn't see through the water, but there was an area near the top where the falling water separated. He pulled a block from under the closest wagon's wheel, it rolled out slowly, stopping when it's shaft and yoke hit the wall near the gate's lock. He climbed on the wagon and looked through the opening in the falling water and was amazed.

Outside the cave's waterfall, the mountainside next to him was all stone, maybe seventy feet tall. It stretched out quite a distance to a log stockade wall at the far end, where he saw part of a large gate next to what could be a gatehouse. He moved along the wagon's bed for a better view. A few horses were in a nearby pen, it was on lower ground beyond the waterfalls pool and connected to a house. Past that was a fenced in cornfield and a few small buildings. As he started to leave he saw a young boy. He was running along the massive stone wall and the cornfields fence, he was looking around like he was doing something he shouldn't. In a sneaking manner, he approached the back of a very small shed or outhouse; it was just beyond the horse pen. It looked like he was talking to someone inside.

# Chapter 60

Earl climbed down, took a bandanna from his pocket and wiped a thin coat of water spray from his face. He looked over his gear, making sure he had everything, but as he started to leave he heard voices nearby.

He started to climb back on the wagon, but saw colors moving across the water. He turned and ran back into the cave. He leaned behind an outcropping where he could still see the water falling and part of the gate at the lock. Two men walked from the side of the falling water up to the lock, as dry as a bone. They were talking as one of them unlocked the gate. When they pushed the gate in it stopped at the wagon.

"What the hey?"

"Wheel block must-a come loose."

"Mm."

They squeezed around the gate and stepped over the yoke.

"This is our only way out, I thought we weren't to blow this?" One of them said.

"We're gonna light this one on the way out."

"You sure they don't know it's here?"

"Yeah."

The one man was untangling a fuse from its spool.

"Well, I don't like ride'n by powder kegs that's set and

ready to go," the other said.

"Relax, it can't hurt you till it's lit—last man out will do that. Besides, it's a 'slow match', burns very slow—we'll have plenty of time to get away."

# Chapter 61

Martin was standing behind the shed when he saw Clayton and Dirty Frank walk from the back of the house behind the horse pen to the wall. There was a gate there, which lead to a short wide path to the pool in front of the waterfall. Frank was carrying a large cloth bag with writing on it, Clayton had a small keg under his arm. They opened the gate and walked down the path to the pool and turned out of view. Martin thought his eyes had fooled him. He always thought the big stone wall ran back to the corner where the waterfall was, but they turned out of view. He looked hard at the stone wall. It was choppy back in the corner, unlike the rest of it. It had five or ten foot sections that stuck out along the short, but wide path near the pool. Mr. Clayton and Frank just turned at a hidden corner. What could be back there, he thought.

Martin heard the front door of the house close, someone stepped off the porch and walked in his direction. He jumped to the ground and rolled under the shed. He got on his stomach and looked out the side, between the dirt and the bottom boards. It was one of Cane's old friends, one of the brothers. The man stopped at the corner of the house and leaned there rolling a smoke and looking at the waterfall. The horses in the pen moved away from the man and Martin could see past him. Clayton and Dirty Frank had reappeared across the pool right next to the waterfall, then they walked behind it. The man shook his match out as he stepped away from the house, he took one more look at the waterfall before walking back inside.

Not feeling safe, Martin crawled out. The man could bring his brother out, or Clayton could come from behind the water.

"What is it?" Susanne asked.

"Ah—nothing, I'll be back later."

"Martin, please don't come back, besides they'll be letting me out for dinner, I'll see you then," Susanne said.

Martin was already gone, running along the stone wall. He looked over his shoulder to see if Clayton was coming out of the waterfall when something hit him on the arm. He fell, rolling in the gray sand. He sat up quickly looking at the ground down the path; he didn't understand. He walked a few feet back and looked down at the head of a snake looking up at him. Its jaw was open, its fangs were long and white. He got goose bumps. Martin looked up the stone wall to the high ledge. He'd had nightmares of snakes coming out of the crack in the wall, but never from above. There was a crack in the wall, which he called the snake hole, it was two feet wide at the base and got narrower as it went back. It was dark in there, too dark to see where it ended. He knew they lived back there, down some little tunnel that led to a snake family or two. Whenever he walked by the snake hole, he would run his hand along the fence on the other side of the path making sure he was as far away as he could be as he rushed by. He looked back down at the ugly head and kicked it under the fence into the corn and ran off.


Dirty Frank looked around as light danced across the walls. Clayton knelt and tossed a tin spool down the cave floor, it rolled to Earl's feet. Earl noticed the label on the spool said 'High Quality, Slow Match Fuse.' Clayton knelt and cleared a wide crack in the stone wall by dragging sand and dirt out with both hands and pushed it behind him. He set the powder keg on its end and pried out the stopper with a knife. He pushed the end of the fuse in and put the stopper back to hold it in place while he rolled the keg into the hole in the cave wall. He removed the stopper and Earl could see black powder pour out on top of the dirt.

"Run down and straighten the fuse along the wall."

That's when Earl slowly walked away backwards keeping his eyes on the moving light across the wall. When he was near the big curve he turned and ran out. Just outside the cave's entrance, he hid behind a massive fallen rock. Dirty Frank turned down the cave.

"Hey!"

"What?"

"Did you see that?" Dirty Frank said.

Clayton was trying to stop more gunpowder from pouring out. "What?"

"I saw something move down the cave," he said.

Clayton looked over. "Probably a deer."

"I'm not so sure," he said.

"Well, go take a look," Clayton said.

Dirty Frank walked into the cave, picked up the end of the fuse and pulled it tight, he set it on the sand along the base of the wall.

"See anything?" Clayton asked.

"Nah."

# Chapter 62

Leroy Burton sat in a chair near the guard on the gatehouse porch waiting for his brother to return. He was carving a small dog from a piece of apple wood he'd found in the pile near the firepit. It was rough, but anyone could see it was a dog, or he thought, a young black bear. He set it on the deck when he heard someone ride up. The guard stood and walked up to the peephole and proceeded to unlock and open the gate.

"Brother," Leroy said.

"Lee," said the man on the horse.

"I thought we wasn't to leave the compound."

Clifford Burton looked down at his brother for a few seconds. "I do what I want." He said shaking his head.

Leroy was walking alongside the moving rider.

"Well, where you been?"

"Hunt'n in the hills."

"We need to talk Cliff." He looked around and said quietly. "Right now."

"Well, can I drop off these rabbits and birds to the kitchen?"

He shook his head saying, "No."

Cliff dismounted, and they walked between gardens to the stone wall where they talked in whispers.

"I think they's fix'n to run."

"What?"

"Yeah, Clay and Frank was carrying a sack of fuses and a powder keg into the waterfall cave, came out without it."

"How do you know it was fuses in the bag?"

"They had five or six of the same sacks in the back room and they all had fuses in em."

"Yeah, I saw the sacks back there, but why would they blow up the best way to sneak out?"

"I'm think'n they's gonna blow it all up, and that's just the one they'll set on the way out."

Clifford rubbed his temples thinking.

Leroy said, "Let's just get."

Cliff was silent.

"You don't even have to take your saddle off, let's go now."

"And forget the big payday?" Cliff said.

"Yeah, what if there ain't no big payday?"

"Mm, let's give'm till dark to say something, if they don't let us in on what's go'n on we'll raise some hell tonight, get our share and then some and head south through the waterfall. Maybe light that fuse."

# Chapter 63

Jersey was waiting at the horses when Earl started up the slope to the trail, Jersey tossed his rope down. They had a lot to talk about on the ride back, but the only good news was finding a back door through the cave. They got to the camp just before dark and had a meeting with everyone to discuss how to proceed.

After they floated many ideas, Jersey spoke up. "With them lay'n explosives in the cave, it could be a weak point and they're setting it for us. What way was the fuse set, Earl?"

"It would burn from outside back into the cave, the blast would be at the waterfall gate. It was a long fuse, slow burner."

"Mm, sounds like something they'd light as they leave," Jersey said.

"That's how it looked to me. They even said as much." Earl said.

"Let's just get there, leave now and get as close as we can."

"Sun's almost down, can we find it in the dark?" Ben asked.

"I know where we can stop and wait for first light, no fires, but we can rest for a few hours. A few of us can head in just before sunrise, take out the high guards and have a view to warn you as you go down the main path.

Ben and Otis, you get the rest of the men to the gate."

"I didn't see the entrance, did you Earl?" Jersey asked.

"I did—it was in the wall at the other end, probably just past the lookout. It was like a stockade wall of very thick logs standing upright. It looked like old Fort Necessity, but taller," Earl said.

"Yeah, that's the wall I saw, we could use a little gunpowder explosion ourselves," Jersey said.

"Oh, I could make us up a little something Bill, I mean Jersey," Fred said.

"Let's use that as a last idea," Otis said. "Unless you're really good at it, we could bring the whole mountain down on us, and them inside."

"We need some kind of signal that Earl's in place before we rush in," Ben said. He looked around. "Well what's the signal gonna be?"

"I'll think of something, at least a gunshot," Earl said.

"Let's give each other plenty of time to get into position," Ben said.

"Yeah, I'll need an hour," Earl said.

"So let's head there now, the men are well rested." Ben looked around. "Mount up."

# Chapter 64

Cane looked around the table of outlaws and smiled. They were yelling and drinking, and food was everywhere. Cane didn't want to stop the fun, but soon he'd have to, at least for the ones leaving before sunup. It might be best, he thought, for the rest to keep drinking until they passed out.

"As you know we doubled the guards today, we need everyone to stay inside the gate tonight. Frank spotted some movement down in the valley, could be nothing but we don't want to give this place up, okay?"

The men reluctantly agreed. He went to the front door and called the guard in; they walked to the kitchen and talked with the guard there.

"When dinner is done I want you two to take them." He pointed at the cooks and Jamie, "and the rest, and put them in the bunkhouse, bolt the door and put a guard in front and at the back. Somehow they been getting out at night and we don't have time to figure out how, but I want them in there until Frank comes and gets you in the morning," Cane said. "Don't leave until Frank or Clayton come to get you."

He reached into his vest pocket, pulled out a few folded bills and gave each man twenty dollars.

"Tomorrow will be a big payday," he said.

"Do you want us should wait till they's done in here?"

Cane looked the room over, it was a mess, then he saw Martin washing a few big pots.

"No. They don't have to clean up tonight. We'll get them on it in the morning. Hey Martin, I forgot about you, how are you doing over there?"

Martin looked at Cane and forced a smile. "Oh, I'm fine, sir."

Cane went out on the front porch and signaled to Clayton, they walked to the horse pen.

"I know, I know..."

Cane raised his hands. "Not so loud."

"I'll set the powder kegs after dark."

"Good. Watch out for the guards up there."

"I'll send em to the front ledge while we get it done, they won't know," Clayton said.

"I'm think'n we take the boy, could use him if we have any trouble."

"Oh, why not the woman too," Clayton said.

Cane gave him a look, and Clay looked away.

"It's time to let the Burton boys in on things, you want to tell 'em or should I?"

"I'll do it," Clayton said.

"Okay, but let me know if you see any sign of mistrust. We don't want them packing up and leaving tonight."

"I think they'll be pissed off, but they gotta know the best way out is together."

# Chapter 65

The slaves were stretched thin and exhausted. They were all brought to the large bunkhouse next to the blacksmith shed; it was a long building going all the way back to the path at the stone wall. They locked everyone in, and extra guards were posted. When he could see the guards had fallen asleep, Martin took a few things for Susanne in a small sack, tied it to his rope belt, lifted a floorboard, and squeezed out. He headed through the side garden, keeping low.

Some men were passed out on the ground. He knelt in the dark shadow of the corn, looking around for any guards. When he felt safe, he crawled to one man, felt around for a gun, but didn't find one. He took what he could from the man's pockets, as far in as he dared reach. He moved to the other man, but this one woke. The man sat up, looking around. He saw his friend and some child sleeping next to him, then he laid back down.

Martin took the path between the blacksmith building and the corn garden. He heard a noise and slowed his approach to the big wall. A man was walking in his direction along the wall, so he laid down and rolled under the corn fence. Clayton and Dirty Frank were whispering and fiddling with something along the wall. Clayton walked backwards, unrolling a cord onto the ground and Dirty Frank covered it with sand as they went. Martin edged up, watching them. They were talking softly and fooling with something—after a few minutes they walked back by, along the wall, around the shed and into the house.

Jamie was snoring when Martin shook his arm.

"Jamie, Jamie," he whispered.

It shocked him when the old man's hand quickly grabbed him at the neck and held tight.

"This had better be good boy!" he said.

It took Martin a few seconds to speak.

"It's not good at all," he said.

They had to pry up another floor board for Jamie to get out, Martin loudly coughed to cover the noise. They were hunched over, sneaking along the corn garden's path to the wall. They peeked around the corner, no one was in sight, the guards chair behind the long bunk house was empty.

"Be careful the guard can come back anytime, if he does get to the shadows."

Martin continued along the wall slowly. Jamie wanted to open the lantern to show more light but couldn't chance it. Martin turned to him pointing at the ground near the stone wall.

"Well?" Jamie said.

Martin got down on one knee and picked up a thick string from the dirt. Jamie looked closely at it.

"Oh no—that looks like a fuse." He took it in his hand. "It is a fuse, a slow burn kind-a thing."

He pulled on it and it came away, Martin followed him along the wall until the line stopped. They got on their knees, and with the little stream of light looked into the snake hole. Martin hung back, Jamie jumped away holding his lamp out, he was off balance and fell on his seat. Martin came to him, kneeling at the fence.

"They mean to kill us all." Jamie said.

Martin looked at the dark snake hole—a chill ran down his back.

"Can't we just pull the string out?"

"I believe we can Martin, I think so. I'm sure it takes a flame to set it to blow'n up, so we keep this lamp away, understand?"

Jamie was shaking, the little lantern started to rattle, he handed it to Martin.

"That little keg is full of black powder, I never been this close before, what if it blows up? Now—I seen these things go off from a distance, barrel this size can split this wall and that would take down the whole thing, and us with it."

They walked slowly to the shed, peeking around it they saw two men talking, one had just walked back from the outhouse, after a minute they walked inside.

Susanne spoke low through the knothole. "I heard them doing something down the path and then they were talking on the other side of the house, they were there for a while," she said.

"They's lay'n explosives. Not sure what to do," Jamie whispered.

Martin was on his knees with his ear against the shed wall. "Let's just take some and blow up the house," he said.

"Too big, a blast that size would bring down the wall, kill us all." Jamie said.

"What about cutting the fuses?" Susanne asked.

"When they find em cut, they'll just fix'm and..."

"Do you think they put some other powder kegs out? Cause I saw 'em go behind the waterfall today." Martin said.

"What?" Jamie was too loud, he pressed against the shed. "They's blow'n up the waterfall too."

"They're not gonna kill themselves, right?" Martin

said. "So that means they plan on leaving soon."

"Probably in the morning." Susanne said.

Jamie looked at the falling water in the dark. "We better take a look around."

On the other side of the house, Jamie and Martin found where the fuses ended up. One was much longer than the other. Carefully they followed each fuse, one led to the snake hole, the other went past it, they edged up to the empty chair behind the long bunk house and quietly moved by. Walking hunched over, they stayed close to the wall. The fuse led into the little mystery shed behind the gatehouse. Now they knew what it held, and why it had two locks. A guard was on the porch of the gatehouse, so they moved between the mystery shed and the wall to go over options. Jamie slid the little opening on his lantern to let out just enough light to see back in the dark corner.

"This here shed is built strong, I can't see any way to get it open without make'n a lot'a noise. We can toss the other keg in the pond, but what can we do about this."

"I'm bet'n they got more powder kegs, we need to get um think'n everything is fine, so they light'em and ride off think'n it's gonna blow up, but nothing blows up." Martin said.

They stopped talking when they heard a guard step off the porch; he walked back and relieved himself on the wall. He was only a few feet away, they could see his outline from the large lamp at the gatehouse porch. Jamie's lantern was between him and Martin. He reached for it, closing the little opening all the way. The guard looked in their direction, it was a very dark corner, but he was looking right at them. He turned facing them and did up his trousers. He tilted his head as he looked at them. Something was different back in the corner, the shadows didn't look quite the same as every other night. He felt for his matches, then he remembered they were on the porch. He walked along the building, got his matchbox and returned. When he struck his match, the corner lit up, but was empty. A spark from the match flew bouncing off the shed. He remembered what was inside and jumped back; the spark was out before it hit the ground, and he hurried away.

Jamie and Martin were standing in the path next to the corn garden when one of the men laying on the ground out front moaned and rolled over. They rushed into the cornfield and stood quietly, looking down the rows at the man as he fell back asleep.

"Now—I think you're right Martin," Jamie touched Martin's shoulder and they both knelt in the dark. "If we empty that keg and put it back they'd not know any better."

"What about the shed?"

"Well," Jamie scratched his rough chin. "We could cut out a few feet of the fuse and cover it with sand. We just need to find someth'n to cut it with—might could break it."

"I got a knife." Martin reached into his pocket and held out a small folding knife. Jamie quickly held the lantern up and opened it just a crack and twisted the beam at Martin's hand.

"A pocket knife!" He moved the beam of light to Martin's face. "Where on earth boy?"

Martin nodded down the corn row and said. "Off one of those men, he was drunk and sleeping."

Martin saw Jamie's smile in the reflected light.

"You can have it Jamie, do you want it?"

"I surely do—but you deserve it boy, that took a lotta guts. Now let's get to work."

After cutting the fuse to the shed, they walked to the snake hole. Martin was uneasy and stood back.

Jamie whispered, "You head back, I'll be there shortly."

Martin didn't argue, he lay waiting under the building.

After a while a guard walked by to the back of the long bunkhouse, his lantern gave a glow to the dark wall. Martin was startled to see Jamie's face directly across the path glowing in the lanterns light, he looked afraid. The lantern went out, it was dark and quite but for snoring from inside. Jamie waited for the next big snore and crawled quickly to Martin. A guard stood from his chair out front and stretched. They both lay quietly beneath the long building waiting for the guards to fall back asleep.

"It's done boy," he whispered. "We did it."

"What about the waterfall?"

"I went to it, they's a tunnel behind it, but the gate was locked. We can only hope it's far a-nuf away."

They hunkered down as they heard a man running. Jamie put his finger to his lips as he closed the lamp all the way. Someone quickly walked by, Martin thought it looked like Dirty Frank's boots.

"We gotta get back inside, you go first and help me up."

Jamie looked around as best he could, the guard out front looked to be sleeping and Dirty Frank was sneaking around. It was all unusual, on a very unusual night. They's leave'n this place right now, he thought, and not all the guards are go'n with.

Once inside Jamie had to leave the boards off the opening when he heard a key in the door's lock. He dove into bed and tossed a blanket half on as the door opened, Dirty Frank walked in. He was holding a lamp high looking at each bunk. When he found Martin he grabbed him by the back of the neck, lifted him and tossed him to the door. The guard woke, and Jamie heard Frank tell him to go back to sleep.

# Chapter 66

Before sunrise Cane was eating jerky and drinking coffee with Albert in the office. They filled cases, canvas bags and saddlebags with everything they had.

"All the other papers burned?" Cane asked.

"Yeah, last night."

Albert took off his glasses and sat back. "You know, I'm not gonna miss this place."

"Hell, you're only here a few times a year."

"And I hate it every time."

"You still pissed we sold Deloris?"

"You—sold Deloris. She was the only good thing in here." He took a sip of coffee. "Why didn't you tell me? I mean, as close as we are..."

"It was the money, you know that, it wasn't about you."

"Felt like it was."

"Well, it wasn't."

"You should have never left school, we were close back then, the best of friends. You wouldn't have done that back then."

"School was a waste of time and boring. And all those stiffs, they were idiots."

Albert was never that much of a friend to Cane back then. Cane saw him as a smart guy that would bend the rules, if it improved things in his favor. Cane liked his dishonesty very much, and he learned from it. Albert's talent with money was genius, Clayton didn't even know about the land and other investments in Pittsburgh that they owned through Albert's ingenuity. When they met back up after school, that was when Cane truly connected with him and they became real friends. Over the years, all the time they spent apart helped as well. It was a small dose kind of friendship; he knew if he saw him daily he couldn't take him.

Cane did worry about Albert stealing from him. He'd go up there twice a year to go over the books. It was more going through the motions than checking up. After an hour or two the numbers kind of blended together, and he'd start rushing things. Before long he'd close the books and act like he was done, so they could go out on the town. He regretted it on the ride back, but he never found any problems. But then, that's what he expected to find from his numbers man. Now though—he needed to fix things.

"I'm sorry about Deloris." He lied. "Looking back, it was just wrong to do it like that."

Kaden walked in, sat in the tall back chair and started cleaning his fingernails with a small knife from his boot. Dirty Frank pushed Martin in the office and looked the room over. Albert looked up at Cane, put his glasses back on, and concentrated on a ledger on the desk.

"Where's Clayton?" Frank asked.

"Never mind about him, I need you to take Martin to the outhouse, then help him get into these." Cane tossed Frank a paper-wrapped package. He looked at the boy. "Hey Martin, gonna take a little trip, got ya some new clothes. Okay?"

Martin nodded and Frank grabbed him by the shoulder and pulled him into the hallway, they passed Clayton.

"Brother." Clayton stepped into the room.

"Clay."

Cane was looking out the window. "We got a couple men smoke'n out there?"

He could just make out small glows from a few men standing near their horses.

"Probably the Burtons, they's ready to go."

"Hm, looks like a few with them." He looked at Clayton. "We got alliances forming?"

"Always."

"We may need their guns tomorrow."

"I know, they wanted to head south, but I got em with us until the pass, then they're off."

"Okay, that'd be fine."

"They got more money come'n." Clayton said.

"I know, Albert's got it already split and in a bag, I just don't want to give it to them now cause they'll take off."

"Good." Clayton said.

Cane looked up from packing money to see an uncomfortable look on Clayton's face.

"What now?" Cane asked.

Clayton looked at Kaden then back at Cane. "I want to take more of my things, been here a while and I can't fit everything on one horse."

"Well, you can't take everything."

"You should have told us sooner, could've fixed and greased a wagon."

"Yeah—I got a lot I wann'a take too." Kaden said. "Some of it expensive."

"You two aren't looking at the whole deal, it's just stuff, you can buy more stuff. We're rich now and it's time to live like it. We're heading to Pittsburgh, gonna stay in the nicest hotel, spend lots of money and live well-to-do for a time. Albert here has got all our money in the Pittsburgh Bank and Trust, and..." He stretched out his arms showing all the packed and stacked treasures. "We divide up all of this.

We'll just sit back thinking about what to do next."

Cane could see on their faces they were starting to come around.

"It's time to have some fun, put this place behind us."

"Okay," Kaden said. "But I'm gonna get another pack horse." He looked at Clayton. "You can have half."

They nodded at Cane and moved to the door.

"Quickly though, we have to leave." Cane got close to the window and looked up at the sky beyond the cliff's edge. "Oh!" he grabbed his side.

"Bleeding?" Clayton asked.

Cane look under his waistcoat. "No." he looked back at the two men. "Within an hour, we leave."

Clayton bobbed his head a few times as they left.

"Hey get those two drunks off the ground and..."

Clayton interrupted him. "I already did."

# Chapter 67

By the time Jersey and Harry Johnson made their way up to the lookout's cliff, the sun had taken the nip off and the rock was well lit. They rounded the corner from the mountainside with guns out, but no one was there. Waving down to Ben, they signaled to come ahead. Jersey led the way down the narrow ledge where they found the guard laying above where the log wall met the mountain. He was unconscious, a bullet burn across the side of his head was bleeding. He slapped him a few times, waking him.

"Who are you, wait a minute," the lookout said as he quickly got to his knees with a look of concern. "Fuse," he said.

"Oh no," Harry said. "Where?"

"They's gonna kill us all," he yelled.

A bullet hit the wall next to them. Harry jumped down as Jersey pulled both guns and shot, hitting the ground on both sides of a guard in the open out in front of a long bunkhouse.

"You're outnumbered," Jersey yelled.

The man raised his hands as another guard came out from another building.

"Hey," the lookout yelled down to his friends, "Jimmy lit a fuse to the little shed." He pointed just below, behind the gatehouse. "And—he shot me in the head."

"When did he light it?"

"Not sure how long I been out."

Fred was standing at the gate, he yelled up. "How long was the fuse?"

"Heads a-spin'n..." the man said.

Harry said down to Fred, "I don't see anything burn'n down there, but this one said it was a long fuse."

"Still can't be burning, can it?"

"Jersey, look there," Harry said.

He pointed down in the distant valley, riders were kicking up dust. "Is that them?"

"Must be, I didn't hear any gun play, Earl must have just missed 'em."

"What?" Fred asked from below.

"Looks like they just left through the back door. We gotta check that shed," Jersey said. "Hey, toss up a rifle." He turned to Harry. "If one of those men down there touches a gun, shoot'm."

Jersey eased over the small wood railing, climbed down from the small ledge, and stepped to the top of one of the wall logs. He jumped to the roof of the guardhouse, breaking through and falling out of sight. Dust came out of every crack as he burst through the front door plowing over the guard who was hiding there. He ran to the gate and shot the lock off. He turned to the guards, two more were there now.

"Throw your guns down and help, you're outnumbered."

The gate opened. Otis, Fred, and the rest filled the entrance—the guards dropped their guns.

Jersey ran to the shed. "Nothing burning here." He pried the lock brackets off with his knife. Inside were three powder kegs sitting on a pile of gunpowder and a fuse leading out and along the tall stone wall. He heard the men going through the compound opening buildings and yelling back and forth. He ran down the narrow path pulling at the fuse until it ended. He held it in his hand and saw ten feet down the path a burnt line running the rest of the way along the wall, he followed.

Earl and his men were rounding the corner of the massive wall in the valley when they saw a large group of men riding out and turning north. They continued, but a lone rider was coming from the cave in the mountain's corner. They hid as he rode by at full speed trying to catch up with the others.

"We better hurry boys." Earl said.

They ran the rest of the way, but back in the dark recesses of the tall corner the others slowed and mumbled about the strange and eerie area. Earl was in the cave when they ran to join him. In the tunnel they smelled smoke. Earl stopped and looked at his watch.

"You smell that?" someone said.

"I hear a fuse."

"Na, we're safe," Earl said, as he shook his watch and put it to his ear.

"That is a fuse," another said.

"Hey—I think my timepiece stopped,"

He shook it a few times as he walked, when he stopped he was standing next to a burning fuse. The men were half turned to run, but had to see what this crazy man was up to.

"Come-on Earl let's go."

The fuse had passed Earl and was farther into the cave; the men started running for cover. Earl gave up on his watch and turned, the others had left, so he walked back out.

"Hey, come on, who's got the time? I'm think'n we're late."

"Are you crazy? Find some cover."

"What? Oh, no—no the fuse is okay I cut it yesterday. We're good."

They stood up slowly.

"I thought I told ya bout that—you know last night when we was plan'n? Sorry, but we gotta run."

Jersey ran along the wall and found the snake hole, he pulled the fuse and the keg rolled out; he found it empty. He saw Tracker Earl and the others walk from the waterfall; they met up behind the horse pen next to the back of the house.

"Any trouble?" Jersey asked.

"Nah, but we saw em, they's high-tail'n it through the valley. Left a lone rider to light the fuse, and he rushed by us try'n to catch-up with the rest."

"Yeah, we saw em from the lookout."

"What's Otis do'n over there," Earl asked.

Jersey looked across the pen to see Otis help a woman from a little shed. He walked her along the front of the house. Jersey and Earl walked between a flowing stream and the back of the house and saw him help her into the outhouse. Otis looked over and saw Jersey and Earl.

Jersey nodded and said, "After you get her to Ben give us a hand we're gonna check the house."

Otis nodded. Earl had found a cold storage entrance that led under the house. Jersey waited while he looked inside, he came out squinting.

"They's a side of beef in there, but I think it start'n to turn."

Jersey nodded then he waved to Ben, he was in front of the long bunkhouse. Ben saw the woman step out from the outhouse, he couldn't believe his eyes, he ran to her yelling, "Susanne. Susanne." They hugged and Ben turned to Jersey, "It's Becky's mother."

He walked her back to the group.

Otis walked to Earl and Jersey at the front door of the house when three guards came out from behind the corn garden on the stone wall path. The guards saw them and pulled their guns, the men scattered. Lead hit the shack and the house and the ground. Otis snuck closer, keeping the shack between them. Earl was on the porch, and Jersey was on the ground in front of the house. They all stepped out with guns drawn, but the guards were running for the waterfall.

"Follow em?" Earl said.

"Na, they got a long walk to nowhere. Let's check the house, then get after Cane."

The house had the look of a fast departure, it was empty, drawers were stripped and left open or on the floor. A few cheap items were tossed about and broken. The kitchen was large and all the cupboards were locked. Earl broke the lock off one, it was full of staples such as flour and sugar. Jersey looked through the office, the only thing he found was a reference to Pittsburgh. He walked back through the house and found Otis on a bed looking at a photo.

"What's that?"

"Chloe."

Jersey stepped up to the bed, Otis handed him a photo.

"She's in the back there with a rake."

It was a photo of Cane and Clayton standing in a line with a few other men posing in front of slaves. Mostly black men and women in one of the gardens, but for a single white woman and what Jersey assumed was her young son, his back was turned from the camera.

"How would they forget this, it's incriminate'n."

"It was under the closet."

Jersey sat down in a corner chair across from the bed,

he could see Otis was upset.

"She isn't here?"

He shook his head. "Na, looked at everyone. They say she was taken away and sold a year ago."

Two gunshots were heard and men were shouting, Earl ran by the door. Otis looked at Jersey like they should go, but he said, "They got it."

"This room is a lot like a room I lived in for a time." Otis said.

"Where was that?" Jersey asked.

"Vicksburg."

"Yeah, Mississippi? Never been—nice?"

Otis nodded, "It was." He smiled and set the photo on the bed. "I had recently collected my papers and was a free man and stopped there for a night or two on my way north. I must a looked pitiful, because an old woman asked if I was lost. We talked for a few minutes and she asked if I'd carry a box to her home and she'd feed me. After three nights in her barn, I moved into the house, in a room just like this. She was the nicest person I ever met."

Jersey saw his eyes were soft and wet as he looked around the room.

"I stayed there for over a year, got that house in the best of condition for her. I loved her like the mother I never had, she loved me right back. My little room was full of things she bought for me. I never ate so good and haven't since."

"Why d'you leave?" Jersey asked.

"She was a smart woman, active in the city politics, ya know. She saw the signs of a uprise'n and was worried about me. Kept me close to home for a time. Then one day there were two suitcases on my bed and a new coat and trousers, also a white shirt and suspenders and a new hat. She made me walk behind her to the train station. She was dressed like she was going to take a trip, men were watching us, I think they were waiting for her to get on the train and leave me. She had me stand next to the bench she sat on and talked to me secret like, while she fanned herself. She explained everything she'd planned, and I understood. When the train pulled in we waited for a time until the whistle blew, after that we hurried up to the train and she said goodbye. She was holding an envelope, and she said 'now give me a kiss', when I bent down she put the envelope in my pocket. Then she pushed me on the train as it started to leave, I looked back and she was crying until two men came up to talk to her. That was the last time I saw her. I ended up in Pittsburgh, then Spring Valley."

"What was in the envelope? If I can ask?"

"A letter and money, lots of money."

"Sounds like a great woman."

Otis couldn't speak, but he nodded.

Earl leaned in the door. "Some old man shot two guards, killed one."

"Can't blame em for that," Otis said.

"Found this in the kitchen." He held up a bottle of whiskey, then he walked down the hall.

Jersey stood up. "Bring the picture."

They followed Earl to the front room just as Ben walked in; he introduced Susanne and Jamie.

"People in bad shape out there," Ben said.

"Some food in the kitchen should feed em before the ride back," Earl said.

"Check the side of beef below the house. Trim it first to see if it's okay," Jersey said.

"I can do that," Jamie said. "Got just the man to

help too."

"Ben, they's two wagons in the cave, you could get a couple men on make'n one ready to roll." Earl said.

Earl and Otis sat at the long table, then Jersey joined them. Earl filled a small glass with the whiskey and looked at Otis, who said no. He slid it in front of Jersey.

"Whiskey? Na, never in the day, it slows me down."

Jamie and Susanne started for the kitchen, Ben looked out the window.

"They just brought your horses in, tied em off at the pond."

"Okay, we leave in..." Jersey looked around at the faces, "fifteen?" they nodded.

"Ben, three of em got away through the cave, probably head'n to Spring Valley, we may see em on the way north."

"I can't go with Jersey, I got..."

Jersey stopped him. "You got your hands full Ben, a long day ahead of you, we're good. If we cross those men, we'll take their guns, so don't worry about them."

Susanne and Jamie stopped at the kitchen door, listening.

"A few men want to tag along," Ben said.

"Any of them not married or childless?"

Ben thought about it. "No."

"Well I'm done get'n good men hurt or killed."

"We could use another man though," Otis said.

"Hmm, if Fred wants to come tha'd be good," Jersey said.

"We'll be fine Ben, you take care of things here," Earl said.

Susanne and Jamie were talking at the kitchen door, they looked at the men sitting at the table. "Are you Jersey Smith?"

"Yes mam, I am."

Jamie walked up to the long table. "He said you'd come and set these boys straight. Well, you done that."

"You're Martin's father?" Susanne said.

Jersey was shocked, he swallowed and said, "What?" the word broke as he said it, he sat up. "Martin is alive—he's here?"

The old man spoke up. "They took him from the bunkhouse this morning."

Earl took a sip from the little glass and looked across at Otis, they both looked at Jersey. He stood up, he felt a pain in his chest and his temples tightened, a pounding came to his head as he turned away thinking. Pulling his hat off, he scratched his head.

"Now wait." he turned. "Did Cane kill my wife and daughter?"

Susanne moved next to Jamie at the edge of the table. "Kaden killed them, but Cane was right there."

Jersey took the little glass from Earl's hand and took a small sip—he nodded and took a bigger sip. He put the glass back in Earl's hand and picked up the bottle. "Old Crow, Kentucky Bourbon. Hmm."

He looked at Ben. "All this time he was right in front of me."

"And me!" Ben said.

"Otis, can I see that photo again?"

Otis slid it across the table, Jersey picked it up and looked closely at it.

"He's getting big."

Jamie said, "You gotta good boy there Mr. Smith. He's a smart one."

"Call me Jersey."

"He saved my life." Susanne started crying.

"Thank you, both, for look'n out for him."

"I think the good Lord used him to look out for us. He spotted the powder kegs, we worked all night to keep this place from blow'n up."

Jersey tossed the photo back to Otis, and said, "It's time to go."

"You can bring that, but only for after." He pointed at the bottle.

"That's good JS."

# Chapter 68

They stopped at the first river north, Cane rode through to the other side with Martin in tow, he turned facing the others as their horses drank. It was shallow there and all the riders took a break. The water was fresh out of the hills, cold and fast, it ran west from there through Spring Valley.

"What the hell Clay, I expected to see half the mountain roll into the valley!" Cane said.

Clayton said nothing.

Jimmy spoke up, "I lit the fuses, just like you said to."

"Mm. Well we're too close to Spring Valley, let's get going," Cane said.

Clayton was patting his horse and looking at the other mounts.

"Give-um five minutes and we'll get an extra hour out of em when we need it," Clayton said.

"Oh—words of wisdom, please share another," Cane said.

"Look, I don't know what happened, do you?" Clayton said.

He tightened down a line on one of the packhorses and looked at Cane.

"Well, do you? He lit the fuses and left, they must have seen..."

"They're idiots," Cane interrupted. "We hired them because they were idiots, they would have run, not gone looking for the powder kegs—and then defuse them."

Jimmy knew one guard saw a fuse being lit, but he took care of him and he'd never wake up.

"What if someone else was there?" Dirty Frank said. "I heard gunshots as we was head'n through the valley there."

Cane looked around and thought. "Yeah, I heard it too."

"What?" Clifford Burton said. "Well if that's true, we may have men after us right now."

Cliff looked at Leroy shaking his head.

Cane sat up on his saddle and looked south. "We should have brought the guards along, if they're on our tail we could use a few more guns."

"And we didn't because why?" Leroy said. "It was too many to split the money with? Well, we can't spend it if'n we're dead."

"Plus—we gotta haul around the kid," Clayton said.

"Yeah, that's right and he could be useful, now more than ever."

Clayton thought about it, then nodded.

"That's fine, but where we head'n?" Clifford asked.

"North. Let's keep along the hills, stay out of the valley for a while. When we get to the rail-tracks at the pass, we'll have a few options."

"The pass is too far north," Clifford said.

"Well, we can't head south," Clayton said.

Cane looked south from where they'd come, at the mountain which should have tumbled into the valley. He looked at Martin and thought, at least I brought the boy along, I think I'm gonna need him.

"I got a bad feeling. All right—let's get going."

# Chapter 69

They'd ridden north through the valley for hours when Earl stopped on a high point.

"See something?"

"Hard to tell JS, let's see your long glass."

Jersey was squinting to see what Earl was seeing as he handed him his spyglass. Otis rode up and tried to see what they were looking at.

"What is it, I don't see anything," Otis said.

"I see color up there," Earl said.

Fred pulled up in the rough. "I see something but I can't be sure what."

Earl handed the spyglass to Jersey, he was down giving the horses water from his folding bowl.

"Mm, well I see the bits of color too, if it's them they're not moving," he looked at Earl. "Good time to catch up."

Jersey finished watering the rides, and they took off at full speed.

# Chapter 70

The Burton brothers were riding point yelling across the trail to each other. Not wanting to breathe in their dust, Cane and his men were behind a ways back. It was Cane, Clayton, Kaden, Albert, Dirty Frank and his friend Jimmy riding in pairs, with Martin on a horse tied to Cane's ride. Cane noticed they'd just passed the west trail crossing out into the valley. He saw them stopping ahead, so he stopped. The Burton brothers and the others slowly rode back.

"Where are you going?" Clayton asked.

As they rode through the group Leroy said, "check'n out this here cross trail."

They were all looking at the trail and westerly as they passed by. When they got to the intersection, they turned facing Cane and yelled, Cane's group rode back to them.

"Cliff, if we go out into the valley we'll be in the open, this ways a village and a trading post with a lookout, plenty of places to make a stand. We could wipe 'em out, have a good meal, then split up." Cane said.

"That little village is too far off, they'll be on us before we get there."

As if on cue, all five men pulled their guns.

"Now come on," Cane said.

Cane's group lifted their hands out in the open except for Albert, who was shot as he fumbled for his gun. Cane looked at his old school friend dead on the ground, he nodded to Kaden to get the reins of Albert's horse, which held a lot of money.

"That's just unfriendly Leroy," Cane said.

"He was pull'n his gun, had to."

"Could-a called out, he'd a stopped," Jimmy said.

Martin nudged his horse a little closer behind Clay and Cane, "Cane, this here's a mutiny."

"Shut-up kid," Clayton interrupted.

"Look Cane, I'm sorry my brother did that, but you saw Albert was pull'n. Now, we don't want to split-up on bad terms we just want to go home. Been head'n north too long," Clifford said.

Cane shook his head. "Can't head south now, if the compound didn't blow up." He stopped for a second and looked over at Clayton. "Well, there's probably a posse on our trail."

"We're gonna head across the valley then south when we get to the other side, head for West Virginia."

"Maybe we should head that way, Cane," Dirty Frank said.

"I'm not go'n south," said Clayton.

"I ain't go'n south neither," Kaden said.

"Just hand over the rest of our money and we'll be off," Leroy said.

He raised his gun aiming at Cane's head. Cane thought he saw a flash of light in the distance.

"Did you see that," Kaden said under his breath, he whispered, "we better get."

Cane gave his friends a look and slowly turned back to Leroy and Cliff.

"That's fine," he said.

Keeping his hands in sight, he reached around and untied a large leather bag, brought it to his lap and opened it wide. He grabbed the bottom and flung the contents into the air. Paper currency and bank note's drifted away, coins flew in an arc causing the other's horses to pull back. Cane's horse turned quickly around and the others followed fleeing down the trial.

The Burton Brothers looked at each other shaking their heads.

"Must'a thought we was gonna shoot 'em."

"Well, let's get all we can," Clifford said.

The others were already on the ground grabbing at falling bills and picking them out of the bushes. Cliff and Leroy dismounted and started picking up all they could. Gold coins on the ground were getting covered by dirt as men fumbled around. They'd pocketed just about all they could when one of them said, "I think we got company."

# Chapter 71

The path had become wide; Jersey, Earl and Otis rode
side by side. They saw dust in the distance, a few riders
headed west out into the valley. Jersey nodded to the
others and peeled off after them. He cut a corner by
heading directly at them, but it was across the open field
where he had to slow to a reasonable speed through the
rough. Once on the westerly trail he could see no sign of
them. When he saw blood, he stopped and backtracked.
The blood led to a spot off the trail, it was an area he
knew well, only five or so miles from his old house on
the river. It had a few scattered squared rocks coming out
of the ground and plenty of thick bushes, he'd gotten
many a rabbit in there. This has to be a trap, he thought,
but a trap meant they're nearby. He pulled his gun and
attentively rode up between two stones of five feet. Once
past them he saw a dead rabbit placed across a stone. It
was a trap—a voice came from behind.

"Who are you mister?"
Jersey had his hands up to his shoulders, a gun in one
the reins in the other, as he turned his head to see two
men on their horses. "Jersey Smith," he said.
"So this is Jersey Smith. Heard you was dead."
They were behind him aiming at his back.
"Drop the gun and turn around slow," Clifford said.
Jersey tossed his gun to the ground, lifted his hand

back up, and nudged Blue with his right knee. Blue turned but Jersey stopped him before they were straight-on by a small nudge with his left knee. The Burton brothers were just past the rocks, feeling pretty good.

"Any last words?" Clifford said.

"I want his horse," Leroy said.

Jersey said, "Where's Martin?"

He took his left foot from the stirrup using it to poke under Blue's ribs, something he didn't like which caused him to lift his head as he blew out hard.

"Who?" Clifford asked.

"You mean the boy?" Leroy said.

Jersey's hands were held shoulder high as he nudged him again, this time Blue lifted his head higher.

"My son, where is he?"

"Settle your horse down Smith or I'll shoot 'em."

Cliff raised his gun with a look of determination.

"Dammit Cliff, I want that horse."

"Where's Martin?"

"Smith you're in no position to be ask'n anything, sides you can see he ain't with us."

Jersey did it again, knowing this time Blue should be sufficiently angry to lift up higher still. When his head covered Jersey's left side he reached for the saddle Colt, as Blue's head came down he took the shot at Clifford Burton, who fell to the ground.

Leroy was shocked for a second seeing his brother fall, knowing he was next he ducked, pulling sideways on the reins. Jersey's second shot just missed him. Leroy's horse made a tight circle bringing him back behind the large stone where he looked one last time at the hole in Clifford's chest and his open eyes staring into his. Leroy took off fast, riding west into the valley.

Jersey moved between the big stones, but Cliff's death

grip on the rein's kept his horse from moving, blocking the path. He pulled back and rode around in a circle looking for a way out; all the bushes had grown in thick between the rocks. He rode back, dismounted, picked up his gun, and pulled Cliff up across his horse, tying him on tight. He walked the horses back out to the trail and looked west. Leroy was out of sight. Jersey looked back east up the trail and at the mountain, his mountain. He weighed going after Leroy or Cane, after a moment he said, "Martin."

# Chapter 72

It was late in the day at the Trading Post, Ed was settling up with two of Roger's friends at the counter, and his wife Lizzy was pouring beer from a pitcher for a few of the lake men. Things were moving at the normal slow pace until the four men walked in. The atmosphere in the large room changed. Cane looked at Kaden as he nodded in the direction of the Indians, he was smiling. He moved aside as they walked by to the door. They were talking and Ed thought he made out Roger's name being brought up.

"Welcome to the Trading Post," Ed said. "Sell'n, trade'n, or rest'n?"

"Ah—resting I think," Cane said.

Ed had a bad feeling about them simply because he didn't hear them ride up and they didn't look like they'd walked. He looked around as Kaden sat near the door. Dirty Frank found a spot halfway into the big room against a side wall, Clayton at the wall opposite. Cane walked up to the counter, placed his hands on it leaning over.

Ed glanced around the room, he could see trouble ahead, no group of men ever walked in and separated like that. Cane watched the Indians walk by the side window.

"Don't see many of their like around these days," Cane said.

"Na, they's good men, keep to themselves up in the hills," Ed pointed by swinging his thumb up to his shoulder.

"I thought we drove 'em all out with the 'removal act', heck that'd be twenty years back."

"Well, guess a few slipped through. Some say they's been roam'n the hills since the Turtle war and before."

"Hmm, someone needs to do someth'n about that."

"Nah—ain't hurt no one. Now what can I get you fellas?"

"Ah, what's good?" Cane asked.

"How about a cold beer, keep it out in the river," he said.

Cane looked at the others, and they nodded.

"Sure, how about a whiskey too?"

"No, but I got some white lightning, you know bush whiskey, made right up there in the hills," Ed said, again swinging his thumb up to his shoulder.

"No thanks. Sounds like a lot go'n on in the hills, those Indians got a still up there?" Cane said.

"No, that's a family, they's somewhere just over the other side, bring a barrel once a month or so. This batch is pretty good."

"I'll take some lightning," Dirty Frank said.

Cane looked at him. "Course you will."

He nodded back to Ed for the bush whiskey, as he turned around and leaned against the counter looking the room over. He nodded to a few of the men drinking, he saw a huge mountain lion skin hanging across a wall. His beer came, so he walked over to the skin and read the scribble under it: Jersey kilt me with a knife. He thought for a moment, rubbing his chin. He looked across the big room at Kaden and the drawing on the wall he'd seen on the way in. He walked back to the drawing at the door and looked closely at it. He put his hand across the lower part of the face.

"Hey—Kaden, look at this man's eyes," he said. "Look familiar?"

"No," Kaden said automatically looking down at the table, but he looked back up. "Ah well, kind'a it does," he nodded. "Why?"

Kaden looked where Cane was pointing, under the drawing where it said, 'Jersey Smith'

"Well, it kind'a looks like Bill from Spring Valley," Kaden said.

"That's what I was think'n."

Cane nodded and walked back into the room, sitting near Clayton.

The sound of someone coming down the side stairs caused everyone to see who would walk through the door. It was Jimmy, he was pulling the boy along. Jimmy looked around the room before walking to Cane.

"Hey, do I get a beer?"

"Did you see anything?"

"No, nothing."

"Can you see far from up there?" Cane asked.

"Yeah, it's a good view of the whole valley,"

"To the south though, could you see far to the south?"

"A-ways, yeah."

Cane rolled his eyes. "And noth'n?"

Jimmy nodded no.

"Leave the boy, get a beer and head back up there."

Lizzy came out with a small tray of biscuits and cheese, but dropped it. "Martin!" she yelled. "Oh my Lord, Ed it's little Martin."

She ran to him, dropping to her knees and hugging the boy. Everyone got excited, they stood and started talking. Cane looked around, he felt things were getting out of control; he stood and pulled his gun.

"Everyone stop! Just stop where you are,"

Kaden rolled his eyes and reluctantly stood.

Cane swung his gun in small circles. "Move back, everyone back where you were."

Cane walked through the split in the counter and

looked in the backroom. Everyone quieted down as the five strangers stood scattered about with guns out. After a long silence, Ed looked at Martin, he rubbed his chin and looked at Cane.

"Mister," he scratched his head. "You do know that there boy is Martin Smith, right?"

"So."

Cane looked the room over, he signaled Clayton to keep an eye on a table of locals, he looked back at Ed.

"Well, that's Jersey Smith's son you got there. You know when someone killed his family he went..." Ed paused, taking his time looking for the right word.

"Went where? North, went south?" Cane said. "Went looking for his mommy, come on man out with it,"

Ed was deliberate and slow. "No—no, he went a little crazy, don't ya know. If I was you I'd leave the boy and head for the hills," again with his thumb over his shoulder.

One of the local men spoke up. "I'd stay outta those hills, old Jersey knows 'em like the back of his hand."

Ed nodded. "Well, now that's a fact. Ya know, come to think on it, the only thing can save you now would be a two days head start. And someth'n tells me you ain't got it.

"Shut-up old man."

"I ain't that old," Ed looked around the room. "Mister, we can see you got someone after you and if it's Jersey, well you're in for one hell of a afternoon."

Cane pointed his gun at him, Ed scratched high on his cheek and looked down at the counter. "Well, just a friendly warn'n is all."

"Lady, get away from the boy."

She kissed Martin and backed up down the center isle to the counter.

"Stay outta that back room." Cane swallowed deep, he felt a bead of sweat on his temple. "Just where is this Jersey?"

"Fact is mister, we ain't seen him in a while but..."

Lizzy spoke up. "Hamish says he's always been nearby."

Kaden started to worry, he stood and looked at the drawing again. He glanced out the door, scratching his head he sat back down. Cane saw the look on his face.

"Cane, if Bill is..."

"Yeah, yeah, I got it Kaden."

"What?" Clayton asked. He looked around the room, at the lion, and the drawing on the wall. "Are we in the one place we shouldn't be?"

Cane looked away.

"Oh, well isn't this someth'n, are you saying we're in Jersey Smith's stomp'n grounds. He could be on our trail, and we got his son right here with us? Well hell, follow'n the Burton's south don't look so bad now does it?" Clayton said.

"No! No, we don't even know if anyone is on our trail," Cane said.

"Hell we don't," Clayton said.

"I saw a flash or two from a spyglass when we was back there where the trail splits off. Let's get someone back on the roof," Kaden said.

Jimmy left, taking his beer. Ed saw him through the window moving up the stairs to the overlook.

# Chapter 73

For about an hour the guests of the trading post sat in silence while Cane talked with his men. It sounded to Ed like two of them were leaving to set an ambush.

"Rider! From the east," was shouted from the lookout above.

Everyone stopped when the sound of a slow horse was heard walking through the beer garden up to the door. Cane nodded to Kaden in the direction of the window, Kaden edged up to it, peeking between curtains.

"Some guy come'n in with a pile of skins."

Jimmy ran down the stairs to the front of the building. The door opened, and Earl walked in with a small stack of skins over his shoulder. Jimmy followed with his gun out. To Ed, the skins looked strangely similar to the ones he'd just paid the Indians for, he glanced in the backroom, they were gone.

"Why, Trapper Earl, is that you?" Ed said.

"You lost some weight, Earl," Lizzy said.

Earl looked around. Guns were out everywhere.

"Ed, Lizzy, what's going on in here? I just want to sell a skin or two, but it can wait."

He backed in the direction of the door, all the guns lifted pointing at his head.

"Ah, I guess I could down a beer," he looked behind and saw Jimmy and Kaden. "Or two," he said.

"Get his gun," Cane said.

Earl set the skins down on a table and raised his hands, Jimmy felt around only finding one small pocket knife. Ed found that number hard to believe. He wondered how Trapper Earl got into the back room, took the skins and rode around to the front without being heard—something was about to happen.

Cane looked at his men. "Hell, he just rode on in, a lookout's there to warn about such things." He looked at Jimmy. "What were you do'n up there."

"Well, he just rode in through the tree's to the east, from the hills. I been look'n south. I came right down and walked in behind him, I did," Jimmy said.

"Mm, we need a real lookout on duty."

Cane turned to Clayton shaking his head, the men looked at Jimmy, but he didn't get up.

Earl watched one of them walk to a window and look out.

"You alone?" Clayton asked.

"Yeah, I'm alone. I don't know what's going on here, but no one's with me, I'm just outta the hills. Why not leave and let these good people get back to, ah," Earl looked around. "Ah—drink'n?"

Ed Junior walked in through the front door, when he saw all the guns out he ran back out. Kaden stood up, rushed to the open window near the back counter. When he got there Junior was seen running by; Kaden raised his gun.

"No!" Lizzy screamed.

Kaden took his time. It was a wide open area all the way to the beer garden's gate. Kaden smiled, but his hand split with a spray of blood. The butt handle of the gun broke into pieces as two fingers and his broken gun fell out of the window to the dirt below. The sound in the room was earsplitting. He swung around from the window and stood against the wall reaching across his chest for his arm at the wrist. He held his bloody hand up looking at it.

Kaden spit trying to speak. "Augh."

He looked up to see who shot him. Jersey Smith stepped through a cloud of smoke in the doorway of the backroom. He was aiming his gun at him, a second gun pointed out into the room. Kaden recognized the eyes and the smile, it was a clean-shaven Bill. Jersey's smile faded as he knew he was looking at the man that murdered his wife and daughter. He took another shot, taking the man's elbow off. Another gunshot blast filled the room as Jimmy fell in a corner; Earl re-aimed at Dirty Frank. Ed had his shotgun out from under the counter, aiming at Cane and Clayton.

Jersey smiled at Martin, and the boy ran to his father hugging him. Jersey moved him around to his back.

"I've missed you son."

"Oh—paw, you're here."

Cane started up quickly, but sat back down when he considered Ed's shotgun.

"Ah, y'all can drop the guns to the floor," Earl said.

Three heavy guns hit the floor. Jersey gave Earl a look which meant—you know they have more guns than that and Earl nodded in agreement. Jersey's attention was back on Kaden, who was moaning, staring at his dismembered forearm gripped tight in his hand.

Kaden let go of his right arm and it dangled in a mess of torn sleeve. His back was against the wall as he edged away from the window, his left hand up as knuckles smearing blood across the wall. The defiant look that Jersey remembered from the Highlands was gone; he was cowering but not begging, not yet. Kaden felt the weight of his forearm—he looked down as it rolled out of the cloth falling to the floor.

He looked up at Jersey's face. It was indeed the man in the drawing, and he was looking at his other hand as it moved along the wall. He looked at his other hand as it pushed into the wall pierced by a burning hole in its center. He screamed, stumbled, and twisted around, backing to the center of the room. He was bent over and squeezing his bloody hand under what was left of his arm.

He again looked up at Jersey, smoke still coming from the barrel of his gun.

"You're the man that killed my Catherine, and my little Marie. You're rabid Kaden and need to be put down. Men like you shouldn't walk the earth. It must'a been a power from above that brought you back here. Back to the river where it happened."

Jersey took a small piece out of the man's shoulder, red sprayed up the side of his face, and Kaden moved slowly back a few more steps to the door.

"Tell me what happened in your life that turned you into a monster. At some point you had to cross a line, right? Did you make a decision to keep killing or was it just a natural thing, like walk'n. Or running."

Kaden stood silent.

"Well, was there money in it? Is that why you kept doing it. Tell us how many you've killed? You seem like the kind of man that would keep track of such things.

Jimmy laughed, then coughed. "He's got everyone beat after blow'n up that mine."

"Shut-it Jimmy." Clayton said.

Jimmy moaned and held his side. "Well—just say'n."

Ed took a step at Kaden "So it was you that took out that mining camp down near Cumberland?"

Jersey leaned back on the counter, he pushed the brim of his hat up with his gun.

"Oh my Lord. How can anyone be satisfied." He

shook his head. "How many families have you..."

Jersey raised his gun, Kaden backed onto the door's threshold and waited for the man he knew as Bill to finish him. Jersey stopped himself, I'm no executioner, he thought. Kaden took another step back, and he was outside looking in. He saw something from the corner of his eye and turned to see Otis. His imposing dark figure stood tall leaning on the wall next to him. Jersey saw a large black arm reach across, then pull Kaden by the throat off the ground away from the door.

Jersey put one of his guns away, scratched his forehead and looked at Cane. He nodded to Earl, who eased up on his gun and concentrated on Clayton and the rest of the room. Ed moved around for a better spot where he leaned on a table's edge.

"Cane," Jersey said. "There's something about you that's always pissed me off."

"Hell, we were bringing your son back," he looked at Clayton then back. "Look it was Kaden that, that—well did that to your family."

Jersey looked at him with hate.

"No, really, I told him not to, I wanted to... I ah wanted to just leave," Cane said.

"I think I know what you had planned for them," Jersey said.

"No—you mean? Oh, no that was Kaden he was sell'n people not us, right Clayton."

Clayton was watching Earl close and didn't respond.

"Mister, you better shut it," Earl said.

Clayton pulled a boot gun and jumped up. He was shot by both Earl and Jersey. He fired at the floor as he crashed into the wall hard, elbow and shoulder going through. Cane quickly looked around for a gun, the closest one was in the hand of Ed and it was pointing at his head. He slowly turned to see his brother hanging limp out of the wall, he looked back at Jersey.

"Cane, I want you to tell these good people about the slave trade."

"Why would I do that, I don't know anything about that," he said.

Cane's glass exploded, a piece hit him in the cheek and a large piece stuck in his arm. Everyone jumped.

Jersey looked around the room shaking his head, "I didn't like the man you made me, Cane—you and Kaden. So I tried to change, I moved away, gave myself a new name. Come to find out the men I wanted so bad were right there, right in front of me, you even killed my dog."

"Oh no, he killed Duke?" Lizzy asked.

"You beat Beck almost to death, she could have died last night—I don't know.

Cane played dumb. "Beck? What hap..."

The door burst opened, Kaden was thrown in, then Otis walked in behind him.

"Just in time Otis, Cane here was going to fill us in on the ins and outs of the slave trade," Jersey said.

Cane was playing with the broken handle of his beer mug.

"I just can't help you there Bill—ah, Jersey."

The glass handle exploded in his hand, a line across the back of his wrist smoked and started bleeding.

"I'm very close to using the approach I took with Kaden," Jersey said.

He aimed his gun at Cane's arm.

"Lizzy, can you take Martin in the back room please?"

She pulled the boy, but he didn't want to go.

The Sheriff and Ed Junior walked in the front door, he had his gun out and Otis moved out of the way.

"Okay this is now over!" the Sheriff yelled.

Jersey looked up from Cane as the Sheriff saw him.

"Hey Jersey," the Sheriff smiled.

He looked around the room, Ed and the other men that he'd come to know gave him a look and shook their heads slightly. He looked back at Jersey, lowered his gun and leaned on the center post. "Well, carry on," he said.

Cane pulled glass from his arm and looked around; it seemed everyone was okay with Jersey just shooting people. This guy could kill me and these so called good people would go along with it, he thought. He gave Jersey a defiant look. He's gonna kill me, this wild man is blaming me for what Kaden did, he looked at Kaden, and he's gonna make it hurt.

"Sheriff this here is Cane Gannon, that's his brother in the wall. We've been after Cane for beating a young woman of sixteen almost to death, for all we know she could be dead by now."

"What, no. I didn't do that, I..."

"Roll up your sleeve Cane, let's see what Beck did trying to get away from you." He saw the look on Cane's face. "You thought she was dead didn't you?"

"Okay, now this isn't what it looks like."

"Tell us what happened." The Sheriff said.

"Well, she was after me, has been for a while and I finally gave in."

"So she slashed at your arm and you beat her to death?"

"The man on the floor there, Sheriff, is the man that killed my wife and daughter and together they took my boy as a slave along with many others."

"Now," Jersey looked at Cane. "Unlike Kaden, I'm going to tell you what I'm going to shoot off."

Cane looked at the Sheriff, but he seemed to be waiting to hear what was going to get shot off.

"Okay, right hand," Jersey said.

Cane quickly pulled his hand to his lap under the table, Jersey's gun followed it.

"I don't much care what's under it," he said.

Cane quickly brought his hand back to the tabletop. He looked back at Kaden bleeding on the floor.

"Fine. Okay, fine—what do you want from me?"

"Tell us about the slave trade."

"Fine."

Cane twisted his chair around and looked at the faces. Jersey nodded to Lizzy, and Martin ran to his side.

"The money is..."

He was interrupted by the Sheriff. "Hey this man is bleeding, someone drag him outside. Lizzy, do you think you could take a look at his wounds."

"Junior, help your mother." Ed said.

Junior and Otis picked up a leg and pulled Kaden out. Otis walked back in as Ed Junior tied Kaden's ankles to an exposed root under a near by tree where they propped him. Cane looked at the ceiling rolling his eyes and back at the Sheriff who nodded to go ahead.

"Sorry. Sorry—it was making me a little sick," the Sheriff rolled his gun at the wrist. "Continue."

Cane looked back at Jersey. "Lots of money to make, and for a while it wasn't hard or dangerous."

"How much would you sell a man for?" Otis asked.

"Oh, a man like you could go for well over $1000.00 easy. I didn't buy and sell, well not much; It was more profitable to find runaways—well at first that's what we did."

"We heard you were taken free men and women south to sell," Otis said.

"We did, yes. Finding free slaves was just easier. Runaways were hard to find, they were always on the lookout, but these free ones, well they didn't see us come'n."

He looked back at Otis. "You were lucky you're a good smithy, you'd been gone years ago."

"What about Chloe? Did you take her from the valley south at the Youghiogheny river? Do you remember her?" Otis asked.

"Oh yeah, I remember Chloe, she put up a good fight, we sold her down in New Orleans," Cane said.

Otis fists tightened, he looked at Jersey which calmed him down.

"When did you start sell'n children and white woman?" Jersey asked.

"Oh, a while back. We were down there sell'n, never buy'n unless it was for a big spender that hired us. Anyway, we heard about a closed auction and after a lot of talking and a bit of money they let us in. Now that was an eye opener, woman and children, not a lot of em, oh maybe eight total. Hell, after that we brought that many ourselves. Well, I have to say that changed everything, that's where the money is."

Cane looked up at the disgusted faces staring at him.

"What's the name of that auction house?"

"Oh, I can't remember that..."

"Okay, right hand," Jersey said.

"Fine—yes, it was called Southern Tobacco and Fruit Market, it's on the bay, west of the city. Once in a while there was a special auction and they told us where it was, but it was always a different location. I'm not saying anything else, you want to shoot me then shoot me."

Earl and the Sheriff took Cane by the arms, lifted him and walked him outside. A few of the men dragged the others out. Cane was set on a rock next to Dirty Frank. The doctor was there at an outside table waiting, Lizzy helped him look all the men over. Jimmy would survive, Clayton was dead, and Kaden unconscious.

"Hey, I missed you son, you're a young man now."
Jersey hugged Martin. They talked for a few minutes.

"Let's go see your granddad, he should be at the house. You know he got married," Jersey said.

"What? Grand-paw?"

"Yeah, we'll meet her together."

"I need at least two men to help me bring these men north," the Sheriff looked at Jersey. "I'll take'm to my old jurisdiction, I suppose you'll not be come'n."

"You know what happened—I'll show up for the trial though."

The Sheriff nodded and looked around at the hands that were up volunteering. "Okay—good, you three head home and get ready, we leave in two hours. Junior can you get a wagon set up and ready, we'll be renting one Ed, if that's okay."

"That'd be fine."

Kaden was half leaning on a smooth rock that was wrapped in the exposed roots of an ancient tree, it stretched high overhead. He moaned in pain, his arms were wrapped tight with blood soaked cloth. He felt the presence of someone and opened his eyes. His torturer—the old woman, was sitting crossed-legged in the dirt next to him. She stared at him over the edge of a filthy cup as she sipped from it. He extended his arms and let out a yell, but his feet were tied in place and he rolled head first closer to her. She leaned up to his face and twisted her head taking a close look into his eyes. He reached at her but his hand was gone. She laughed, it was the horrible laugh that had been haunting him. He pushed at the ground to get away, but with only one hand he rolled and squirmed back to the root covered stone.

"Worst coffee I ever ate," she said.

She held the cup away and slowly poured it out, it was hot and dark and looked strong just like he liked it. Kaden wished he could have had a mouthful, if only to wash away the taste of blood and dirt.

"You here from hell old witch?"

He looked at her, he knew the end was near. She looked real, but she couldn't be. He smelled the coffee, it made his mouth water, he spit.

"Well, say something."

She looked into his eyes. "So—I guess you really was a outlaw."

"Well, I guess I was. Why are you here, we burned down your hellhole and you were inside—dead."

"That wern't hell." She slowly shook her head. "No—not even close." For the first time she had the look of a sane person. She teared up, and looked away. "Think I'll take a look around, while I can."

Kaden watched her walk by the trading post then she ran into a stand of trees.

"This one's dead."

Kaden looked up at the trading post man, he was pointing at him.

Otis walked up. "Strange, I didn't think he was that bad, must'a bled-out."

Kaden look down from over Otis's shoulder at himself, his arms were out stretched, his eyes and mouth were wide open.

"Looks like he was scared to death." Ed said.

Otis nodded. "Mm—does indeed."

Kaden saw the old woman waving from the forest, he felt drawn to her.

The Sheriff looked at a few men and asked. "Can you get Cane here tied up while I..."

Cane jumped from the rock running, he got to the worn path down to the river and poured on the speed. Jersey started after him, he saw something in the corner of his eye. He looked over to see Roger running along next to him. Roger smiled and said, "Wing?"

Jersey nodded and said, "Wing 'em."

Jersey stopped and watched Roger take a few more long strides as he tossed his knife overhand into Cane's thigh. Cane screamed, skipped a few times and fell tumbling into the river.

Cane floated face down. He opened his eyes as he drifted, looking at the smooth colorful rocks and pebbles on the riverbed. He saw how the sunlight enhanced their colors as it rippled across them in ribbons. It was something he never thought about, now it was only inches from his face and he was forced to see beauty in it. He kept his head down and held his breath as long as he could. He felt the pain in his leg as he drifted weightless. He thought of Clayton—he saw him dead, hanging in the wall. And of his father, the once great rancher that he brought down to a sniveling old man. At that moment Cane was as close to feeling shame as he'd ever been. When it got deeper and cloudy with blood and a bit ugly, when the sun couldn't reach the bottom as well, Cane took in a deep breath of cold mountain water.

# Chapter 74

Jersey and Martin brought Hamish and Betty for a visit to Spring Valley. They'd been back a few days, but normalcy seemed impossible, friends had died. The street was sparse, and the Highlands was closed, though most of the captives from the compound stayed there until they could figure out what they wanted to do. Ben sent for papers for those that were free, those that weren't were secretly given to Otis to move on through the underground to freedom. No charges were filed against Howard. As soon as he was let out he wisely left town. Susanne never left Becky's side. She and Melissa nursed her back to health, soon they walked her to the cafe for lunch and to see her friends.

The slave trade had taken place right under their noses. Sadness and regret was visible on faces, but there was also a satisfaction that once it was found out, it was stopped. Wayne, Dirty Frank, and all the guards faced Federal charges.

The Sunday sermon was unifying. Otis sat happily, Bible in hand, with the freed men and woman. Pastor Dale warned of paranoia stopping growth and how they still must be the welcoming, friendly town they'd built, or face stagnation. In a way it seemed like the little town was starting over. Though an awareness spread of what could happen and how evil can creep in and slowly destroy everything. The law must remain vigilant so the rest can live without questioning every new visitor or neighbor. Hamish spoke of dealing with loss, and what a joy it was getting Martin back. Ben spoke about slavery and finding Susanne.

It was one of those great Sundays when everyone came to center park after Church. Jersey sat on the grass near where he sat on his first day in town. He leaned against a tree taking it all in, nearly everyone he cared about was near; Melissa, Martin, Hamish and Betty. Beck and Susanne were sitting nearby with Ben, Otis, and Earl. He finished eating Missy's wonderful chicken, undid his gun belt and slid it under the blanket. He closed his eyes listening to Martin telling tales of captivity. Musicians in the gazebo started playing again, this time a waltz, as a few danced in little circles on the side street. He was almost asleep when he heard some talk about an amazing dessert just brought out.

Jersey stood and walked in the direction of the food table, which was always at the park's edge across the street from the Sunny Side, where food could be easily added.

Ben asked loudly. "So what's next for you, Jersey Smith? Or are we going back to calling you Bill?"

People laughed, Jersey turned in the center of the park and smiled at Ben.

"Well?" Ben asked.

"I, ah..." He backed up in the direction of the food table looking at Otis and Earl. "New Orleans I think, Ben."

His friends nodded.

Jersey turned to the table looking over all his choices when a girl hurried out of the Sunny Side, he looked up and watched her run down the street. Jersey's eyes followed her, then he looked to see what she could be running from. It was a stranger in the shadow of the doorway. His foot held the outer door open, as he stood back inside holding a gun in each hand.

The large gathering was unaware. Jersey didn't reach for his gun; he knew it was on the ground next to the tree. He thought about moving away, but with the park full of people behind him, some would get hurt. He stood alone at the long table looking at the smiling face of Leroy Burton.

"You killed my brother," the voice came from the doorway.

"I did. He was going to shoot me, you can't expect me not to shoot back."

Martin had been watching every move his father made since they were reunited. He saw past him, the bad man with his gun's out standing in the door of the little restaurant. Martin took his father's gun from under the blanket near the tree. He cocked it with two thumbs and looked at Jersey standing with his back to the people. Hamish quickly reached for the gun, but Martin twisted round and continued for his father.

Most of the near by crowd quieted as Hamish and Melissa ran after Martin, thinking the boy had gone crazy and was about to shoot his father. The barrels of Leroy's guns lifted as he snapped the hammers back. Jersey stood ready to jump sideways, but knew he couldn't. He thought about who might get shot directly behind him. Martin stopped when he saw the man cock the guns. He lifted his father's gun. It was large and heavy in his hands. He pulled the trigger as Hamish grabbed for the gun slipping his thumb under the hammer not allowing it to fire, he pulled it away. Leroy paused for a moment, looking at the boy from the compound, he was trying to shoot him. The doorway filled with lead balls and Leroy took a few to the body. He shot wildly. As he turned to go back inside, he was hit again, and again. He fell with his foot propping the door open where he lay still.

Jersey didn't have to turn to know who shot, he had so many capable friends. He saw blood on the table in front of him and felt his side, his loose white shirt was ripped and blood stained. The event stunned everyone. People looked around the area, some slowly rose from the ground where they'd jumped. Jersey looked inside his shirt, the ball seemed to have cut shallow through his side and he turned to see if anyone caught the lead behind him. Everyone was looking at him. Otis, Earl, and Ben were holding smoking guns, Melissa and Hamish were kneeling with Martin nearby, they saw the blood on his side.

Earl spoke up. "You okay, JS?"

Jersey pulled the ripped shirt away from his side and looked in. "Yeah, just caught my side."

He held the blood stained rip out for Melissa to see, he smiled at her shaking his head. "New shirt."

# A Letter from Hamish Maguire

To: Aaron Maguire,
Maguriesbridge, Ireland

My son the best of news, our little Martin is alive and well.

He's lived these few years captive only a days ride from here with slaves of both black and white, men and woman. Jersey and a few men from Spring Valley freed them and hunted down those responsible.

The boy has grown so much and has some fascinate'n stories to tell of his adventure. He remembers you fondly and is writing you a letter as I write this.

He keeps the little knife with him at all times now, the one you sent from England that Christmas which seems so long ago. It's funny he has fashioned the sheath on the back of his belt sideways just as his father does. He's been a real joy to Betty and me and he will be stay'n at the house while Jersey heads south for a month or so.

It seems Jersey has found love again. He asked how I felt about it, which was kind but unnecessary. Life here on earth goes on and must be lived. I do like her, she's almost as beautiful as our Catherine.

Speaking of Catherine, I spoke to the congregation in Spring Valley about her and about dealing with the loss, as a few townsmen were killed taking on the ruthless Gannon gang.

Betty sends her love and can't wait to meet you. Her life is so different now, she's really come out into her own. Her husband was a good man but it seems he held her down a bit, she seems so happy now. As am I.

As the trouble around here seems to have cleared up, I was affected by your last letter it seemed different. Is everything okay with you? Please write explaining your situation.

My thoughts and prayers are often of you.
Affectionately, your Father

Glynn L. Simmons lives between Detroit and Ann Arbor in the beautiful state of Michigan, with his wife of over 40 years, Janene. He enjoys photography, fly fishing and the company of family and friends.

Glynn has been writing ideas for film and stories most of his life, only in the last few years has he sat down and put time into his favorites. He has five more books due out soon. The next will be the first of four stories set in Northern Michigan of 1956. About a retired Detroit detective that can't seem to stop working.

The next 'Wild, Wild East' book will be out in the winter of 2020. It's about Jersey's brother James and his friend Aaron, the son of Hamish. *Jersey will return in the third book in the series.*

• For information about 'Jersey Smith' and 'The Wild, Wild East' books, and more - please visit www.GlynnLSimmons.com

• Sign up for The Newsletter 'guaranteed only 5 times a year'. You'll receive - book release information, special deals, articles and much more. (To your in-box only once a quarter, and one special mailing a year—*just 5 emails a year total*)

Made in the USA
Monee, IL
16 December 2020

53305875R10238